THE BLUE CLOAK

THE BLUE CLOAK

SHANNON MCNEAR

THORNDIKE PRESS
A part of Gale, a Cengage Company

GALE
A Cengage Company

Copyright © 2020 by Shannon McNear.
True Colors.
All scripture quotations are taken from the King James Version of the Bible.
Thorndike Press, a part of Gale, a Cengage Company.

Thorndike Press® Large Print Christian Historical Fiction.
The text of this Large Print edition is unabridged.
Other aspects of the book may vary from the original edition.
Set in 16 pt. Plantin.

LIBRARY OF CONGRESS CIP DATA ON FILE.
CATALOGUING IN PUBLICATION FOR THIS BOOK
IS AVAILABLE FROM THE LIBRARY OF CONGRESS

ISBN-13: 978-1-4328-7904-4 (hardcover alk. paper)

Published in 2020 by arrangement with Barbour Publishing, Inc.

Printed in Mexico
Print Number: 02   Print Year: 2022

Dear Reader,

The story of the Harpes rises from the mists of history like the shadows of a nightmare. The first account I read of them was as a postscript to my research on *The Cumberland Bride,* with an incident that took place on the Wilderness Road in Kentucky a little more than four years after the close of that story. When asked about the possibility of doing a novel set against the backdrop of their reign of terror, I readily agreed — but then later, when faced with the necessity of digging deeper for the purpose of developing such a story, I had to seriously pray over whether or not to accept the opportunity. How dark is too dark for a Christian to write? I asked people close to me, whose spiritual discernment I trust. Every single one came back with a variation of the counterquestion, Is God stronger than evil, or not?

And so here I am, on the other side of writing it. I can't say the task was always easy or enjoyable. The telling of the story contains possible triggers for those who have been similarly traumatized. But I am encouraged, and I hope you the reader will be as well, that the Light truly is greater than the dark . . . and no circumstances are ever so terrible or hopeless that His love cannot reach us.

Blessings!
— Shannon

*For Sarah, Susanna, and Maria. I hope
I've done your story justice . . . and that
I may meet all three of you someday,
in heaven.*

*And for others still waiting for
redemption . . .*
God sees, and hears, and is not idle.

Whither shall I go from thy spirit?
Or whither shall I flee from
thy presence?
If I ascend up into heaven, thou
art there:
if I make my bed in hell, behold, thou
art there.
If I take the wings of the morning,
and dwell in the uttermost parts of
the sea;
Even there shall thy hand lead me,

and thy right hand shall hold me.
If I say, Surely the darkness shall
cover me;
even the night shall be light about me.
Yea, the darkness hideth not from thee;
but the night shineth as the day:
the darkness and the light are both alike
to thee.

PSALM 139:7–12

For I am persuaded, that neither death,
nor life,
nor angels, nor principalities,
nor powers,
nor things present, nor things to come,
nor height, nor depth, nor any
other creature,
shall be able to separate us from the
love of God,
which is in Christ Jesus our Lord.

ROMANS 8:38–39

There is no pit so deep that God's love
is not deeper still.

— Corrie ten Boom

CHAPTER ONE

June 1, 1797
Knox County, Tennessee

It was unbecoming to be jealous of a dear friend's marriage.

Rachel Taylor bit her lips together, kept her hands folded, and hoped everyone would think the moistness of her eyes was only a bit of sentimental good will on Sally's behalf. Not the wish that she herself was the one taking vows. Or concern for the circumstances that brought Sally this marriage to begin with.

The doors and shutters stood open all around the cabin, but still the inside felt close and hot with the press of people. Sally's seven younger siblings ranged about the edges of the room, the boys and little ones fidgety and staring longingly outside, the older ones standing near their mother, Missus Rice, big with child and misty-eyed herself.

Only Sally looked unaffected by the heat, blue eyes bright, golden hair upswept, and the moisture on her face and neck managing to lend more of a glow to the flush of her cheeks. Her groom put in a valiant effort but fidgeted almost as much as the children, looking ill at ease in what Rachel suspected was his only shirt and waistcoat. At least he'd combed and tied back his red curly hair and made a similar attempt to tame his short beard, though apparently even a wedding did not merit high enough in his estimation for a shave. At least he didn't resort to bear grease for grooming those unruly curls into submission.

Not that half the males in Knox County didn't, if they bothered with such niceties at all.

The groom's brother — some said cousin, but Rachel wasn't sure she cared about the difference — standing on his other side, or hulking might be more like it, certainly didn't. Although for this event, he too had smoothed and tied back his hair, in garb that Rachel was sure he thought passed for clean.

"Big" and "Little" Harpe, they were called, hereabouts. Micajah and Wiley were their proper names, for those concerned with proper. There seemed to be little enough of that about these two —

Big Harpe's eyes snapped to Rachel's, his dark gaze seeming to bore into her. She suddenly could not breathe, and the heat within the cabin intensified as she looked away, but there was no escape from the weight of the man's regard.

Quite the contrary, from the corner of her eye she could see the curl of his mouth, which did nothing to ease the frank ugliness of the man's visage. Indeed, the smile only drew a shiver from her.

The man standing a little beyond him, serving as witness to the marriage, must have noticed her discomfiture, for he lifted a questioning eyebrow. Now there was one who used only the finest pomade, his clothing immaculate and of the finest modern cut. His regard drew even more of a flush, because although she, as daughter of a well-known merchant near the burgeoning town of Knoxville, knew most folk around, he was none other than Hugh Lawson White, son of Knoxville's founder, General James White — and recently returned from the study of law up in Pennsylvania.

Far too fine to be standing as witness for a lowly Baptist preacher's daughter.

So Rachel forced the briefest smile and turned her gaze toward Sally's father,

11

Reverend Rice. Brown hair combed back, beard falling neatly over his chest, hazel eyes crinkled, and face pinched in what appeared to be more than common soberness at such an occasion.

"I bid you, Wiley and Sally, to turn and take each other's right hand as you pledge your vows."

Rachel could no longer see Sally's expression as her friend angled away from her, but the intent look of her groom was now in full view. The light in Wiley's eyes made him almost handsome.

Could it be that Wiley really did love Sally? He certainly avowed it so to Sally, and her father. Insisted that his pleas, bordering on demands, for Sally to be his wife were because of his great and terrible affection for her.

And with that thought, the jealousy came flooding back. Not that it was Wiley she wanted — heavens, not at all — but for someone to look at her like that. The way Wiley did at Sally.

For a moment, it didn't matter that they knew very little about Wiley and his brother. That they'd seemed to just surface from the wilderness, as so many men did, as if born there. Hadn't they come to church, and not just listened but "amen-ed" at all the right places? And Wiley had even come forward to be baptized. That should be enough to satisfy anyone.

Here Sally was, marrying him, after all, and her daddy and mama wouldn't be giving her up to just anyone. So it was good and right for Rachel to be happy for her friend — and to feel a twinge of longing that she might soon be a joyful bride as well.

Although her own prospects were woefully dismal, despite the fact that near every man in Knox County traipsed through her father's trading post at some point or another, and at least half of them stopped to make eyes at her. It wasn't as though she didn't enjoy the attention, or banter back, or even pretend to be flattered at the ones who dropped a marriage proposal on the spot. Sometimes she didn't even have to pretend. Other times, the attention gave her a squirmy feeling inside, like —

Like being caught, yet again, on the receiving end of Big Harpe's regard.

She glanced quickly away. Some men would view any show of kindness as an invitation to take more than she was prepared to offer. And Micajah — he wasn't just huge, but ugly to boot. Though she'd wit enough to know that a plain face often hid a gentle heart, Micajah had a way of looking straight through a body.

Or worse, like a dog would look at a rabbit, or a cat, a bird.

Hunter, and the hunted.

The wedding was over, and while the men gathered outside and a little apart to enjoy a pipe in the sunshine, Rachel helped Missus Rice and the other girls with laying out supper on the table they'd set up beforehand, out in front of the house. The boards fairly groaned under the load of roasted turkey, venison, gravy, berry preserves, apple pies, greens, and other delights.

Sally and Wiley wandered here and there under the trees, across the steeply sloped yard, holding hands, exchanging looks, and stealing kisses that were suddenly no longer forbidden but somehow seemed just as scandalous. When everything was ready, they came and were seated at a place of honor with the rest of them.

Here, even Sally's mama and daddy seemed happy. Sally's own joy seemed uncontainable, and finally Rachel yielded to the happiness of the day. No misgivings. No jealousy.

Rejoice with them that do rejoice, and weep with them that weep.

If there was ever a better admonition for

the day, she did not know one.

As initial hunger was sated and folk rose up to play, some at a throwing game that everyone said had been learned from the Indians, and a couple of people on musical instruments, Rachel found herself approached by Hugh White. "You are looking well, Miss Taylor. I hope you have been, indeed?"

She dipped what she hoped was a fair approximation of a curtsy. "And yourself, Mr. White." She couldn't stop the smile tugging at her mouth. How strange it was to find themselves all grown and formal with each other, when just a few years back, she'd have been out there begging to play with the boys, and they all simply called one another by first names.

The stiffness between them was formality indeed, since Rachel well knew that Hugh only inquired after her health as a gesture of friendship, and certainly nothing more. It was no secret that since returning from Lancaster, Pennsylvania, he'd been calling on the daughter of Samuel Carrick, the preacher at his family's own church right there in Knoxville. Elizabeth Carrick was a better fit for a man recently admitted to the bar than she, a merchant's daughter, anyway.

15

His answering grin softened the square planes of his face and crinkled his deep-set eyes. "Your father's trading post over at Campbell's Station seems to be flourishing."

"It is, at that. And how does Miss Carrick these days?"

He laughed, but briefly. "Very well. Very well, indeed." Hugh shot her a searching look. "Exchanging pleasantries is all well and good, but I wished to inquire more specifically. Were you discomfited somehow during the ceremony? You looked — distressed."

She opened her mouth then shut it again, thinking better of the words that nearly popped out. How to explain the odd way Micajah made her feel, just being in the same room?

His blue eyes remained on her, cool and assessing. As piercing as Micajah's in their own way, but without making her feel stripped bare.

"I — am concerned for Sally," she admitted, softly.

Hugh's hand brushed her forearm. "We are all concerned for Sally."

Rachel glanced toward her friend, still seated next to Wiley, leaning now against his shoulder and gazing adoringly up at him.

"Then — why —"

The words failed her.

It was not only unbecoming to be jealous of her friend but also to question the validity of the marriage itself, once the wedding day had come.

"It is a sad fact that some marriages come about due to necessity, rather than mutual regard or expediency."

Alarm flared in Rachel's breast. "Then — he has indeed behaved dishonorably toward her?"

Hugh's mouth pressed firm for a moment. "We can only pray that he behaves henceforth with honor." His own gaze strayed toward the couple. "Prayer is our best course under any circumstance."

"That is very so," Rachel murmured.

They stood for a moment, watching the couple snug in closer to each other and exchange a fond glance. In this moment, nothing appeared amiss as far as mutual regard.

"But come, Miss Taylor, we should not be so solemn on such an occasion."

Rachel peered askance at Hugh and found him bending another smile upon her.

"You have inquired after Miss Carrick," he went on, "but I've not had the opportunity to ask whether you've had any callers these days."

Rachel laughed despite the seriousness of the previous moment, though her smile melted into what felt like gritted teeth. "I? Of course not. I'm far too busy helping my father with trade."

"Oh? With all of those men who come through the station, not a one has caught your eye? Or recognized your sterling qualities and become taken with you?"

"Oh, plenty of them claim to be *taken* with me," Rachel murmured, shifting to watch the game at play.

"Rachel," Hugh said, also softly, and she snapped back to look at him. He angled another smile at her. "I had a friend while studying law, a certain Benjamin Langford from Virginia, who is similarly unattached. He wrote to me some time ago, asking about opportunities here out west." His smile turned to a teasing grin. "Should I write him back and tell him he most certainly should come to Knox County and survey its many pleasing attributes?"

A wave of heat swept over her. "Hugh White! Don't you dare." A giggle forced its way up her throat. "Please."

Now his grin was downright wicked — although subdued, because after all, this was

Hugh. "Now I shall definitely have to write him."

For some reason the thought made her heart beat a little faster. "Please do not mention me." She cleared her throat. "Besides, Daddy has been talking about sending me up the Wilderness Road to help Daniel and Anne. So it won't matter a whit if you ask him to come or not."

"Well." The corner of Hugh's mouth remained lifted. "I'll simply have to tell him to go to Kentucky instead."

Rachel huffed and shook her head. " 'Twouldn't matter. If he's studied law — studying? — then I'm sure he'd consider himself quite above me." At Hugh's sudden look and laughter, she found herself blushing anew. "Oh. Gracious. I just realized how that must sound." Hugh laughed even more heartily, going so far as to bend with a hand on his knee. "Besides, you have your Miss Carrick, who is very much above either of us."

Hugh's amusement muted to a twinkle. "Now, Rachel, I would put anyone of the fairer sex above myself."

She met his gaze directly for but a moment and found herself coloring again. "That you would. And thank you."

If only there truly were another man with

similar sentiments, who was yet unattached and would actually, as Hugh said, recognize her sterling qualities — and was not just woman-starved from too much time in the wilderness.

Not that she had an overabundance of sterling qualities. Mama doubtless despaired of making her less outspoken, less bookish, more willing in the kitchen, and less eager to be right at Daddy's side, in the thick of trade.

All good qualities for the wilderness, Daddy insisted, but she doubted it was so.

Amid cheering, Sally and Wiley were cutting the cake Missus Rice and her girls had made. Hugh stood beside Rachel, watching, his smile gradually fading. "I hope he does well by her," he muttered, as if to himself.

At Rachel's alarmed stare, he met her gaze with a tight smile. "If you will excuse me — ?"

"Of course," she murmured, as he moved away to speak with Reverend Rice.

The cake was cut and served, and the scraping of a fiddle announced there would be music and dancing, despite the frowns of Preacher and Missus Rice. But both Sally's parents danced a jig when the tune was right for it.

The hour grew late, and the time came

for Sally to go home with her new husband. Rachel took the opportunity during the goodbyeing to draw her friend aside and hand her a parcel tied with twine. Sally pushed back a stray lock of gold, her eyes going wide. "And what is this?"

Rachel laughed. "A wedding present, of course. What did you think?"

Sally slid the twine off, careful to keep it whole, and unwrapped the brown paper to reveal folds of rich indigo-dyed wool. A sigh escaped her lips as she shook it out to find that it took the form of a woman's cloak.

Rachel held her breath, waiting her friend's reaction.

"Oh Rachel, it's lovely!"

"Do you like it? For true?"

Sally threw her arms around Rachel then drew back to examine the garment more closely. A wide hood, a frog of silken cord connecting the edges at the throat, and its length billowing long enough to cover an entire skirt, and not just to the fingertips. "I ain't never had anything so fine, and that's a fact. I love it! Thank you ever so much."

Rachel let herself smile this time. " 'Tisn't scarlet, and seems like that's the color everyone wants —"

"Oh no," Sally hastened to assure her. "I prefer the blue."

She swung it around her shoulders, and as Rachel suspected, the shade offset Sally's eyes, making them even more vivid than usual. "It suits you, as I knew it would."

Wiley came up at that moment, and Sally turned to him. "Look at what Rachel's given me!"

Rachel thought his expression a little stiff, but he seemed pleased enough. "Aye, 'tis right nice," he said in his thick Scots brogue.

Sally beamed and turned back to embrace Rachel yet again. "Thank you again, my sweet friend. And — for being here today."

"Why would I not?" Rachel demanded, but Sally only squeezed her harder then stepped back, wetness shimmering in her eyes.

"I have never been so happy," she said.

"And well you should be," Rachel murmured.

With all her things packed into a small wagon that Wiley and Micajah had driven to the wedding, Sally was handed up onto the seat by her daddy, who kissed her on the cheek and bid them farewell, after a few words to Wiley that none else could hear. Micajah followed, mounted on his own horse, and they all set off, away over to the ridge to the cabin they rented on Beaver Creek.

Rachel lingered to help Missus Rice tidy up, but before long she found Hugh at her elbow. "Might I see you back to the station before I return home myself?"

She needed only a moment's consideration before responding with a smile. "That would be most welcome."

He set her up on his horse and walked beside, in the opposite direction the Harpes had taken. "I find it passing odd that Big Harpe went along home with the newlyweds," Rachel said, as conversation lagged between them.

Hugh sucked his cheek a moment. "Perhaps he intends to guard them on the way and sleep in the barn once they get there."

She felt her cheeks flaming but pretended that neither of them spoke anything amiss. "The country is far less uncertain than it once was, although — I suppose that could be the case."

Hugh's gaze came to hers. "Is it true they say that the Harpes lived with the Cherokee themselves for a time?"

Rachel's shoulder lifted. "Doesn't necessarily mean anything, if so. Plenty of Cherokee were friendly."

"Plenty more weren't."

"True enough."

She should have felt more eerie about the

woods, which thickened as they ascended the foot of the ridge, but she didn't, not with Hugh at her side. He might be bookish, but she'd seen him shoot. He was more than capable with rifle, knife, or tomahawk, and had ridden against the Indians more than once before going away to law school.

"Much has changed in a few years," Hugh mused. "Although this country is wild yet, and will be for a long while."

Patting the bay mare's satiny shoulder, Rachel scanned the forest, broken here and there by the occasional clearing where newly hewn cabins stood, and fields of corn and tobacco, with smaller kitchen gardens closer to the houses. "A beautiful country it is," she said.

"Very much so," Hugh murmured. After a moment's hesitation, he added, "I hardly blame the red man for fighting to defend it."

"Nor do I," Rachel agreed. Although she had to admit things had been ever so much quieter the last couple of years since August of '94, when General Wayne defeated the Shawnee up at the Battle of Fallen Timbers in Ohio Territory. The men of the Tennessee settlements had led a raid on the Cherokee town of Nickajack later that year. The Cherokee, Creek, and others had been far less of a terror since.

Over the next rise they climbed, and then down the sharp descent of the ridge, at an angle to the slope first one way and then the other. At last the untidy cluster of buildings that comprised Campbell's Station came into view, and stopping outside the one bearing a placard proclaiming it Taylor's Trading Post, Hugh helped Rachel down. "I must hurry on," he said. "Though Eliza had other obligations that prevented her from attending the wedding, I promised to stop in and tell her every detail." His smile flashed a little too sharply for a moment. "And then I may have a letter to write."

Without thinking, Rachel popped his shoulder with the back of her hand. "Oh, you." This drew only another laugh from him, and she gathered her skirts and turned to go inside.

"Rachel."

She hesitated, meeting Hugh's earnest gaze.

"It was good to see you today."

She smiled a little. "You as well."

They'd crossed the ridge north of her parents' home, then cut northwest, where the deepening forest seemed to swallow them. Sally gripped the seat with one hand and clutched her shawl with the other so she was not pitched from her perch by the roughness of the path, barely wide enough for the passage of the wagon.

She peeked at Wiley, sitting beside her, his tall, muscled frame slightly hunched, reins slack in his hands.

Hands that had already touched and known her most secret places. And now, she was his wife not only in body but in word and law as well.

He caught her looking at him and smiled back. "I cannae believe this is happening at last."

The rumble of his Scots brogue sent shivers across her skin. "Nor can I." She scooted closer, and as she leaned into his side, he wrapped an arm around her. Finally they could kiss and cuddle, and no one could say it was unrighteous to do so. "And I cannot wait to see the cabin. Our new home. I get to be mistress of my own household!"

Wiley's smile dimmed then flashed. "Of course you do."

Something about the way he replied niggled at her, but she tucked her head and leaned her cheek against his chest. They were married in truth, and it was all that mattered.

The road grew rough and narrow, and as Wiley straightened so he could take the reins with both hands again, Sally drew away a little, bracing herself once more. The sun had fallen below the tree line, and another shiver made her pull the shawl snug about her shoulders. "Almost there," called Micajah, from behind.

Sally glanced back at her new brother-in-law. People called him "Big" Harpe, and Wiley, "Little," but there was nothing little about her new husband — except in comparison to Micajah. But she refused to call either by their nicknames.

Micajah met her gaze and gave her what she could swear was the most un-brotherly smile she'd ever seen.

Despite the unevenness of the road, she turned around and leaned into Wiley's shoulder again. "So where's Micajah going, now that we're married?"

"What d'ye mean?"

"Well." Sally swallowed. "He's not going to live with us — is he?"

"Aye, why would he not?"

"But — we're married now."

Wiley looked down at her, his expression blank and uncomprehending. Her breath lodged painfully in her throat. "I was looking forward to — well, to us being alone."

At least at first, because babies would undoubtedly follow. "And —" Her face burned now. "Some things do require us being alone."

Her husband of just a few hours shrugged. It was the opposite shoulder, but a shrug nevertheless. "It's his home too. Where else would he go?"

Sally stuttered to silence. Mama and Daddy shared a sleeping space with her younger siblings, but both had been insistent the older ones sleep in the loft. *"For privacy,"* Mama had always said, with a glance toward Daddy that was always met with a twinkle and a little smile.

Micajah's smile looked too much like that, come to think of it.

The forest shadow held a sudden chill her shawl would not allay.

They rounded a bend and turned off a rutted track onto a path that was not only barely traceable through the underbrush but just wide enough for the wagon. Wiley looked unperturbed as he guided the horse down a slope, the wagon's side scraping bushes and weeds, until they emerged into a clearing where a cabin and a couple of rough outbuildings stood.

Humble surroundings, and a yard more cluttered than not, but little else to be expected of a pair of bachelors, Sally supposed. The cabin looked solid enough. And she'd be glad of the opportunity to get down and stretch —

A figure moved behind the cabin's unshuttered window.

Sally smothered a yelp as Wiley pulled the horse to a stop in the yard. The door opened and a woman, tall and rawboned, stepped out onto the porch. A second female figure, more slight, followed her, and they came to the edge of the steps and stared at Sally.

Who were these wild-looking creatures, with hair braided untidily back and dresses that could only be described as slovenly, at best? Were they Indian, or white? Sally surmised white, by the shade of their skin and hair, as well as the cast of their features, but rarely had she witnessed such destitution.

She couldn't even find the words — or voice — to ask Wiley why these women were there, much less who they were.

He set the brake on the wagon and came around to hand her down.

"Look at that!" the taller of the women said. "Passin' her down like she's a fine lady." And they both laughed.

Wiley kept hold of Sally's hand and turned toward the women. "This is my wife, Sally," he said to them, an odd note in his voice. "And, Sally, this is Susan and Betsey."

"Or, as we call them," came Micajah from behind them, "Honey and Tunney." He too laughed. "We could call you Sunny, with the color of your hair."

Sally stared around at the four of them. Only Wiley's expression remained stiff, though he too forced a laugh. "But — who are they? Your sisters?"

At that, all four truly did laugh, long and heartily. Sally stared at them, face heating, the pressure in her breast building yet again.

"Sisters," the shorter of the two women said, wiping her eyes. "Oh, aye. Susan and I are sisters, sure enough."

Somehow, the sniggering tone to her voice belied the words. Sally held her tongue, and turned her gaze to Wiley.

Her new husband. Who somehow had not thought it worth mentioning that two other women lived in the same cabin as him and his brother.

His own laughter died to a mere chuckle, though his mouth still pulled wide in a grin. "Susan and Betsey are, ah, aye, they're family." He stepped to the side of the wagon and pulled out one bundle, handing it to Sally, while Micajah lifted another and a basket that Mama had carefully packed with

30

supper items. Before Sally could respond, he handed it off to the women, who squealed and whisked inside.

Sally did not move. "Who are they, Wiley, truly?"

He drew his shoulders back and gazed at her with marked belligerence. "I told you. Family." His eyes flicked to Micajah, who leaned against the post by the porch steps, arms folded.

She looked from one to the other. "Is one of them — your wife?" she finally ventured, to Micajah.

His lazy smile widened. "Aye. My wife." The ugly features split in a full grin, aimed Wiley's way, and her new husband shocked her with a chuckle before taking her elbow.

"Come on, Sally." Wiley directed her up the steps, as Micajah brushed past them on his way to lead the horse and wagon to one of the outbuildings.

Sally was not sure at all that she wanted to go inside, but his hand on her elbow gave her no choice.

The interior of the cabin lay in as much disarray as outside, if not more. Over at the table, the two women chattered, but quietly, over the contents of her basket. "That is —"

"For our supper?" Wiley finished, with a

little smile.

Sally stood in the middle of the room, gazing around. Besides the table, flanked by two benches, a pair of rope-strung bed frames stood against one wall. A thin, stained tick adorned each one, with a blanket or two. Assorted clothing hung on hooks or lay in piles. She swallowed, and could hardly catch her breath. *Lord God in heaven, what have I gotten myself into?*

CHAPTER TWO

June 1798
Campbell's Station, Tennessee

"Five hundred pounds of sugar, two hundred coffee, six bolts of muslin, and twenty spools of thread. Three pairs of lady's gloves. Two copies of *Gulliver's Travels*." Jed Wheeler, the wagon master who'd brought their latest delivery, scratched his jaw and, blue gaze glinting, fixed Rachel with a hard look. "You sure you can sell those all the way out here?"

"People have need of education," she said. "Did you bring any other books?"

"Aye," he said slowly, "but Reverend Carrick claimed them already."

"Ah." Of course the Presbyterian minister, seeking to establish a university, would receive priority over a lowly frontier station.

"I have my doubts about those gloves as well."

Rachel looked up from the list she was

compiling for his next trip, and flashed a smile. "We pay you to bring the goods, Mr. Wheeler, but is selling them not our business?"

Behind him, the eyes of the wagon master's lanky son widened, despite the teasing note in her voice, but his father only laughed. "That it is, Miss Taylor."

She chuckled along with him and went back to her list. "Now then. Where are you headed from here? To Charlestown or Savannah?"

The older man set his hip against the tailgate and folded his arms. "Actually thinking of making the trip to Philly this time. Anything in particular you want or need from there?"

"Ooh." The possibilities were endless. She glanced over at Daddy, just emerging from the back of the post building, with an unfolded letter in hand. "Mr. Wheeler says he may be going all the way to Philadelphia. What would we want most for him to bring back?"

Her father stopped, blinking behind his spectacles before the dark eyes narrowed. "Let me think on that a bit. In the meantime —" He lifted the letter and fluttered it. "Dan and Anne are requesting your presence a little sooner than expected, Rachel.

But likely better now than once winter sets in."

Rachel clutched her list and pencil to her middle. "But I'm not yet ready for the journey. And who will escort me? You can't yet get away."

Pa rubbed his bearded chin as Mr. Wheeler opened his mouth to speak, but it was his son Isaac who snapped to attention first and sputtered, "Why, we could carry her up the road to Cumberland Gap and over, couldn't we, Dad?"

Going that route was still a novelty, since opening the year before last to wagon traffic, and the boy had obvious wanderlust to be fed in the process.

"Mebbe," Mr. Wheeler said, evenly, as if he didn't care, but Rachel had already seen the twinkle in his eyes.

It was a done deal, she knew.

Preparation took surprisingly less time than expected. Mr. Wheeler expressed his willingness to stay an extra day, beyond the accustomed rest of the Sabbath, but Rachel had been planning this so long that packing was a rather quick affair. And Sunday meeting afforded her the opportunity to say farewell to nearly anyone she might wish.

Except . . . Sally.

After her wedding a year ago, Sally had

attended Sunday meeting more and more seldom. The perplexity of her family over such a thing was obvious — and at first it was said that the distance must simply be too great, but then the looks became more pained, and the questions died to whispers.

Rachel herself had thought little of it — living on the frontier often meant occasional attendance at best. And she'd heard that Sally's new husband and brother-in-law were doing brisk business, supplying John Miller with sheep and hogs for meat.

Then came the day when Sally visited the Taylors' trading post, and while looking at a display, shied like an unbroken yearling at Rachel's approach. But when Rachel threw her arms around her, Sally held on, trembling, like she was drowning.

"My dear friend! What is it?"

"Oh." Sally drew back, her once-bright and direct gaze falling, shifting, going anywhere but to Rachel's. "It is — nothing. Truly. I am — well."

With her hands still on Sally's shoulders, Rachel peered into her friend's face. "You don't seem well. Is aught amiss?"

A better question would be, *What is amiss?* She knew this.

Sally glanced past Rachel. Her face went pale, then her blue eyes met Rachel's, wide

and imploring. "Pray for me. Please. Just —
pray for me."

Her hands pressed Rachel's for but an
instant before she scuttled away, to where
Wiley stood near the door, with an expression somewhere between distress and a
glower.

And in the months following came the
whispers — that Big and Little Harpe's
business was not entirely on the level. News
of one neighbor's barn burning down, then
another. Occasional glimpses of Sally were
never without the presence of two other
women, one tall and gaunt and the other
smallish like Sally — and as the weather
grew colder, the tall woman wore the unmis-
takable blue cloak Rachel had given Sally as
a gift.

Why that seemed more troubling than
anything else, Rachel could not say.

She'd not been able to get close enough
to Sally after that for conversation, but some
said that Big Harpe had himself married.
And then, closer to summer, it was said the
Harpes had all simply disappeared.

*God in heaven, keep her safe, wherever she
is.*

Benjamin Langford stepped inside the tavern and scanned its close, dark, smoky interior. The object of his search sat at a table over by the far wall, the angle at which he leaned in his chair and the way his arm encircled the tankard giving away just how long he'd been there.

Without a word, he marched across the room, hauled his cousin up by the scruff of his coat and one arm, and dragged him outside.

Thomas knew better than to do much besides twitch and sputter — at least until they were outside. There, he shook himself free and, between glares, straightened his coat and brushed off his breeches. "Blast it all, Ben, why must you be such a killjoy?"

"For the same reason I'm always tasked with fetching you, I suppose." Ben folded his arms. "I like it no better than you, but you refuse to listen to anyone else."

"So what is it this time?"

"Your father bids you home."

Thomas released an actual growl.

"What? You know he isn't well. Have some consideration for your own sire."

His cousin continued to glare, weaving now on his feet. "Just because you are his

38

namesake, you think you can push me about?"

Ben had the strongest desire to roll his eyes — or just thump his cousin insensible and save himself the trouble. "You're cross only because you've drunk too much." Or more honest about his true feelings because of it, but his normally cheerful cousin often grew morose with too much strong drink.

At least whenever Ben appeared.

"And my father summons me." Thomas's voice took a mocking edge. "Or so you say."

"In truth," Ben said. The exasperation was beginning to erode his patience. "He is not well and wishes to speak with you."

"More like, he has a task he wishes accomplished, but will not discommode you." Thomas sighed noisily. "Very well, let us be on our way. Now, what might I have done with my horse?"

"You walked," Ben answered evenly, nudging his cousin into motion.

"Ah. So I did. How convenient."

Thomas wobbled, and Ben took his arm more firmly. "Steady now. And you wonder why I feel the need to come after you."

"I don't wonder," he muttered, but Ben let it go unanswered.

Perhaps another bit of honesty seeping through.

They arrived back at the Langford town house with no further incident. Thomas's mother, Henrietta, a petite, plump woman dressed in the latest high-waisted fashion, her hair carefully curled but covered with a proper pinner cap, met them, clucking over Thomas's unsteady state — which was much improved by the walk. "Your father is in the garden," she said at last, and despite her warm smile to Ben, he could read the worry and dismay in her features.

A quick embrace and buss on the forehead did much to soften the look, however, and then he followed after Thomas.

A stone path weaved amid the sculpted hedges, red now with autumn, banks of lilies artistically placed to seem as though they'd sprung up on their own, and clumps of still-fragrant herbs. At once like the gardens he'd wandered during his year in England, and yet unlike. Near its center, bending to smell a lone white rose bloom, stood his uncle, "Pitt Ben," the graying sheriff of Pittsylvania County, Virginia. Thomas stood a few paces off, shifting from one foot to another, hands sliding into pockets.

At least he had the good grace to be ill at ease.

Ben held back, but his uncle straightened

and beckoned him closer, all the while regarding his youngest with obvious frustration.

"I have been considering, Thomas, what you told me you'd be most interested in doing with your life," Ben's uncle said.

Thomas straightened, just a little. His father definitely had his attention.

Clasping his hands behind him, Ben's uncle walked back and forth a few steps. "I have been concerned for Mary and the children, since Richard died. She assures me that her situation with her brother-in-law Judge Todd is yet beneficial to all of them, but, as a father, I'd like more than her letters for reassurance. So, Thomas, I have decided to approve your request to travel to Kentucky, on the condition that you first visit your sister and write me immediately regarding anything she may need." He fixed the young man with another hard look. "And whatever you do, aye, look for a situation for yourself. Perhaps your brother, Stephen, will take pity on you and assist you in finding something."

"Thank you, Father," Thomas said, in tones of astonishment.

"And you." The penetrating gaze swung toward Ben. "As much as I would prefer your accompanying him, I think it best to

41

send you a little after. That is, if you are willing."

Ben found himself with the urge to fidget as well, as his uncle's words only seemed to lend credence to Thomas's assertion that he was the favorite. "I am," he answered mildly.

Thomas, of course, only shot him a baleful glare. "Told you," he mouthed.

But it was to Thomas that his uncle turned and ushered away with a hand upon his shoulder, strolling down the flagged pathway toward the house. Ben lagged behind, allowing them their privacy.

There were things he'd wanted as well, truth be told. Some of them involved venturing west, and exploring that vastness referred so often to as "the Wilderness," populated by wild animals and even wilder men.

And that included white men as well as red. Perhaps even more so.

Ben absently patted the pocket of his coat, feeling the crackle of the letter inside. *"There is great need for law on the frontier,"* Hugh White had written. Half raised on the frontier himself, yet with a strength and gentility to rival anyone in Ben's own family, his school chum spoke often of his beloved Tennessee while they attended law school together, and how he longed to return and serve the folk there. Ben envied Hugh's vision and passion. Could he himself find a sense of purpose out there in the wilderness, at least something greater than looking after a wastrel cousin?

He snorted softly and watched said cousin and his father tread the path ahead of him. Hugh had also alluded to a particular feminine personage he found particularly worthy of notice — a veiled hint, no doubt, that Ben should also find her of interest. Perhaps if Thomas settled upon a place and occupation out in Kentucky, Ben might find the leisure to go and see what Hugh found so interesting. He surely wouldn't have any such luxury until then.

The Tennessee wilderness, north of Knoxville
It had been a warm enough fall day, but evening was coming. And doubtless with it, the frost.

And there might be rain.

Please, Lord, don't let there be rain.

As if God would listen to her prayers. He hadn't seemed to be paying any attention at all this past year and more.

Sally drew her knees up closer to her chest, and wrapping her arms around her legs, curled as tightly as she could. A bed of moss and leaves softened the timber floor,

43

and tucked here in her little nest, surrounded by brush, she could almost pretend
she was yet a child, innocent and carefree.

Before Wiley. Before any of the Harpes,
and the mockery they made of marriage.

A flutter in her lower belly startled her.
She flinched and looked down. It came
again, first the sensation of something tiny
brushing against her insides, then — a most
definite *tap, tap-tap.*

Oh. Dear Lord, it's true.

A rush of emotion flooded her — panic,
joy, terror, elation — and wetness flooded
her eyes. She'd known for weeks, with the
cessation of her monthly woman's time, that
she was likely with child.

Whose, she could not say.

A wave of nausea, hot and heavy, rolled
over her, with the memory of Wiley's voice,
cursing.

*"She's mine! You agreed it would stay that
way."*

*"I agreed to no such thing. We share.
Everything. As we shared Honey and Tunney.
And in return I keep us safe. Do not forget the
Cherokee. Or Dunn."*

*More cursing, such as Sally had never heard
in all her born days. "You are a filthy son of a
slave, Big."*

Micajah's smile was slow and terrifying.

44

" 'Twould be sad to leave your little wife a widow."

Wiley caught his breath then released one last curse before turning away.

"See? It's better this way. You still have a chance at getting a child on her for yourself."

He didn't only take her — but he did it in plain sight of everyone, with muttered endearments borne on what felt like the hot breath of hell itself.

After, she dragged herself outside to the necessary and heaved until only bile came up.

And after, Susan and Betsey were nicer to her and began to include her in their conversations.

She was truly a Harpe now, they said. And at least Wiley had been her first. He was the gentler of the two.

But woe be upon any of them if they conceived a child. A baby's life would be worth nothing, especially to Big. When the men weren't about, the women slipped her seeds that they promised would keep her barren. It must have worked, because their courses came as expected all through the first fall and winter.

But then, come spring, their supply of seeds ran out. And there was no time to find more — or think about what to do instead

45

— because the men came home from selling hogs, all in a lather, ordering them to pack up. While Sally scrambled beside Susan and Betsey to gather what they needed, the men left again and returned with a brace of horses. Fine ones.

Sally knew they couldn't have been purchased honestly.

In less than a day, then, they launched into the wilderness, headed straight north from Beaver Creek, on a path so faint and narrow it could hardly be called a track — but Big and Little seemed to be familiar with it, and to have no hesitation about wherever they were going.

The cabin they'd left behind seemed a mansion now.

Just a few days later, it became apparent that someone was in pursuit. A mounted party led by men Sally thought she recognized overtook them, and in the scuffle, Susan and Betsey dragged Sally away into the brush. "Naught to do now but hide," Susan muttered, as they found a place to huddle together, deep under cover of the wild forest.

And here they'd been, for three days. Susan insisted the men would be back. She and Betsey talked of finding their way northward, to Big's father, Old Man Rob-

46

erts. Sally contemplated slipping away southward, to her own family, and something of her thoughts must have shown on her face, because Susan looked at her then leaned in and hissed, "Don't even think about running away. He'll only find you again."

Sally didn't have to ask who "he" was.

But Susan couldn't stop her from at least thinking about it. Or wishing she could have one more conversation with Daddy and Mama.

"Be a good wife," Daddy had admonished her, *"and he'll be good to you."*

If that was true, she must be doing something horribly wrong, for Wiley to treat her so. Maybe she only needed to try harder to be what he wanted.

Maybe then he'd have found her worth fighting for, and wouldn't have just handed her over to Big.

And now — here she was, with child. What would become of them?

The thoughts were still swirling, back and forth, ebb and flow, like floodwaters on the river, pulling her along with a strength she could not deny, when Big and Little reappeared.

Just as Susan said they would.

Both filthy and reeking, yet possessed of a

47

strange, dark jubilation. They'd escaped from Tiel and his men — just slipped away out from under the posse's noses, Micajah crowed.

Sally doubted that detail but dared not question it.

The men had next gone to a tavern west of Knoxville, intending just a drop of refreshment, but wound up in a scrape. Wiley proudly displayed a knife wound to his chest. "Take more than this to bring down a Harpe," he growled.

Sally fussed over him as the two men continued their story, but what had begun as merely a tall tale fell sharply into horror.

"Johnson sure willnae ever rat on us again," Micajah said, laughing, his Scots brogue thicker than ever.

She could no longer bear listening and walked away into the forest, limbs shaking so that she could hardly stand. Heavy footsteps followed her.

"Sunny," came Wiley's voice, but she refused to turn.

His hand came down on her shoulder, hard and painful, yanking her around. His face was cruel and thunderous.

"Dinnae you be walking away from me," he said at last, in menacing tones. "Dinnae you ever walk away." When she didn't reply,

48

he went on, "You are my wife. Part and parcel of this."

"Am I still your wife?" she whispered, barely above a whisper. "You handed me over to your brother."

He leaned in close. "Which makes you even more part of this."

Oh, he stank — and of something more than hogs and man-sweat. It was blood and death, she was sure. But when she turned her face away, unable to bear the smell, he grabbed her jaw and pulled her back again.

"Look at me, Sunny."

"My name is Sally. And you stink."

His fingers squeezed until she thought her bones would crack. "I dinnae know what kind of fancy you thought you was getting here, but we are man and wife before any court in the land, and before God Himself. You cannae get out of this."

She pulled in a long, slow breath, lifted her eyelashes to meet his furious gaze, and gathered every ounce of her courage. "You are not the man I married. And God would not approve of your use of me."

With a growl, he let go but only to backhand her. She fell, a squeal escaping despite her best attempt to muffle it. She tried to scramble away, but he overtook her, both hands rough upon her body.

"I'll show you 'use,' " he snarled, and proceeded to prove just how futile were her thoughts of escape.

CHAPTER THREE

December 11, 1798
Moddrell's Station, Kentucky

Rachel tucked the shawl more tightly about herself against the chill lingering at the edges of the room, stacked high with goods, and went to peek out the window at the gathering clouds, bringing evening gloom earlier than usual. There'd be snow tonight, unless she missed her guess. The air held the cold tang of it.

Out at the hitching rail, a man was dismounting, and glancing this way and that, tethered his horse before heading for the door of the trading post. Rachel reached for the broom beside the window and started sweeping. It was always better to appear busy when folk walked in, but she'd perfected the art of observing from the corner of her eye.

Well dressed and young, with an open, handsome face, the man surveyed the interior of the trading post, his gaze lingering for a moment on the chess game taking place over by the hearth — or perhaps it was the fire itself he looked at so wistfully, before bringing his attention back to her with a bright smile and widening eyes. "Good evening, miss! Who might I have the pleasure of addressing?"

Oh, one of those. Rachel could feel the pinch at the edges of her own smile as she pretended to be startled by his regard. "I am Miss Taylor. My brother owns this post, but I've been helping these past several weeks."

"Well. You are not the first businesswoman I've encountered upon this journey, but you almost certainly are the most comely."

He favored her with an admiring glance from head to toe, which she could not help being all too aware of, despite the effort to appear distracted. She shot him another small, sidelong smile. "Thank you, sir."

He beamed as if he'd done her some grand favor. Rachel shifted away, under the guise of sweeping, and indulged a small eye roll.

But she must remember her manners. "How can we help you, sir? And who might you be?"

He looked around again before leveling

that smile upon her once more. "I am Thomas Langford, lately of Virginia, but I am here to survey the situation in Kentucky and visit my sister with an eye to settling, for myself."

The name struck her as familiar, but in the business of trade, and out here on the Wilderness Road, people came and went with such frequency that it was impossible to recall when and where the connections might be. "Welcome to Kentucky then," she said mildly. "Feel free to browse our goods or warm yourself at the fireplace." She tilted her head toward the men at the chess table.

"Thank you, Miss Taylor." He hesitated, seeming awkward for the first time. "I was wondering if you might recommend a place of lodging hereabouts. The last one I stayed at was — less than desirable, in the quality of food or accommodations."

"A common dilemma here on the Road." She leaned on her broom, the smile a bit less forced this time. "There's a respectable enough ordinary here, but it's small and stays pretty well filled up, even this time of year. I hear, though, that Jim Farris's tavern, just down the road a piece past Hazel Patch, on the Little Rock Castle River, is a solid establishment. Good food, and beds as clean as can be expected." She flashed him

53

a teasing grin.

He blinked and looked a bit dazed. Rachel sighed internally. She did not need this green youth going all calf-eyed over her. No matter how rich or hopeful he was.

She returned to her sweeping, and he wandered over to the fireplace, spreading the tails of his coat to the heat as he peered between other men's shoulders at the chess game in play. The others greeted him with gruff voices and moved aside. Within minutes, he was talking and laughing along with the rest of them.

He seemed a bright enough youth, and would likely do well for himself here on the frontier.

She swept the entire aisle, then over by the door, and gathering her sweep pile, carefully caught that into her dustbin. She'd just go toss it off the side of the porch —

Out the window, over across the road, a flash of blue caught her eye. Rachel leaned to look more closely. It was indeed a woman swathed in a cloak, in the company of two men and two other women, with a pair of rail-thin packhorses in tow.

Sally? Here?

Still holding the dustbin, she dashed to the door and outside, then to the edge of the porch as the group trooped on down the road. "Sally!"

It was not the figure in blue who stopped and turned, but one of the other women, ragged and wrapped in a blanket.

Rachel's pulse stuttered. "Sally?"

The blanket fell a little, revealing a face she thought she recognized, but thin and pinched with obvious fear and doubtless the cold. A flash of recognition, even of hope, then one of the men and the woman in blue snatched her arms and dragged her along.

December 12, 1798

It was a cold morning, after an even colder night. As every night before, Sally slept only from sheer exhaustion, curled against Betsey, both of them shivering under the lean-to they'd cobbled together from fallen branches. It wasn't even full daylight before Big and Little hustled them out of the woods and back on the road.

"My feet are so cold," Susan said. "Big, could we mebbe find a tavern and stop a bit, just to warm ourselves?"

The taller man threw her a glare and lengthened his stride. Beside him, Wiley yanked the leads of their poor, thin pack-horses, forcing them to a faster walk.

"Please, Big."

Sally would not grumble or argue with

the request. Although, how did Susan have room for complaint, after claiming the beautiful blue cloak Rachel had given her?

Rachel. A pang rippled through Sally's breast. What a shock, to have seen her old friend, all the way out here — and worse, to be seen by her, in this condition —

"And slow down a little," Betsey chimed in. "We can't go that fast."

Micajah turned, his expression thunderous, and regarded the three of them. "Waddlin' like ducks, you are."

"It's y'all's fault we're this way," Susan snapped.

Was it Sally's imagination, or did something in Big's expression soften, or at least flare to pride?

Despite the pinch of hunger, her stomach rolled.

But it was true, they did waddle. Susan and Betsey a little more so, being a bit rounder than Sally.

They trudged up a hill and crested the rise to the growing sounds of a settlement, and a river rushing over rocks just beyond. Sally stopped, one hand on the small of her back, stretching a little. Encountering other folk at all these days seemed a matter of both surprise and dread.

Micajah and Wiley also stood for a moment, looking this way and that, then Micajah led off, making toward the sign of a tavern as if it had been his idea all along. Sally let herself sigh, quietly. Perhaps in addition to letting them warm themselves before the fire, the tavernkeeper would be kind enough to offer a crust of old bread, or even the rind of a ham. Folk generally were kind, all across the wilderness. Some more than others, true, but none would dare refuse hospitality to travelers in need.

Which always worked to their advantage, Wiley said with an ugly laugh.

Sally swallowed back the sudden bitter taste in her mouth and tucked the blanket more tightly about herself.

FARRIS'S TAVERN, the sign said. A paper tacked to the door announced it as a meeting place for travelers along the Road, encouraging them to not travel alone but wait there for others, so to form a larger party for the purpose of safety against robbers and savages.

Sally glanced about her guiltily. Sometimes those two were one and the same. Would she never escape this nightmare?

She trailed after the others, head tucked, as they tramped across the porch. The warmth enveloped her as she stepped inside and shut the door carefully behind herself.

Silence fell for a moment while Big and Little glanced about the common room. Then, "Good morning, and welcome!" came a hearty male voice.

"Morning," Big answered, and the rest of them echoed.

They did, after all, know how to mind their manners in company.

Susan led the way to the wide hearth, where a cheerful fire blazed. Sally thought she might die of bliss, soaking the heat into chilled hands and feet and — well, everything. She stood for a moment, hands extended, then turned and carefully bunched the back of her skirts to get the full effect on her lower legs.

A young woman was just unloading platters of johnnycakes and a rasher of bacon onto the sideboard. The tavernkeep stood behind a counter, reaching for a brace of earthenware mugs on a shelf. "Help yourselves to breakfast! Will you have ale with your meal, or coffee?"

"Oh, we've no money," Big said, "so we'll just warm ourselves and be on our way."

Sally knew the melancholy tone was completely put on. But it had the intended effect — while the tavernkeep looked perplexed, a young man in new-looking clothing sauntered over. "That's no trouble.

58

I'll pay, and happily." He gave a nod to the tavernkeep. "Set them all a cup of their choosing."

Sally swayed a little on her feet. A real meal, and drink, at a table. They'd been scrabbling for food for so long, having to content themselves with game roasted over a fire in the open woods. Occasional hospitality they enjoyed, but it always startled her.

"I am Thomas Langford, from Pittsylvania County, Virginia," the young man said, beaming as they all lined up at the sideboard. "Our good hosts are Jim Farris and his daughter-in-law Jane. And who might you be?"

"We air the Roberts family," Micajah said, speaking for the group as he always did. "And we thank ye for your generosity."

Mr. Langford's gaze skimmed them all, but his smile remained undimmed. "Are you traveling up the Wilderness Road? I'm headed to Mount Vernon primarily, but am in need of companions on this lonely road. I'd right enough welcome your company."

A fresh pang rippled through Sally's breast at the young man's jovial smile and bright eyes. She too was so innocent and trusting, once.

They seated themselves around the table,

the women shedding outer wraps and the men setting rifles and tomahawks on the floor or against the table, and fell to like starving creatures. Which, by all accounts, they were.

Mr. Langford, himself eating at a much more leisurely pace, regarded them with wonder. He pulled a flat bottle from the inner pocket of his coat and took a sip. " 'Pon my word, it warms my heart to be able to share breakfast with such appreciative folk."

Big and Little both shot him wolfish grins, but Sally kept her chin tucked.

"You may come with us, and welcome," Big pronounced in grandiose tones.

"Excellent!" Mr. Langford tippled from his flask then held it out to Micajah. "Care for a drink?"

But Big just gazed at him impassively, as if he'd offered a bowlful of grass and asked him to partake.

A memory, from days before, flashed across her mind's eye. Two other travelers, glad for their presence, sharing a campsite for the night. Setting out with them the next morning. Then Big and Little, coming up behind each of the men, the pop of gunfire and billowing smoke from the shots, and the men went down in the road. . . .

The hot and painful beating of her own

heart. *No . . . oh, no no nononooo . . .*

The johnnycake in Sally's mouth turned to dust, and the bacon in her fingers dropped to her plate. Susan and Wiley shot her sharp glances, and she covered the fumble with a wipe of her fingers on the tablecloth before reaching for her cup. She'd chosen coffee, but even that tasted like ashes as it wet the dry crumbs in her mouth and swept them down her throat.

The road was astonishingly wide and well traveled, with ruts that bespoke scores, probably hundreds, of wagons pulled by various draft beasts, but what amazed Ben the most was the trees. Huge, graceful, bending and singing in the breeze, even with leaves fallen. And such leaves — large and colorful, lying in drifts across the hillsides, beneath thickets of some tall, abundant bushes. Ben knew already from his study that these were either mountain laurel or rhododendron, and he wished it were spring already so he could see them covered in blooms.

Even so, with winter fast approaching, and a brisk wind under gray skies, Ben was in love. Majestic trees standing guard over the steep, rugged hillsides. Craggy mountain-tops with breathtaking views of valleys and

61

farther hillsides. Caves tall enough for a man to stand in, nestled among the crags and hollows — some visible enough to beckon a traveler with promise of mystery and adventure. He'd turned aside from the path more than once to investigate, and not found himself disappointed yet.

And the deep quiet, aside from the patter of Ivy's hooves as she kept as fast a running walk as the road would allow, broken only by the occasional flutter of a leaf or bird, or a squirrel foraging in the leaves. A crow called, distant and echoing, then was swallowed up in silence once more.

Ben drew a deep lungful of the air, clear and cold, and slowly let it out. It reminded him much of home, in Virginia, and yet more rugged. More — wild. Much more.

Regardless of what Thomas did, he just might settle here himself.

He'd ridden through Cumberland Gap just a couple of days before and currently was not far from what the map told him was the Rock Castle River. After an indifferent stay at a rather ill-kept ordinary, he hoped the next station had better accommodations, because aside from the cold, he'd rather camp in the open than face another establishment such as the last.

The road snaked along beside a creek,

made its way up the side of a hill, and emerged on the other side, nearly without warning, above a small station. As he descended the hill, he could see nothing that denoted a tavern or ordinary, but one largish building held a placard that read, TAYLOR'S POST. Perhaps he could turn in here and find directions at least.

He tethered his mount to the rail in the company of a rangy brown thing that barely lifted its head at the presence of his bay mare, and tugging off his cocked hat — a relic from his late father's Revolutionary days — he pushed open the door and stepped inside. A warm, cinnamony fragrance wrapped him about, and the cheer of lamps well situated to provide the best advantage of the light they offered.

A group of men clustered about the hearth over to the right, and behind a counter stood a tallish man about his own age, dark hair grown long and pulled back in a simple tail at his nape, and with a thick but well-combed beard. He conversed with a pair of Indians in threadbare but embroidered coats over leggings and moccasins, while a woman set a platter of small cakes nearby. Ben's stomach gave a sudden growl.

As if she'd heard it, the woman's attention swung toward him. Abundant dark hair, of a shade so closely matching the man's that she must be a sibling and not wife, lay piled in an untidy knot that yet managed to look elegant, the wisps framing a strong, squarish jawline, and lending a wistfulness to equally dark eyes. Her gaze swept him head to toe and back in a moment, and a full mouth pursed ever so slightly.

Now what about his appearance could possibly draw such censure? He offered a half smile and walked toward her.

"Welcome," she said, tipping her head, expression barely warming. "What might we help you with today?"

"I'm in need of information — and supplies for my journey, I suppose, since I'm here."

A dimple flashed in her cheek, and her chin lifted. "And I suppose we might be able to offer some of both."

A grin pulled at his mouth. "First, where might I find a good supper and lodging? And second, I seek my cousin, a young man, rather well to do, named Thomas Langford of Pittsylvania, Virginia."

Recognition and thoughtfulness sparked those dark eyes. She gave a little nod. "He stopped by just a few days ago. And you are his cousin, you say?"

"Aye, Benjamin Langford, of the same county." He lifted an eyebrow. "And you are?"

He asked it more out of courtesy — and perhaps to meet that element of challenge in her demeanor — than from genuine interest. And she took it equally impassively. "Rachel Taylor, of Knox County, Tennessee. My brother Dan" — she tipped her head toward the man behind the counter, still deep in conversation with the Indians — "owns this post, but for many years I've helped my father run trade at Campbell's Station near Knoxville."

The sudden realization of connection swept away any other comment he might have had on that. "Knoxville, is it? Do you happen to know a Hugh White?"

A genuine smile, if slow, curved her lips at that. "Who from Knoxville does not know Hugh? But, yes. I am well acquainted with him."

He studied her for a moment. A sober, sensible dress of brown, long of sleeve and neckline modestly draped in ivory linen, yet modishly cut in the latest high-waisted styles and a slight pouf at the shoulder. And the smile, even as she regarded him curiously in return, transformed her from eye-catchingly pretty to stunning.

65

"White and I studied law together in Pennsylvania," he said. "In fact, I have a letter from him, inviting me west to visit. I've been much occupied with other business, however."

To his astonishment, color rose in her cheeks, and the dark eyes flew wide. "Langford," she murmured. "No wonder the name seemed familiar. Hugh mentioned you, at my dear friend's wedding summer before last." She laughed a little, as if in apology for the fact.

Consternation turned to the first inkling of suspicion. Could it be — no, that would be just too incredible for belief, if this Miss Taylor was the one that White had hinted he should meet.

"It is, indeed, most remarkable that we should encounter each other here, up north of Cumberland Gap, on the Wilderness Road," she added, laughing again.

Well. Perhaps not so incredible after all. "Remarkable indeed," he answered. "I can scarce believe it."

If this truly was the female White had written him about, it was no wonder he had found her worthy of notice.

Cheeks still burning, Rachel tucked her head and smoothed her skirt with both

66

hands. "My apologies. You must think me very odd."

Why she cared about such a thing, she could not fathom. Except that she found it most unsettling, the way he studied her, half smiling, as if he knew something he would not admit, but found it more pleasing than expected.

The feeling went both ways, if so. She'd not expected him to be so — pleasant — either. And it ought not matter that she found him easy on the eyes, with brown hair framing his face in slight waves, and blue eyes that caught the lamplight and twinkled in a countenance somehow both scholarly and rugged, the strong jaw clean shaven with otherwise unremarkable and even features.

In short, he looked as she might expect of a dandy from the East who'd studied law with Hugh White, and yet — more interesting. Both buckskin breeches and long coat, with cavalry boots, were travel stained but of a good cut, mostly practical for the frontier. Rachel caught herself wondering how he'd look in hunting shirt, leggings, and moccasins.

She could still hardly believe that of all the places across the frontier, unbeknownst to either of them, he'd happened upon her brother's trading post while she was here.

It must be the sheer incongruity of it that tied her tongue and snarled her thoughts, because suddenly all she could think to do was turn and indicate the platter she'd just brought in, and say, "Would you like a cake? And perhaps some coffee?"

The boyish grin returned, his eyes lighting even more. "Both would be most appreciated. If it would not trouble you, given that you are not a tavern or ordinary here." He glanced around, seemingly for the first time, but his regard was curious rather than critical.

She waved for him to help himself to the cakes, but he waited while she weaved around the men at the hearth to the coffeepot they always kept warming and poured him a mugful of the steaming but likely too-strong-by-now brew. He cradled the cup in one hand, scooped up a cake with the other, and had just taken a sip and a bite when the door swung open and another man stepped inside. This time, a greatcoat over a hunting shirt and leggings bespoke this visitor's having more time in the wilderness than Mr. Langford.

He stepped to the hearth to warm his hands then turned his head to address the room at large. "Been another murder up the Road. Y'all heard aught about it?"

Instant quiet fell, and even Dan looked up this time. "That's what — the fourth in a month or so? Not at all uncommon for this area of the country, but —"

"Waal, they's saying this one is connected to a ragged bunch that passed this way but a few days ago. Two men, rough lookin', and three women, heavy with child."

Recognition tickled yet again at Rachel. *No . . . truly this time it could not be . . .*

"Victim is a man they say goes by the name of Langford. Thomas, or Stephen, or somesuch —"

Rachel's body went cold, and Mr. Langford wheeled toward the speaker, his face suddenly and completely white. "Which is it? Thomas or Stephen?"

"Thomas came through here a few days ago," Rachel said, though she'd already passed that information to Mr. Langford, his cousin.

"Stephen owns a bunch of land up around Mt. Vernon way," one of the men playing chess said, slowly. "And I remember that lad, passin' through the other day." He exchanged a glance with the other men. "Did seem a mite green to survive the frontier, now that I think about it."

Mr. Langford edged nearer the group,

69

looking hard at all of them, but setting his gaze at last on the man who'd brought the news. "Tell me all you know about this, please. Thomas Langford is my cousin."

The man gave him a pitying look. "I'm right sorry to hear it. Man's body was found stripped and right butchered near the Road over past Rock Castle River yesterday. Bunch of drovers said their cattle was shyin' at a particular part of the road, so they's went to investigate and found the body. Jim Farris went up to help identify it, said young Langford was staying at his tavern a coupla nights before —"

Rachel's knees went soft, and she half-fell against the counter. That was the very tavern she'd recommended to the younger Mr. Langford.

The man by the hearth continued his tale. "Farris said Langford was waitin' on more travelers, you know, like folk rightfully oughta. But the travelers what come along — these two men and their pitiful-looking wives, although what kind of men would keep three women and use them in such a way —" He spat into the fire.

Rachel reached for a chair. The image was branded on her mind of Sally, pulled along between Wiley and the other woman — the woman wearing the cloak Rachel had given Sally.

Her heart hammered in slow painful beats. For that cheerful, bright-eyed young man to meet such an end . . . and for Sally to be tangled up in such a thing . . .

She looked up at Mr. Langford, standing transfixed, the mug still gripped in his hand.

"They're organizin' a posse," the man at the hearth was saying. "Farris says he's no doubt those two rascals are responsible, ill-favored as they were, and lookin' so closely at young Langford while he was payin' for breakfast, flashin' his money about and all."

"I want to join," Mr. Langford said, his voice near a growl.

The man gave him a long look. "Well, won't do you any good to go tonight, and you'd be placin' yourself in grave danger as well, under the circumstances. But Farris's Tavern is an easy half-day's ride from here. Tomorrow's plenty of time."

Mr. Langford glanced about, as if undecided as to his course, and Rachel found her strength and voice again. She rose from her chair. "I don't see any reason why you shouldn't lodge tonight with our family, Mr. Langford." His gaze shifted to her and he started to shake his head, but she hastened to add, " 'Tis the least we can do for a

71

friend of a friend, in your grief." She swallowed. "And — I have a request to make of you, if you'll be riding out with the posse."

CHAPTER FOUR

Thomas, murdered. He could not believe it.

He *would* not believe it, until he saw evidence.

And yet the certainty that his careless cousin had met a terrible end soaked into his very bones, stealing all rational thought.

Merciful God, what shall I tell Uncle Ben?

He'd say nothing until he'd further investigated the matter.

Miss Taylor led him through the smallish back room of the trading post, stacked high with goods on one side and empty crates on the other, to a staircase that led to a tidy apartment above. A young woman, dandling what looked to be a newborn babe on her shoulder, peered at him with wide and frazzled eyes while Miss Taylor explained, but her smile was kind once she understood her sister-in-law's request on Ben's behalf. "You are welcome, of course, and no mistake. We turn away no one on the Road, if

73

we can help it. And friends are always welcome, no matter the need."

Ben sketched her a bow. "That's very kind of you, Missus Taylor. I'll not forget your hospitality."

She dipped her head in response and patted the baby's back. "What a terrible thing, about your cousin. I am so sorry to hear of it! Kentucky is less wild than it once was, but travelers must still be wary."

He nodded. That fact was well known.

Miss Taylor directed Ben to set his baggage over by the hearth then helped her sister-in-law lay the trestle table for supper, and while Ben stood, wondering if he should offer to help, Daniel Taylor came through the door and approached, offering his hand. Ben shook it.

"Your horse is well tended for the night," Taylor said. "I'm most regretful to hear about your cousin, and you are welcome to share whatever we have."

"Thank you," Ben said, and meant it more deeply than he could say.

Taylor took the baby from his wife so she could finish with supper, and shortly the meal was set upon the table. Ben sat down with them, taking the seat next to Miss Taylor at her invitation. " 'Tis but simple fare," she said, but surveying the venison roast, sweet potatoes, winter squash, corncakes, butter and jam, he shook his head.

"On the contrary, this is as fine as any I've seen offered in stations along the Road so far," he murmured.

Finer, perhaps, for being given in simple hospitality, and in light of his fresh grief.

In his cradle, the baby began to fuss. Missus Taylor sighed and rose from her bench. "He always knows when we're about to eat." She shot Ben and the others a tired smile. "Pray continue without me."

Picking up the little one, she tucked herself into the rocking chair in the corner and prepared to feed him. As Ben straightened in his seat, Miss Taylor's gaze lingered fondly on mother and babe before lifting to his as she reached for the platter of corncakes. "Do you have family, Mr. Langford?" She faltered, her cheeks coloring. "I mean, aside from your cousin, of course."

He took one of the cakes and passed the platter to her brother. "If you mean a wife and children, Miss Taylor, I do not." He accepted the bowl of squash, fragrant and dripping with butter and nutmeg, and spooned some onto his plate before speaking again. "Thomas was the youngest of a rather large family, all of whom are married and moved away, and his father and mother

75

were kind enough to stand in for my own, who died several years ago. I was their only surviving child."

He stopped, holding the sweet potatoes this time, spoon in hand, and swallowed back the thickness of his throat. Pray God these tidings would not fell his uncle and aunt.

A light touch landed on his sleeve, and he looked from Miss Taylor's small but square hand to her gaze, full of moisture. "I am so very sorry for your misfortune," she whispered, her voice cracking. "And unfortunately what I have to share may make it worse yet."

Her brother frowned, cutting a bite of his venison. "Are you talking about Sally?"

Miss Taylor nodded. Her brother's expression deepened to a scowl. "I knew those fellows could be no good." He shook his head, once, before popping the chunk of meat into his mouth. "Can't understand what Preacher Rice was about, letting Sally marry that one."

"From what Hugh said," Miss Taylor said, "it was — needful."

Another shake of the head. "Figured."

Miss Taylor glanced up at Ben. "A year ago last June, my good friend married the younger of the two men they suspect killed your cousin. Hugh and I stood up for them."

Ben laid down his knife and fork. "That was the wedding you spoke of earlier?"

She nodded, stirring her squash with the tip of her spoon but making no move to eat. "Nothing seemed greatly amiss, at first — other than they courted and married in about, oh, six weeks' time, but such things aren't unheard of on the frontier." She flicked him a glance. "Next we know, the older brother had married as well, but what times as they'd come to town, it would be in the company of Sally and two other women." She hesitated. "Word got around, early last year, that the brothers — Micajah and Wiley Harpe, they're called, though they often go by Big and Little — were doing a bit too well in their hog-selling business. Folks' barns burned mysteriously. Then one of our neighbors found his horses missing and tracked and arrested the Harpes, only to have them disappear into the wilderness. A bit later, we heard of a murder west of Knoxville — gruesome bit, that. Some said it was done by the tavern-keep at a particular rowdy groggery in the area, while others said it was the Harpes, who'd showed up there a few days before and gotten themselves into a scrap. The Harpes themselves disappeared, until —"

She drew a deep breath. "I saw them, not a handful of days ago, passing through the station here."

Her brother lowered both hands to the table. "You didn't tell me that."

"There was nothing to tell," she said, her voice somehow at once thickened and sharp. "It was late evening and I was sweeping the floor, but caught a glimpse of the cloak I'd given Sally for a wedding gift. It was blue," she explained to Ben. "No missing it — nor mistaking Wiley and Micajah. But when I called out to Sally, it wasn't her wearing the cloak at all, but one of the other women. Sally herself turned around — she'd only a blanket to serve as wrap against the cold." Miss Taylor's voice broke again. "Wiley and the woman wearing her cloak grabbed her and forced her along before she could say aught to me."

Taylor returned to cutting his meat, but more slowly. "There were three other murders on the Road as well, all within the past few weeks. I wonder if they're connected."

Miss Taylor's already-pale cheeks went even more bloodless, and her eyes shut tightly. "I'd not thought of that."

Ben looked at her, and at her brother, and the spread before them. Over in the corner Missus Taylor rose, tucking the babe into his cradle, and returned to the table, but no one else spoke or moved for a moment.

With a sigh, Ben lifted his fork and dredged it through the sweet potatoes. "You say your friend's father is a preacher?"

With the question, everyone else was back in motion. Miss Taylor nodded stiffly but still did not take a bite. "Of the Baptist persuasion. They were but recently come to Knox County as well, but folk have been hungry to hear the Gospel. And well they might, with how wild Knoxville herself is."

He shook his head slowly. It was nearly beyond comprehension. Not only Thomas falling to such a fate, but a young, innocent girl entrapped in such a situation.

"Baptists are known to be a lively bunch," Missus Taylor said.

A slight smile curved Miss Taylor's lips. "They are. And it is, if I might say so, a refreshing change from those stern Presbyterians." She cast Ben a quick glance. "My apologies if you are yourself a Presbyterian. Some have even said, though, that it served Preacher Rice right, teaching a way that alters from the tried and true, to lose a daughter in such a way."

Ben chewed and swallowed a bite of venison. "Rather mean-spirited of them." He'd refrain from specifying his own denominational leanings in the moment.

"But true enough to human nature," Mr. Taylor said.

"Very true." Ben took a bite of squash. "So, Miss Taylor, you mentioned a favor."

"Aye." She straightened a little, her eyes lifted to his once more, imploring. "If you ride with the posse, and — you do catch up with the Harpes — please tell Sally that — that I am still praying for her. If," she added softly, "you have the opportunity."

"I will make every effort to see that I do," he said. "And — I'll also do what I can to see to whatever needs she has."

The color came back into her cheeks. "Thank you."

After dinner, while the women cleared the table and washed dishes, Ben helped Taylor carry up water and haul in wood for the night and next morning. "Please, call me Dan," his host insisted. "No need for formalities here, and under such circumstances."

They stoked the fire, and Ben bedded down in front of the hearth, with extra blankets offered him by Anne Taylor. With a last glance his way, Rachel Taylor lingered in the doorway of a side room that was apparently hers. "Good night, Mr. Langford."

Did the lack of formality extend to her as

well? "It's Ben. Please."

Her dark eyes widened a little, then with a nod, she disappeared inside and closed the door.

He stretched out and lay for a long time, staring into the near-darkness, listening to the settling of the building and the wind howling outside.

Ah Thomas! What last predicament did you put yourself in that was your undoing? And was it something I could have prevented had I been there?

Rachel readied herself for bed, her hands going through the motions of undressing to her shift, then taking down her hair and brushing it, while her heart continued to beat painfully and her stomach did tiny flips at the thought of the terrible end Mr. Langford's cousin had met with.

And Sally . . .

Oh Sally.

Could any of this have been different if Rachel had prayed more? Harder?

And why hadn't Sally asked for help?

As quickly as that thought came, Rachel shivered. There was not only Thomas Langford but the matter of those other recent murders. And all the barn burnings that had taken place around Knox County not long

81

before Rachel had made the journey to stay with Daniel and Anne.

It was possible Sally hadn't felt safe confiding in anyone, under the circumstances.

The tears came then, and Rachel pulled up her quilt to stifle the sound of her weeping.

When Rachel rose the next morning, their guest was already up, his things neatly piled near the door, himself seated next to a fire stoked and ready for the day, and a pipe in his hand. He looked up from his contemplation of the flames as she crossed the room. "Good morning, Mr. Langford," she said, softly.

Sounds of the baby fussing came from the next room, but neither Daniel nor Anne had made an appearance yet.

He nodded and lifted the pipe. "Good morning. I hope you don't mind —"

"Oh — not at all." The fragrance of pipe smoke reminded her of Daddy.

"And I believe I asked you to call me Ben."

Measuring roasted coffee beans into the grinder, she threw him a thin smile over her shoulder. "Then I expect you should call me Rachel, given that we're thrown together as friends in such an unexpected way." Her smile faded, and she applied herself to turning the crank. "I hope you slept well."

She looked up to find him suddenly beside her. "Well enough," he said. "Might I help?"

"Oh, I've — got it. But thank you." She angled him another look, one that she hoped conveyed sympathy if naught else. "Ben."

He watched her grind the coffee with nary a flicker across his grave, handsome features. "You and your family have been very kind," he said, softly, once she had finished.

A lump rose in her throat. "How could we not? Hugh spoke very highly of you, and any friend of his is a friend of ours." She fought for more words. "And this — this must be unspeakably difficult for you."

His blue gaze held hers for a moment before he turned half away and leaned against the counter. "I cannot help but wonder, if I'd been there —"

She tapped the coffee grounds into the pot and laid her fingertips lightly on his arm. "If what Dan said is true, and those other murders are also the Harpes —" She clenched her teeth on the words. *Oh Sally!* "Well then, they killed two men, or several, and likely would not have hesitated even were it both you and your cousin."

A muscle flexed in his cheek, but he made

no further comment.

She poured in water and went to hang the kettle over the fire.

"What else can you tell me about these Harpes?" he asked.

Thinking, she measured out cornmeal and reached for two eggs out of the stoneware bowl on the back of the counter. "They weren't the wildest around Knoxville, by a long shot. At least — not at first. They wagered a heap on a horse race earlier in the year and lost. I'm sure that didn't help their humor any, but those two were both so ill-favored . . ." Rachel bit her lip, stirring. "I often wondered what Sally saw in Wiley. She went on about how sweet he was, at least before they were married. After . . . I suppose it's telling that I've only had occasion to speak with her once since."

"Once?"

Rachel nodded. "We thought it was just how far out they lived from the station, but they never even came to Sunday meeting. This from someone who made a big to-do about getting baptized a few weeks before their wedding."

Mr. Langford blinked with obvious surprise. Rachel carried the bowl of batter to the hearth and knelt to position the cast-iron pan in the coals. While it heated, she

84

sat back on her heels and sighed. "I suppose, looking back, it makes more sense now. The Harpes likely never were God-fearing folk. But Wiley played a good role, making Sally's family think so." She waved toward the countertop. "Could you bring me a spoonful of bacon grease from that crock up there?"

A look of confusion slid across his face, but after a moment's hesitation, he found what she'd asked for and carefully scooped some with a wooden spoon. She thanked him and put the dollop into the warming pan, angling the spoon so the rest would melt off.

Mr. Langford crouched on the other side of the hearth and watched as, when the bottom of the pan was coated, she poured batter for corncakes. "So, they've been accused of stealing horses and other livestock. Suspicion of arson. Suspicion of murder, already." He chewed the side of his cheek. "White — Hugh, that is — mentioned the law out here is tenuous at best, but I presume there are courts at the county seats, at least?"

Rachel sniffed. "If you could call it that. Knoxville has so much to contend with already, but horse thieving and a murder certainly make everyone sit up and take notice. Although, both there, and out here, seems there's a shooting a week, from one thing and another."

Their guest continued to look thoughtful. "That platter on the table, please?" Rachel said. "And the spatula, where you found the wooden spoon."

He fetched both without hesitation.

She turned the cakes and slid them off onto the platter as they finished, then poured more batter as Anne emerged, carrying the baby, and came to stand at the hearth. Rachel greeted her sister-in-law with a smile. "Thank you," Anne said. "I'd intended to be up and about before now, but little Jesse was especially restless last night."

She gently bounced the infant, and Rachel glimpsed the beginnings of a grin on the baby's face. "It's no trouble, honest and true."

Dan came out as well, and Ben joined him in bringing up more wood and part of a slab of bacon, which Rachel set to slicing and frying in between batches of corncakes. The men sat to partake of breakfast. For a moment Rachel missed the conversation between herself and this stranger who suddenly was not such a stranger anymore. Although, he'd likely want to be on his way very soon.

His errand was most pressing, and she was but one personage on his journey, after all.

Such a sober meal, and yet satisfying, Ben had never experienced before. Simple fare, yet prepared with obviously expert hands. Ben found himself watching Miss Taylor — *Rachel,* although it felt too familiar to say so — with fascination. None of his acquaintance but servants handled cooking with such ease, and this young woman had a sharp mind and good understanding to go with her industrious hands. A tender heart as well, for this friend of hers who had fallen into such unfortunate circumstances.

The four of them were at table together but a short time before he and Dan Taylor pushed back their plates, but Dan seemed in no hurry to leave his chair. "I've a need to get downstairs and open the post for the day," he said, fastening a searching look on Ben. "But I'm thinking we've a greater need to pray before you go any farther on your journey."

"I'd be most grateful," Ben said, and it was the truth.

They all properly bowed their heads, and Dan prayed, taking his time with deep, thoughtful tones, his words not read from a book but no less heartfelt, asking the Almighty's provision and protection and guidance over Ben and those who would be seeking the men responsible for his cousin's demise.

After, Ben thanked the Taylors and went to collect his baggage from the door. To his surprise, Rachel trailed behind, with corncakes and bacon wrapped in a cloth. "These are for your ride. And . . . I'll walk you out, if you don't mind."

Minding was the least of his thoughts, but he'd not say it. "Thank you most kindly, Miss Taylor."

A smile glimmered at the corner of her mouth.

"Rachel," he amended, and ignored the warmth rushing into his face.

She led him back down the steps and out to the stable. Leaden skies were only just beginning to lighten in a winter's dawn. In less than a week, it would be the shortest day of the year.

Fitting, for how his heart felt, facing the task at hand.

Ah . . . Thomas.

Miss Taylor scooped Ivy a fresh armload of hay while he packed away the provender she'd offered. "What a beautiful creature," she murmured. "What breed is he — or is it she?"

Ben reached for a brush to smooth away the night's roughness from Ivy's russet coat before he saddled her. "She's what they call an American Horse. Her dam was a Narragansett Pacer. Beautiful single-foot amble, very smooth under the saddle. Ivy inherited both of those."

Smile widening, she stroked the mare's nose and neck. "Ivy — how lovely." She left the horse and fetched a scoop of oats, pouring it into the feed bin at the corner of Ivy's stall. "Extra for the journey," she said, almost as if in apology. "With our compliments."

"You are entirely too helpful." Setting aside the brush, he slanted her a glance and reached for saddle and blanket.

The answering smile she flashed held a bit of an edge. "What, should I not extend hospitality as I can? Or should I be merely decorative and useless, here on the frontier?"

Settling the blanket in place on Ivy's back, he laughed, despite the day's somberness. "Obviously not. And your generosity is much appreciated."

A frown flitted across her lovely features. "I must confess, however. I feel — somewhat responsible."

He stilled, holding the saddle in both hands. "What?"

No hint of humor this time in her glance. "I was the one who told him Farris's was to be recommended as lodging."

"You could not have known," he said, too quickly, and his voice roughening. He cleared his throat and lifted the saddle to its place, then bent and reached under Ivy's belly to grab the cinch. "Besides, if it's the Jim Farris of whom I know, another cousin of mine and Thomas's is wed to his son."

It was her turn to go completely quiet. He glanced over while looping the latigo through the ring on the end of the cinch, and to his consternation, her eyes welled.

"Miss Taylor." He dropped the strap, mid-pull, and leaned toward her for emphasis. "This was none of your fault. You'd no cause to suspect anything amiss, either with my cousin, or — or with your friend Sally."

She swiped at the tears with the back of her hand. "I know this, with my head, but my heart says otherwise."

He stared at her for a moment, as an untoward impulse rose up in him to pull her into his embrace. 'Twould be as comforting for him as her, he'd suspect, but they were of too new an acquaintance for such a

90

thing. "God is greater than our heart, and knoweth all things," he quoted.

Hope glinted in her gaze, at the truth of his words. He reached for her hand and clasped it between both of his. "I promise you again, I'll make every effort not just to relay your message to your friend, but if anything at all may be done for her, to accomplish that as well."

She sniffled and swallowed, her fingers stirring against his palm. "Thank you, ever so much." Her eyes came back to his, dark and luminous even in the dusk of the stable. "And I'll be praying for you, every day."

Who was he to this girl, that she should care? But he'd likely need every one of those prayers.

CHAPTER FIVE

Yesterday, the wilderness had been cold and forbidding, but with a wild beauty that entranced Ben. Today it held a definite air of menace. Every crackle of leaves brought his head around, and every fellow traveler earned second and third glances, with suspicion layered generously into casual greetings to strangers.

The station on the Little Rock Castle River came into view, and Ben easily found Farris's Tavern. His gut clenched. This — this was the last place Thomas had been seen alive. If indeed the reports were true, that is.

And he was about to find out.

He swung down from Ivy, looking about. It was yet full daylight, with a handful of folk going about their business. They eyed him with the same suspicion he'd been regarding others with all day — and was doubtless regarded with in turn.

Slinging his saddlebags over one arm, he stepped onto the porch and took off his hat before entering. A middle-aged man in shirt and waistcoat over worn breeches stood near a sideboard, setting down a tray of sliced breads, but the abruptness of his turn toward Ben betrayed an unease as well. "Welcome, traveler," the man said, but with no hint of humor. "Come in and warm yourself."

Ben nodded with a word of thanks, and set his baggage and hat on a nearby table before approaching the hearth. "Jim Farris, is it?"

The man didn't even blink. "Aye."

"I am Benjamin Langford. Cousin to Thomas Langford, who lodged here recently, and I believe to your daughter-in-law Jane as well."

That did bring a response — instant stillness on Farris's part, and a sudden paleness of his otherwise ruddy countenance. "I — deeply regret — have you already heard the news?"

Ben nodded. "I have. I'd appreciate hearing your telling of it though."

"Of course." Farris turned toward the back of the room. "Coffee, or something stronger? I'll be but a moment."

"Coffee is fine, and much appreciated as well."

To the sound of the man's retreating footsteps, Ben put his head down and sighed.

So, it was true.

A pattering footfall came from the rear of the building, and a light, feminine voice. "Ben! It *is* you!"

He looked up to see the pale but glad face of Jane as she ran to throw her arms around him. With a little laugh, he embraced her in turn. "It is, indeed. And how are you faring, my cousin?"

"I —" She caught her breath and stepped back from him, a shadow falling over her gaze again. "I am well enough. But so very grieved over Thomas!"

"Aye, 'tis why I've come. I was supposed to be meeting up with him soon."

Her hands knotted in her apron. " 'Tis so terrible, what happened. But Papa Jim said he'd tell you all that."

And here came Farris now, bearing two steaming cups of coffee. He handed one off to Ben then reached for a chair and indicated Ben should sit before grabbing another for himself. Jane whisked the platter of sweet bread off the sideboard and offered that to Ben before taking a slice as well and settling nearby.

Farris sipped his coffee, regarding Ben over the rim of the cup as Ben tasted his own. "How much do you know already of the matter?"

"That Thomas met up here with a rather ill-favored group of travelers, two men and three women, and that he bought them breakfast before setting out with them on — what day was it? December 12? And that his body was found by cattle drovers and brought here."

"Found by drovers but taken to Stanford."

"Oh, my mistake," Ben said.

Farris nodded grimly. "Understandable. I went up there to help identify his body. Man by the name of David Irby was there as well, and helped in the task."

"I know Irby, yes. They were supposed to be traveling together."

"Well, Irby had gone on to Frankfort a few days before. He told me how they was particular to keep track of expenses, but that account book has not been found as of yet. Young Langford was tomahawked, and his body stripped and mutilated. But we knew him by a missing tooth, here." Farris pointed to his own lower jaw.

"That's Thomas, to be sure," Ben said

95

softly, and stared at the sweet bread in his hand.

"We buried him again — your other cousin in Stanford, Stephen, can show you where."

"Buried again? You mean — ?"

"Aye, we had to exhume the body to identify it. Cold as it is, thankfully the job wasn't as gruesome as I'd have feared, although it was bad enough."

Ben swallowed heavily. This circumstance was becoming more and more gruesome. "I thank you — most heartily — for all of that." He finished the bread, hardly tasting it, then downed another gulp of coffee before curling both hands around the cup. "The folk he left with — I met someone at a station up the way who discovered an unexpected connection and offered some clues as to who they are and where they came from."

"Oh?"

"They call themselves the Harpes. Micajah and Wiley, and they lived for a while in Knox County, Tennessee. The wife of the younger is named Sally, and is a minister's daughter."

Jane gasped, exchanging a shocked glance with Farris. "That poor thing. Who'd have thought it?"

Farris scowled. "Harpe, you say? They introduced themselves as the Roberts family. How's this other person connected?"

"It's Rachel Taylor, at the trading post by the same name. She was friends with Sally and actually attended their wedding, with a schoolmate of mine who stood as witness for the same."

"Huh. Fancy you meeting up here, under such circumstances. No more unlikely, I suppose, than you and Thomas Langford and all your connections hereabouts."

"No," Ben said, and sipped at the bitter brew, already cooling beyond his taste. "So, I was told that Thomas was careless in showing his money when paying for breakfast that morning."

Farris nodded, gazing into the fire for a moment. "He was careless in more than that, and little wonder. He'd purchased whiskey the evening before and sipped at his flask all through breakfast. Offered some to the men as well. He was very generous," Farris said with a roll of his eyes.

Oh God . . . Ben shook his head slowly. "He was ever too fond of strong drink."

"He was also quite loose of tongue," Jane added. "He'd said some trifling thing that got the other men's dander up, and which I hadn't the patience for either, but he was

97

quick to offer apology and assure me that he'd not offend me for all in his saddlebags, which was worth five hundred pounds."

"I warned him he shouldn't be so free to show all the contents of his purse. And the other travelers heartily concurred and made a great show of their gratitude for breakfast in including him in their party that day." Farris grimaced. "Just recalling how they watched him makes me shiver. I pulled him aside and cautioned him against going with them, but he assured me all would be well."

Releasing a slow breath, Ben stared into his coffee then set the mug on the hearth, leaning his elbows on his knees and covering his face with his hands.

If he'd but been here . . .

"I hope you don't blame yourself," Farris said, very quietly. "Judging by the looks of these men, they'd not have hesitated in murdering the both of you."

Straightening, Ben scrubbed his hands across his face, then up and through his hair. "His father feared this sort of thing would happen. He was to stay with Irby, or wait for me."

Farris's eyes narrowed. "He was of age and should have been sensible to the dangers."

"Not quite of age. And *sensible* never

entered his vocabulary," Ben said.

"How old was he?" Jane asked.

"Eighteen."

She tsked and shook her head. "Old enough to know, aye."

The coffee and sweet bread lay heavy in Ben's gut. *Lord God, what do I do now?*

The obvious answer was to continue with the plan he'd already come up with, to join the posse and do what he could to find the Harpes and bring them to justice. A strange task for one who'd read law, perhaps, but it felt right.

He'd not be able to face Uncle Ben unless he'd done everything he could to see these men answer for their crimes.

Not to mention the promise he'd made Rachel regarding Sally.

"What a perfectly wretched circumstance, to be sure," Farris said.

"Absolutely," Ben muttered. He almost could not bear the pity in their faces. "Is it too late then to join the posse?"

Farris shook his head, more slowly. "I think not. You'll need to ride for Stanford right away though."

Ben chewed his cheek. "And that section of the Road holds its own perils, from what I've heard."

The other man nodded.

So he could either go on his own and risk being waylaid, or wait for someone else to come, and then possibly find himself in a situation similar to Thomas's, or arrive too late to do anything useful.

He blew out a breath. "I will wait until morning and then go, regardless."

Farris nodded briskly. Jane, however, just shook her head, frowning.

Rachel woke from a troubling dream to the sound of the wind howling around the corner of the building. Seldom did she hear it, for the snugness of their log building, but tonight, when every little creak and moan put her on edge, she supposed it was no wonder.

She lay there, wide awake, listening. A tendril of light shone through a crack between the shutter — moonlight. The full would not be for several nights yet, but still it beckoned, despite the wind and chill. Rachel slipped out from under the covers and, pulling off the topmost quilt, flung it around herself then tiptoed to the window.

Easing back the shutter, she was careful to stay to the side and scan everything within sight before shifting, very slowly. The other buildings of the station, the stable, the street beyond — all were still, no one in sight, and the trees beyond the only things in motion.

Somewhere out there, in this moonlit, windblown night, was Sally. Not just in the company of very bad men, but expecting a baby soon, by the sounds of it. Had they anywhere to go? Had she a woman to be with her when her time came, besides the other two in her company?

And where was Mr. Langford this night? Had he made it safely to Farris's?

The image of his grave, handsome face rose before her, followed by one of him riding into peril, with Micajah and Wiley swooping from the forest to pull him from his horse.

She sank to her knees on the icy-cold plank floor and leaned against the rough wall below the window. *Oh Lord . . . protect them both! Let Your shadow cover Ben — Mr. Langford — as he goes with the posse. Protect them all, and lead them to these men, to bring justice to those who were killed. And deliver Sally as well.*

There she stayed, how long she couldn't tell, heedless of the discomfort, pouring out prayer in soundless, wordless feeling.

Ben rose before dawn — not a difficult thing, since once again he'd barely slept,

101

and sunrise came late during the winter. Gratefully accepting provisions from Jane and offering his thanks to her and Jim Farris for all they'd done for Thomas, be it ever so much too late, he set out from the tavern. The wind remained brisk, after rattling the shutters of his window all night, but the sky was clear, with a few stars still standing against the lightness growing in the east. After packing his saddlebags and securing them behind his saddle, he pulled his hat down low, snugged his greatcoat around his neck over the woolen muffler, and mounted Ivy.

"Be safe," Farris said, from the back door the of the tavern.

"And, please, take no foolish chances," Jane added. "You'll be in my prayers."

"Thank you," he said with warmth.

Prayer might just be all that preserved him on this journey.

He set Ivy's nose to the road and set off at a brisk pace.

This morning, the sense of peril was stronger than ever. Up until two days ago, the patter of Ivy's running walk was nearly a song. Now it held only the rhythm of impending danger. He needed to get to Stanford as quickly as possible, and her unique gait naturally provided the easiest and best way to accomplish that, but how would he ever hear an approaching attacker?

He loosened both of his horse pistols in their saddle scabbards and kept a hand resting upon one of them. Such a stance was like to become tiresome, but beyond constantly surveying the road ahead and woods all around, he could think of no other defense.

Perhaps it was a foolish venture to want to ride with the posse, but again, he could not return to Uncle Ben with such tidings and not do all in his power to see these men brought to justice.

God, protect me, indeed.

It was thirty miles and a bit to Stanford, Farris had said. An easy ride for Ivy, with her amble. And she was handling the roughness of the road with no difficulty at all.

A short distance out, he and Ivy forded the main branch of the Rock Castle River, and a little after that, at the edge of a ravine, he drew Ivy up short to gaze around. Here, Farris had told him, describing the spot in great detail, the drovers had found Thomas's naked, mutilated body, at the bottom of the ravine. A terrible thickness rose in Ben's throat, and his eyes burned. He scrubbed a sleeve across his face, and still the wetness came.

Oh Thomas. Would that it had been me instead. Or even that I'd fallen beside you, because then I wouldn't have to tell your father that I'd failed to look after you.

Ivy tugged at the bit, and Ben gave her her head, letting the cold breeze dry his tears before they fell.

As dawn broke over the hills, the clouds cleared, leaving the sky a pale blue above a sun that managed to be brilliant despite winter's chill. Before long he passed through Spout Springs, where his cousin and Thomas's older brother Stephen had surveyed for a settlement they were already calling Mt. Vernon. He followed the sign to Langford's Station, a little off the road and into the wilderness, stopping at a tavern there to inquire, but as he'd suspected would be the case, Stephen was not there — he was either guiding emigrants somewhere along the road or at his home in Stanford, farther on.

Around midday Ben passed Stigall's Station and, by his reckoning, would soon be nearing Crab Orchard. Fellow travelers were not as plentiful as he might have liked, and he dared not linger with the two he overtook who were traveling in his direction, with the need to reach Stanford as soon as he could. For the most part, Ben let Ivy keep the brisk pace she'd chosen. But at last, in a stretch of small, rough hills not far beyond Stigall's Station, flecks of sweat marked her shoulders. He slowed her to a fast walk and leaned to pat her neck.

Just ahead, the road cut close to a river, with a narrow track leading down to the water's edge. He turned Ivy aside and to the riverbank to water her. At this pace, they'd easily reach Stanford by nightfall, and perhaps he could ask Stephen for supper and lodging before setting out with the posse.

Ivy put her head down, plunging her muzzle into the current, blowing noisily under the surface and drawing a laugh from Ben. He patted her neck again while she drank deeply, shifting a little, ears pricked.

Her sudden leap sideways nearly unseated him. Gripping with his knees, he looked to where her attention focused, ears flicking back and forth, nostrils dilated.

There was nothing — no sound, no sight amiss —

Two men rose from behind a boulder that seemed hardly large enough to hide one. Shaggy, ill-dressed, rifles in their hands with tomahawks dangling from their belts, and a bow and arrows strapped across the body of the tallest. A bolt of fear like lightning shot through Ben's body, head to toe.

God — no! Save me!

With astonishing swiftness, the bigger man stepped out onto the road ahead, while the other angled toward Ben's rear.

Ben turned Ivy's nose, heels in her side, and hissed, "Hie!" Straight into the freezing current she plunged, the icy shock of the water taking away his breath. Please, God, that this riverbed be mostly level and not the rocky treacherousness he'd seen elsewhere — but it was either the risk of Ivy breaking a leg or surrendering himself to being butchered as Thomas was.

Because by all descriptions he'd heard, these two were none other than the Harpes themselves.

Two cracks sounded, in quick succession, and a splash on either side attested to how narrowly the shots missed him. Still Ivy pressed on, half galloping, half swimming, until her hooves found purchase on the other side — and then it was straight into a stand of cane, taller than his head, even mounted, which whipped cruelly at both of them.

They burst out the other side. Ben drew Ivy to a prancing halt, listening over her labored breathing and the pounding of his own heart. Were they pursuing? A crash and rattle from the other side of the cane would seem to indicate so.

This time, Ben sent Ivy galloping for the nearest hill and up, between the boulders and through the patchy cover of rhododendron or some other brush. Two more cracks came from behind him, and the whine of a ball to his left. He flattened himself on Ivy's neck, standing in the stirrups and clinging to her mane as she bounded and scrambled up the rough incline.

Up, up, and over. He dared not let her stop, though he could barely guide her and ought to at least try to keep as many trees as possible between them and their attackers.

Another set of pops echoed from below. Splinters showered them as they passed a hickory, but they'd gained the ridge, and Ben could collect the reins and direct Ivy down into a small hollow.

He pulled her up short once more. Blast it, he'd lost his father's old hat, but he'd sure not go back for it. A faint rustling and crunching came to his ears. He picked a direction, down through the roughest part of the hillside, and set Ivy in motion again.

Down a long hill with tangled underbrush, which Ivy forged bravely through, up a short draw, and over another thickly wooded hill, where a view spread before him of a river bottom, mostly wooded with a small farm in the distance, smoke curling from the chimney of a cabin. At the foot of the hill lay a narrow road, nearly a path, and Ben turned Ivy upon it.

And still she kept going, putting all her heart into the gallop he asked of her, with never a hesitation.

The trace appeared to roughly parallel the river, so Ben stayed with it, stopping only where it crossed a small creek to let Ivy drink and rest while he consulted his map. It hadn't enough detail to be helpful, but it seemed to him, if the river had been on his right, and he'd left the road and turned north and then a little west, that the road should be on his left and they would at least parallel it, if not intersect it again at a certain point.

Folding away the map, he nudged Ivy across the creek and on down the trace. They should be far enough away now that two men on foot could not follow. Not with him leaving the road and forging on where there was no path. Not with the hot pace that Ivy had kept.

Even so, Ben could not keep himself from scanning the hill on one side and the fields on the other.

A cabin came into view shortly. Ben

turned aside and called out, "Halloo the house!"

As a dog barked, one of the shutters eased open and the muzzle of a rifle poked out. "What you be wantin'?"

"Only to ask how far it is to Crab Orchard, or Stanford, and which direction?"

A voice hushed the dog, then, "Just up the trail a piece. You be going the right way, over to the west."

"Thank you kindly," Ben called back, and lifted Ivy's reins.

If people hereabouts had heard of Thomas's murder, he didn't blame their suspicions. Still, it was hard to not even see a friendly face at the moment.

He set Ivy at a comfortable clip, in her easy single-foot gait, and again watched closely.

The rest of the ride was so uneventful that by the time Ben rode into Stanford, halfway through the afternoon, he wondered if he'd imagined it all.

This little settlement was, compared to others he'd rushed through today, almost — pretty. Although most of the buildings were log structures, not a single brick in sight.

A few inquiries, and Ben found himself

outside a house that managed to be stately despite its humble construction. Stephen was home, but greeted him with the expected blend of shock and weariness. "Come in," he said, after his initial surprise. "Do you need lodging? Aye, we've room. I'll send someone to stable your horse."

He called out, and a strapping young black man emerged from the rear of the house. He gave a nod as the task was communicated, and slipped away again. Stephen swung back toward Ben. "Come. We'll sit to dinner in a bit, but I've spirits and more to refresh you, if you wish."

"That would be most appreciated." Ben followed him down the hall.

They settled before a fire in a very comfortably appointed drawing room. Stephen offered Ben tobacco, and he filled his pipe, feeling Stephen's eyes upon him.

At last, as Ben lit the bowl by a splinter from the fire, Stephen sighed. "It's been a long time, cousin. A very long time. I'd not have known you."

Ben gripped the pipe stem in his teeth and smiled thinly. "How long since you emigrated here?"

Stephen stared into the flames. "Fifteen years since I left North Carolina." He released another heavy breath. "But I'd not go back, despite the hardships."

"I'd say you've done well for yourself if you've purchased fifteen thousand acres, in addition to your home here."

His cousin nodded. "Well enough. I was — unsurprised to hear from Thomas that he had interest in resettling here and finding his own situation."

Ben savored the sweetness of the smoke his pipe produced, then blew it out. "Your father sent me along to make sure he did not fall into trouble." He shook his head. "I failed that task, miserably, and am not happy about the circumstances in which I'm here."

Stephen thoughtfully puffed at his own pipe. "I've had concourse with my father but a handful of times over the years." The corners of his mouth lifted. "It took him, oh, a good ten years to forgive me."

Ben gave him a searching look. "For?"

The smile widened, still wry. "Come now, I'm sure you've heard the stories. For choosing the cause of the Crown over that of the colonies, of course."

Ben studied him still.

Stephen's eyes met his, ruefully. "They confiscated my lands in Rutherford County, you know. Which is why I came here." At the slow shake of Ben's head, Stephen's brows went up. "Nay? Well, that's a surprise."

"You have indeed done well for yourself then."

Stephen acknowledged the compliment with a tilt of his head. "So, this matter with Thomas." He sighed heavily again, set the hand with his pipe against his knee. "He was but a babe when I left. And my father seemed already old at that time. This news can do him no good, I'm sure." He measured Ben with his steady blue gaze. "So what will you do now?"

"It's my intent to join the search party, if it isn't too late. I'll not face your father with less than my full effort to bring Thomas's murderers to justice."

Stephen nodded slowly. "I believe they intend to leave tomorrow. I can send a message over to inquire. In the meantime, our full hospitality is yours. And I'll write my father to let him know where you are."

"While you do that, could you — no." Ben thought better of the request. "I'll write it myself, if you'll but post it."

"Of course," Stephen said. "But what is it?"

Ben turned to gaze contemplatively at the fire. "On the way, I met someone with a connection to those they think responsible for Thomas's death. I need to thank her for her prayers."

True to his word, Stephen made the necessary connection, and it was all arranged. Early the next morning, Ben rose, baggage packed once more, and handed off to his cousin the folded and sealed missive to Rachel. Ignoring the speculating gleam in Stephen's eye, he fished for a coin to cover the post, but his cousin waved him away. "I reckon I can pay for a post or two. You just do your part to bring those men in."

The posse was set to rendezvous at the courthouse, a sturdy log building in the center of the settlement. There Benjamin introduced himself to a Joseph Ballenger, captain of the local militia, a Thomas Welsh, presumably brother to Stanford's sheriff, and a handful of other men, all of varying degrees of roughness and eyeing his more refined dress. "Ya might wanter change to a hunting shirt for this ride," one said, but Ben offered him a cool smile.

"I might, on another day. But should we not be on our way?"

Ben detected a curious reluctance mingled with the eagerness in the atmosphere — and a good measure his own, he was sure. He'd lain there long after retiring the night before, reliving the incident in the forest with the two men. Were it not for Ivy's fleet sure-footedness, Ben might also lay butchered on the trail, even if those two men weren't the Harpes.

Farris's descriptions of the state of Thomas's body were enough to make him shudder, even now.

"Gather round!" Captain Ballenger's voice boomed. The man's sharp gaze fastened on Ben. "Langford tells me you might have aught to add to our search?"

Ben told the group who he was and the little he knew of the party Thomas had last been seen with — and then of his encounter on the Road, the day before. "They may or may not be the same men, but their description seemed to match."

There was as varied a response to this as men present, but Captain Ballenger scratched his bearded chin and said, "We might as well start with that then. Mount up!"

CHAPTER SIX

The ride was easy enough at first, back down the Wilderness Road, stopping to ask along the way if anyone else had caught a glimpse of the suspicious party. The other men took turns questioning Ben about this and that, and he learned names and professions and, in most cases, places of origin.

Some were as rough-spoken as they appeared, but others surprised him with their wit, understanding, and apparent education. The way Uncle Ben had spoken, everyone out on the frontier was ignorant and half wild — but since so many had emigrated from the eastern states, that could not possibly be true.

Ben was a little ashamed to think he'd absorbed that assumption, even when he thought he had not.

In matters of law, he was required to work with all manner of men. He knew already that the amount of a man's coin did not necessarily correlate to the amount of wisdom he possessed, nor gentility equate completely with pedigree. Out East, however, the lines seemed more sharply drawn. He thought about Uncle Ben, serving as sheriff of Pittsylvania County for so many years. When a matter like this one came up, he'd call on others to serve but never rode out himself. So unlike this band of men who, despite their lack of association with Thomas — except perhaps through Stephen, barely acquainted with his own brother and himself unable to ride out due to physical infirmity — were more than willing to go on the hunt for what seemed a hardened killer — or two.

He thought of Hugh White. *"There is much need for law on the frontier."* Was this a taste of his upbringing? If so, no wonder he'd appealed to Ben to come practice law here and not in Virginia.

The image of Miss Taylor's face came to his mind's eye then, dark eyes wide and shining, her rounded cheeks flushed, the strong jawline softened with a grin some might deem unladylike, but to his eye, it was fresh and genuine. Like everything about Miss Taylor. He thought of her quiet, capable industry that morning after they'd learned the news about Thomas. He'd only ever observed servants preparing a meal, and never assisted — at least not past his boyhood.

Here on the frontier, though, might it be possible to not even need servants?

That truly was an idea he'd never seriously considered — but it held much appeal.

They rode most of the morning with no word of Thomas's fellow travelers reappearing, and it was early afternoon before they reached the spot where Ben had encountered his would-be attackers.

Three of the men dismounted and, handing their horses off to others, ventured off the path, examining the ground where Ben told them the two brigands had made their appearance. Back and forth, then in ever-widening circles, but they all shook their heads. "Nothing here to judge by," one said. "I wish to God there were."

Ballenger fixed Ben with a hard look. "Are you sure this is the place?"

"Yes, I'm sure."

Ben wheeled Ivy about, took her down the path to the edge of the river where they'd plunged in the previous day, and while she drank as before, gazed across the current to where they'd made their mad dash through the cane. "I crossed over and rode away, over there — you can see marks of my horse's passage there. I was certain I heard them pursuing."

"They forded the river in the cold?"

"Well, who knows what they'd do," another countered.

Ben gritted his teeth. If they could detect no sign of the ruffians' passage, or of his encounter with them, how was he to prove helpful?

"Hie now," Welsh said, "I think I've found something."

Rachel took the bundle of letters from the post rider, handed him the ones that had been waiting the last three days, then tucked the required coin into his palm. While he examined both, she riffled through the stack he'd handed her. Familiar names, some of them, and others not —

Her own name leaped out at her, in an unfamiliar but beautiful, even hand. She turned it over to find *"B. Langford, Esq."* and *"Stanford, Kye"* written on the other side.

"Will this be all?" the post rider asked.

Rachel looked up, her heart pounding a guilty rhythm for — well, for the simple act of quickening at the sight of that name. "Sorry — aye. Did I give you enough?"

"Aye." After stowing the letters in his bag,

he leaned from the saddle, his gaze warm with an appreciation she wished was not so very familiar. "Unless — you'd wish to add a kiss to sweeten the day and speed me along."

She forced a laugh and flapped a hand at him. "Be off with you, Johnny. You know I don't give those away."

He smiled, slow and lazy. "I could make it worth your while."

Rachel stepped back. "Most emphatically not. Now go."

Holding the smile, he touched his fingertips to his hat brim and turned his horse toward the road. "One can always hope. And ask. Good day to you, Rachel!"

Shaking her head, she retreated back inside and set all but the one letter upon the counter for others to find when they came in. But hers — she found herself trembling a little, and unwilling to open it in sight of others, much less share the moment with them, so she slipped it into her pocket for later.

All afternoon, however, it seemed to burn there, and finally, stealing a moment where no one seemed to need anything, Rachel stole away, through the storage room and out the back door, where the light was already fading into evening but she could

still easily read without a lamp. She broke
the seal, red wax imprinted with an embel-
lished *"L,"* and unfolded the vellum.

Expensive stuff, for a simple note. But
then, she knew what kind of family Ben
came from. And hopefully this meant he'd
found his cousin, and Thomas's older
brother.

Stifling the sudden little catch to her
breath, she focused on the script.

Stanford, Kentucky, Dec. 19, 1798

Dear Miss Taylor,
I am writing to inform you I arrived
safely at my cousin's house in Stanford.
I have learned that it was indeed my
cousin Thomas who met such an unfortunate end.

I covet your prayers as tomorrow I join
the posse riding out to seek those suspected of his murder. Thank you for
those you have offered on my behalf
already, for they have doubtless been all
that kept me from a similar end today,
on my journey here.

A chill struck Rachel. Was that the very
next day after she'd felt such urgency to
pray for his protection — and had God

120

answered that prayer so immediately? One hand stole up to cover her mouth as she quickly read the next lines.

I do not know, of course, when I might have opportunity to write again, but I will do all in my power to keep you apprised of our progress. Your friendship is greatly appreciated at this time, and even more so for its unexpectedness.

Ever your servant,
Benj. J. Langford, Esq.

Rachel looked again at the date. Three days ago. He'd been riding about, then, for the last two. Christmas would be in three more, hence. Would they find Sally and the others before then? If not, would Ben miss being with his family?

Christmas was a quiet affair at best out here. Maybe a little *feu de joie,* more these days since the Shawnee were less of a threat, she was told. The Cherokee, now, were still something else, but even they seemed to enjoy Christmas festivities back in Knoxville — probably a little too much.

She scanned the letter again, refolded it, and tucked it back into her pocket then hurried back to work.

She'd most certainly be praying. Every

121

spare moment.

They'd found a clear trail at last. And even Ben thought he could follow this one.

It was a marvel how these sharp-eyed frontier men could discern what was amiss and what was not in the lay of the forest. From their conversation, he caught bits and pieces of what went into tracking, and though he wanted to know more, he felt it best to leave them to what they knew while they were on the hunt. And so he did a lot of standing back out of the way, holding the reins of other men's horses, during their stops to examine a particular location.

After finding faint sign where Ben was nearly waylaid, the search party had combed what seemed every square inch of wilderness between that portion of the Road and southwestward for almost four more days, finding trails and losing them again. But still they pressed on.

He'd also watched them bear the hardships of making camp with humor and a resignation that Ben supposed simply came with living out here on the frontier. He of course was subjected to much teasing about sleeping on the ground, wrapped only in a blanket with saddlebags as his pillow, but Ben assured them he was willing to endure as much as they, under the circumstances. It was true that his coat and breeches were looking worse for wear, and a casual hand across his own jaw attested to the sore lack of opportunity to use a razor.

Captain Ballenger caught him scratching at the scruff on his chin and shot him a wry grin. "Another day or two, and you might have promise of a real beard there."

Ben laughed. If such a thing would give him credibility among these men, he'd gladly forego shaving.

Today, however, on their fifth day on the hunt, there was a decided lack of humor. "Happy Christmas to us," one man muttered as they shared coffee around the fire.

Ben counted the days. Surely enough, it was. He lifted his tin mug to his lips. "And how do your families observe the day, here on the frontier?"

As they had with other questions, they narrowed their eyes at him, as if to discern whether he meant it a criticism or was simply making conversation.

"It's an honest question," he added. "If I consider settling, it's good for me to learn the ways of the folk who live here, and even if I don't — I ask out of curiosity."

"Some folk don't hold with much celebratin' at all," Welsh answered. "And those what

123

do, well, it's anything from a simple dinner with family and mebbe neighbors, to enjoyin' a bit of spirits and a feu de joie."

Ben nodded. "It's much the same where I come from, in southwestern Virginia. There's more gaiety in cities farther east, however." He offered a rueful smile. "I suppose it depends as well upon what church you align yourself with."

A few chuckles greeted his statement. "Aye, that has some to do with it," Ballenger said. "And whatever our views on church, well, we can agree that these men need to be brought to justice."

With a hearty sound of agreement, they broke camp and were back in the saddle shortly after.

It made Ben contemplate, though, where folk did sit on the matter of religion. Did people on the frontier still respect the laws prohibiting travel on the Sabbath? How many were irreverent, or were they simply more private about their faith? He suspected the latter, with how quick most were to speak of prayer, or express gratitude for offers of such.

He supposed too that their courage and determination in facing the task before them had no small thing to do with it as well.

Thank You for this company of men who

have given themselves to find Thomas's murderers, whatever their standing before You. Only — please give us favor in the actual finding! They need to be home with their families.

To his surprise, it was not long before the cry went up that fresh sign had been found of a small party's passing.

They went forward with more caution until, as the ground grew rougher and the vegetation more tangled — notwithstanding the lack of summer foliage — someone called a halt and Ballenger sent two of the men ahead, creeping through the underbrush. They returned in short order. This time everyone dismounted, and securing their horses at the bottom of a gully, all gathered up their weapons and filed up the slope as silently as they could, skirting one hill before climbing a bit, and then —

Suddenly, there they were. Five travelers, huddled around a fire built half beneath a tree, no doubt to help diffuse the smoke. With a silent signal from Ballenger, the seven men rushed the camp, arms at the ready. Ben carried one pistol but had holstered the other under his coat.

Heart pounding, he kept his place between two of the other men as they converged upon the party, lifting his pistol to sight at the bigger of the two men. Cries came from the women, and all raised their hands as they gazed, openmouthed, at their assailants.

Three women, to be exact. All obviously with child.

Ben hardened himself to that, for the moment, and kept his attention on the men. Both bareheaded, shaggy, looking as if neither had seen a comb, much less shears, for at least half a lifetime. The bigger man was of darker complexion, his hair an indeterminate black and several weeks' worth of beard obscuring rough features. It could not hide the cunning in that face, however, despite an obvious attempt to look unassuming, nor the way his gaze flicked this way and that before at last settling on Ben.

Those dark eyes met Ben's. Recognition flared. A slow smile curved the man's mouth.

Ben could not keep himself from a quick, hard swallow, and fought the urge to dry his palms on his breeches.

Lord God, You are my hope and confidence, and will keep my foot from being caught.

"You are under arrest for the murder of Thomas Langford," Ballenger was saying, while he drew out lengths of rope. With the

126

assistance of the others, he began to bind the men.

"Good morningtide to you as well," the big man said in a heavy Scots brogue, a smile still playing about his mouth.

Ballenger made no comment but turned to the women. "My apologies, but I'll have to bind y'all also."

The woman wrapped in what was no doubt the cloak Rachel had described gave a grave nod. And she was almost certainly, also by Rachel's description, not Sally.

The other men appeared to be treating the women with deference, so Ben could take his time, continue to watch and listen while he considered how he best could assist in the situation now.

And not betray how much he knew of these people, without good reason.

They performed a quick search of the ragged party's belongings and found items that had definitely belonged to Thomas — among them, the account book that Farris had mentioned. And tethered next to two scrawny packhorses, Ben recognized Dandelion, the chestnut gelding Thomas had favored, which was a half sibling to his own. The evidence was enough to confirm they'd found their men and were well justified in hauling them back to Stanford to be tried for murder.

Hands bound behind them, said men were made to walk while heavily guarded. The women, however, would be mounted on the three horses, but when the tallest, wearing the blue cloak, would have claimed Thomas's horse, Ben took it and approached the smallest of the females.

She stood back, head down, still clutching a ragged blanket about herself with her bound hands, although the edge had fallen back to reveal hair that might have been golden, or could be again, with a good washing. Ben could scarce believe any female would let herself become so unkempt.

"Will you allow me to help you up?" he asked.

The poor creature gaped at him as if he uttered a foreign tongue. Was she that unused to being spoken kindly to, or — ?

"You would prefer riding to walking, would you not?"

Her mouth closed, and her cheeks washed red. "I would gladly ride," she murmured, so softly he nearly did not catch the words.

He bent to give her a foot up into Dandelion's saddle. While settling herself, her eyes flicked back to him, suddenly sharp. "Have a care in showing me any favor. They've killed a man, before, for appearing too solicitous of their women."

The chill of her words struck where the morning air could not. He resisted the urge to look over at the men they'd apprehended. "To appear less solicitous would be ungentlemanly," he said.

She blinked then drew the blanket more firmly about herself and turned a little away. "Well, pray don't talk to me less'n you need to, at least."

He so wanted to speak, if only to ask her name and about the cloak. The woman wearing the garment was seated now on one of the other packhorses, leveling a narrow-eyed glare upon the girl riding Dandelion, behaving as though she were queen despite having her hands tied before her.

Perhaps, in this party, she was.

The shorter of the two men — and he was not small by any means, topping Ben's height by a finger or two — looked none too pleased at Ben's attentions himself. The bigger man, however, met Ben's gaze and once again smiled.

This time Ben held the look, first with one man then the other, until they were both prodded into motion by others.

Patience. He'd plenty of time to speak

with the girl.

Still, Rachel's request pressed upon him, and mounting Ivy, he let the others go ahead until only Ballenger's second-in-command remained and motioned him to take the next-to-last place in the line. Leading Dandelion, with the rest of the girl's party safely beyond earshot, Ben looked back. "Are you Sally?" he asked, keeping his words quiet.

Her head snapped up, the blue eyes wide again.

"I am acquainted with your friend Rachel."

"Rachel Taylor?" Her voice quivered, pitching dangerously high.

"Shh — you don't want the others to hear. But, yes."

Tears welled instantly in her eyes. "I — saw her. Or thought I did. Days ago, before —"

She bent in the saddle, as doubled as her belly would allow, and pressed her forehead to her fists. An answering pang echoed through Ben's breast. Glancing ahead to be sure they weren't watched, he said, "Do not speak of that here. I am only bid inform you that Rachel has been praying for you."

A strangled sound escaped the girl, and her shoulders shook with weeping.

Why? Why would God be so cruel as to send her a reminder of that last conversation she'd had with Rachel, now? When all was completely ruined?

Unless — unless He meant it as a reminder that He truly was with her, and this was not ruination but the beginning of her rescue, as she'd prayed for, herself, for so long. Could it be? Dare she even let herself contemplate it?

And how could Rachel be thinking of her, after all this time and all she'd doubtless heard of their misadventures? Sally saw the looks, everywhere they went. Knew what folk thought of them. It wasn't like Sally was fine folk before, but she'd been a good girl — until Wiley. Now she was a mere step above offal. Maybe not even a step.

She scrubbed at her face with her sleeve and straightened but could not bring herself to look at the handsome, well-dressed man leading the very fine horse she rode — a horse that Micajah had himself claimed through such foul means — and riding another that was clearly of the same quality. "How fares Rachel these days?"

"She seems well."

"Was it her brother's trading post where you saw her?"

He nodded and hazarded her a glance. "You should probably know I am also a friend of Hugh White, who Rachel tells me served as witness to your wedding."

She couldn't help it — but just found herself gaping at him. "And how on earth would you know him?"

Except — another glance at his fine apparel, and she could guess it had something to do with both of them being of society.

"We attended school together," he said, quietly.

School. Which meant —

"You're a man of the law?"

He nodded again, shortly.

She swallowed back a hard lump in her throat. Should she be heartened by this knowledge, or threatened?

"I'll do all in my power to aid you," he said, his gaze suddenly severe. "But I must have your cooperation."

And what would that require of her? To turn on Wiley? She stared ahead at him, and he must have felt the weight of her gaze, because he turned and looked back. His mouth curved in something halfway between a smile and a sneer, then his guard yanked him back around.

Wiley, who had given her away to Micajah without a fight, who she'd seen step up and deliver a killing blow with as much relish as his brother. Gritting her teeth against the sick feeling wrenching her gut, she hardened herself.

"I'll do whatever's necessary," she whispered.

Perhaps this really was the beginning of a rescue.

They arrived back in Stanford with their charges by late afternoon and proceeded to the jail, a small but stout log building located just beside the courthouse in the center of the town, right on the Frankfort Road, once called only Logan's Trace. Ballenger sent and summoned the clerk from Christmas dinner to sign the prisoners in. Ben stood by, listening, while the men gave their names as Micajah Roberts and Wiley Roberts.

"Not Harpe?" he asked.

Micajah, the bigger of the two, swung around to level a stare upon Ben. "We air the Roberts family," he said at last.

The clerk glanced uneasily between Ben and the prisoners and Ballenger, who waved a hand and growled, "Record it as Roberts for now."

Ben nodded, and the women were herded forward. The tallest stepped up. "I'm Susanna Roberts."

The other that Ben had not spoken to gave her name as Elizabeth Walker. And lastly was Sally, clearing her throat. "Sally Roberts," she said, when prompted.

The men were put in one of the jail's two rooms, about twelve-by-twelve square, women in the other. Several men set to the task, Christmas or no, of fortifying the men's side. While Ballenger oversaw the making of shackles for the two men, Ben helped see that the women's needs were tended to, a fire built and pallets brought, then stepped aside to speak with the clerk of court. The man's eyes widened when he explained not only his relation to Thomas but the unexpected connection to the situation through Hugh and Rachel.

"I don't see any reason not to allow you to sit in on the questioning," the clerk said. "I'm sure we could use the perspective of another man of law."

Ben thanked the man and excused himself to find Ballenger.

"Thank you for all your help," the other man said, giving Ben a hearty handshake.

"It's my intent to linger awhile," Ben said, "so if I might assist in any other way — ?"

"I'll let you know, thank you." Ballenger scratched his jaw. "So they're insisting the name is Roberts and not Harpe."

Ben shrugged. "Little we can do about that for now. They'll be tried either way."

"Aye. 'Tis curious, though."

At last, there was nothing more for Ben to do, and taking Ivy and Dandelion from the hitching post, he made his way to Stephen's.

Over food and a glass of spirits, Ben related the hunt to his cousin. "And what will you do now, return home?" Stephen asked.

Ben dredged his spoon through the crumbs of his Christmas pudding. "I am determined to see the trial through but would be glad to find lodging elsewhere if my presence is a burden for your household."

"Oh, certainly not! 'Twould be an affront if you stayed somewhere else."

"My deepest thanks, then."

Stephen released a long breath and sat back, clasping the handle of his cane. "I can still hardly believe this has happened. I never truly knew my brother, but . . ." His head came up. "You said they found clothing with these people, and various other articles that appear to have been Thomas's? And his horse?"

"Yes. They're sending for both David Irby and John Farris to come identify his effects and give testimony at the hearing."

"They plan to bring them before the Quarter Sessions next week?"

Ben nodded.

"Stay at least until then, and we'll see what's done."

At last, when he'd eaten and drunk, and they'd discussed all that could be, Ben retired to his bed. It was good to stretch out on a cot after several days on the cold ground, and he simply lay there for a few moments after blowing out the candle, listening to the sounds of life all about him, in murmurs and footsteps and general creaking of the house. He thought about the faces of the five they'd found that morning and brought in. About Thomas, and his quick grin and generous nature.

Lastly, he thought of Rachel, and her gift to a friend on her wedding day. If not for that cloak, he'd hope that perhaps they were all mistaken, and there was no certainty of connection at all. But — no, there it was.

Rachel. Hugh White. The Harpes.

Thomas.

And now, himself.

Sally lay curled, her feet to the hearth, her

back to Susan, who claimed the center spot between her and Betsey, when a nudge came to her hip.

She ignored it.

It came again, harder. "I know you ain't asleep."

"Leave off, Susan."

"I saw you talkin' to that man who led that horse you were ridin'. Need to be careful, you know."

"I know," she murmured. "And I told him so."

"You talked an awful lot though."

Sally sighed. "He knows two of the folks who were at mine and Wiley's wedding."

That met with a moment of silence, then, "Huh." Another silence. "Surprised he didn't tell me to give up this fancy cloak."

Sally curled more tightly, bringing her knees up snug beneath her belly. The baby inside squirmed, seeming to protest the squeeze. "I told him I'd passed it on to you, when you and Big got married."

Another soft "huh" escaped the woman. "What would you do that for?"

Mostly to not make more trouble, but Sally wasn't going to say it. And Susan's theft rankled, especially on a night such as this one.

"I s'pose you're just tryin' to make nice, if

he knows you're a preacher's daughter and all."

Sally snorted softly. "Don't make no never mind anymore what I was."

Susan gave a chuckle. "And don't you forget it."

CHAPTER SEVEN

Though the Court of Quarter Sessions was not to meet for a little more than a week hence, it was still a busy few days. Ben saw the summoning of witnesses and sat in on the questioning of the women, one by one, with his own paper and ink to hand, alongside Mr. Green, the clerk.

They brought in the taller first, who also appeared to be the older. She swept in, wrapped in blue wool as if she'd a right to it. A burn rose in Ben's throat. He didn't for a moment believe Sally's assertion that she'd gifted the thing away, so soon after receiving it herself. Her response to his mention of Rachel was too strong to not affirm more sentiment than she was willing to admit.

He'd not yet revealed his connection to Thomas to the Harpes, but most likely it was but a matter of time before someone mentioned it in their hearing. Would he even be allowed in on the proceedings if they knew he was a blood relation? Perhaps best to remain quiet about it and just say he was there as additional counsel.

"And you are — ?" asked Ballenger, seated beside Ben.

"Susanna Roberts," she said. "Wife to Micajah Roberts."

Ben studied her. Black hair, braided roughly, once-pale skin roughened, no doubt, by the cold and wind. She was not pretty, could not even be called handsome, but she smiled at Ballenger as if she thought she were.

"When and where were you married?"

"September 5, 1797, in Blount County, Tennessee."

"Do you understand why you and your husband are being held?"

She tipped her chin until she was fair looking down her nose at all three men. "I do."

Green twirled the quill between his fingers. Ballenger snorted. Ben held his peace.

"Did you help in the murder of Thomas Langford?"

She just gazed back with that maddening little smile. Ballenger shook his head, and Green bent to write again.

Ben kept his eyes on her. This one would

yield nothing, he was sure.

"Did you *witness* his murder?"

No response.

"Did your husband murder him?"

She shifted her gaze to Ben, and the smile widened. Again, as if she thought she were pretty and could somehow sway him.

He refused to look away, refused to move. Doubtless those dark eyes had indeed witnessed the hapless Thomas's last moments — but seeing justice done meant keeping himself objective.

At least in the face of the accused.

"Is there aught you require for your comfort at this time?" Ballenger asked.

Her gaze came back to the militia captain. She shook her head.

"Very well." Ballenger motioned to the guard. "Return her to the jail, and bring the next."

The second woman once again introduced herself as Elizabeth Walker, then with a coy smile, "You can call me Betsey."

Betsey was smaller and more delicate than Susanna, fair where the other woman was dark. Ranging the wilderness had not been kind to her either. Her blue eyes lacked the brightness of Sally's, and her face some of the younger girl's winsomeness.

"And whose wife are you?"

141

Her smile went almost predatory. "Either, as it suits me."

Ben's stomach turned, and the guard at the door shifted. Green's quill fluttered, then he dashed down a word or three. Ballenger sighed, more heavily than before.

He asked her the same questions he'd presented the first woman, with a similar lack of response, except that she denied having participated in the murder. Ballenger sent Betsey back and had Sally brought.

She glanced around the room once when entering then seated herself and kept both hands and gaze in her lap.

"Name, please?"

The slightest hesitation, then, "Sally Roberts."

"And you are married to — ?"

"Wiley Roberts."

Ben watched the color rise in her cheeks and noted the shudder that shook her. What must she have endured in the short span of such a union?

Ballenger must have had similar thoughts, because he clasped his hands before him and leaned forward a little in his chair. "Tell me, Missus Roberts, how did you find yourself in such company?"

The blue eyes snapped upward, wide. "I did not know he was bad until after I married him."

The militia captain tapped his thumbs together. "Did you help in the murder of Thomas Langford."

A simple shake of her head.

"Did you witness his murder?"

The woman's face went completely white, and she tucked her head.

"Did your husband murder him, or assist in the murder?" Ballenger had gentled his voice this time.

If she could have folded in on herself, Ben thought she would have.

"Would you be willing to testify against him?" Ballenger asked softly.

A tremor coursed through her, but again, she gave no answer.

The big man blew out a heavy breath. "We cannot help you if you aren't willing to work with us."

Her eyes flickered to Ben, and he gave her the barest nod. Still she kept silent.

"What of your family, child?"

Her lips parted, trembling for a moment. "My daddy — he would tell me to be a good wife and do as my husband bids."

Ballenger swallowed so forcefully Ben could hear it. "No daddy worth his salt would want you to stay in such a situation. Not when there's murder been done."

Her eyes lifted, met his, then Ben's. It was like a mask had slid over her features, for now she was calm, almost emotionless. Not with the same degree of detachment the other women had displayed, but very nearly.

Ballenger leaned forward again. "If you aren't willing to speak for your own sake, what about for the babe you carry? Do you not want better for the little one?"

Tears welled, and she bent her head once more. At last, she shook her head, scrubbing her cheeks. "I can't. They — won't let me. Susan watches me, even when Wiley and Micajah aren't around. You just — don't know how bad it is."

Ben had to unclench his teeth and force himself to take a deep breath. Ballenger was shaking his head again, and Green looked stricken.

After a long moment, Ballenger sat back. "I hope you will reconsider and let us help you." He nodded to the guard, who stepped forward to usher her from the room.

Sally rose, started to turn, then hesitated and looked at Ben, her blue gaze still swimming. "Tell Rachel I'm sorry."

"We are praying for you, still," he said.

He wasn't sure what prompted him to say that, but the words seemed to bring her comfort. Her mouth firmed, then with a

144

quick nod, she let the guard lead her away.

The three of them exchanged glances after the door shut. "Should we even bother to question the men?"

Ben shook his head slowly. His stomach soured at the very prospect. "I think not. Let us gather evidence and speak with the witnesses when they arrive, and then present all of it in court." He pushed back from the table, capped his ink, and wiped the quill while Green did the same with his own then gathered everything into his satchel. "If you need me, I'll be at Stephen's. I've letters to write."

He stared at the sheet of vellum where he'd penned the date, *"Dear Rachel,"* and nothing else. With a deep sigh, he raked one hand through his hair, slowly, massaging the scalp in an effort to relieve the ache there.

It should be a relief that they had the Harpes — or Robertses, or whoever they were — in custody. That Rachel's friend Sally was here, in relative safety, with deliverance from her situation within reach. But the cold knot in his belly would not ease, and he knew not why.

He closed his eyes, but those tear-filled blue eyes haunted him. *"They'll never let me . . . you just don't know. . . ."*

Gritting his teeth, he dipped his quill and began writing again.

I pray this finds you well. It is with mixed feelings I relate to you that we have apprehended the party of which we spoke. They claim to go by the name of Roberts, but the youngest woman is indeed your friend Sally. She is as well as can be expected, and most grateful for your continued prayers.

Quill still in hand, he scrubbed the other palm across his face.

What was he doing, trying to help a woman who could be party to the murder of his own cousin?

God . . . You are my God. My soul thirsts for You, my flesh longs for You in a dry and thirsty land. . . .

He knew that wasn't the exact wording of the scripture, but they were the only words his heart could seem to find in the moment.

Help me here. Give me the words I need, not only for Rachel but Sally as well. And — if it is possible — do deliver her from this circumstance.

Another swipe across his face, and fingers

146

through his hair, and he returned to the letter.

Her situation is precarious, to be sure. The case is to be heard next week at the Court of Quarter Sessions, and I will know more of what shall be done for her, after, but in the meantime, if I may ask a favor — please do write to her family and see if they are willing to welcome her back, should the opportunity arise.
In the meantime, I remain
Yr most obednt srvt
Benj Langford, Esq.

Rachel scanned the words, sank onto a stool, pressed the page to her breast for a moment. Sally — found, and safe, or reasonably so. *Oh Lord, may it be so!*

She read the letter again, more carefully. She would be glad to write to Sally's parents, of course. And — would it be possible for her to visit Sally, perhaps? Ben didn't say outright that Sally was in jail, but Rachel knew already, since all the news from up the road was about nothing but those ragtag travelers who had been caught and brought in by the posse from Stanford. Speculation was rife over how many more deaths might be attributed to the rough pair of men.

Some were shaping up to be more than speculation. It still turned Rachel's blood cold to think that Sally's own husband could be a murderer, not once but several times over.

And that Sally herself had likely witnessed the horror.

Ben hadn't expected to hear back so quickly, but Rachel must have written and sent her reply the moment she'd received his last letter. It came the day before the Court of Quarter Sessions was to convene, and although he might have taken the time to dash off a quick reply of his own, tomorrow would better inform him on what that reply should be.

The next morning dawned gray and somber, a reflection of Ben's own mood. He'd reminded himself a dozen times that nothing about this hearing depended upon him. These folk had proven themselves more than capable this past week, assembling witnesses and weighing evidence. At best, Ben had merely supplied confirmation of what others recognized, and yet — he could not bring himself to sit idly by and let others do all the work. Not with the knowledge of

Thomas so freshly in the earth, and the horrible state in which he was found. Nor of Sally's ghostlike countenance and demeanor since the questioning.

After the arrival of David Irby from Frankfort, Thomas's traveling companion for the first five days of their journey, and the Farrises from over the Rock Castle River, all the Robertses' belongings were once more collected and laid out, and between Irby, the Farrises, and Ben, various personal effects and articles of clothing were positively identified as Thomas's. The pocket book, where Thomas had faithfully recorded all expenditures made between himself and Irby, so that they might settle them evenly. A shirt, breeches, and short coat, marked with Thomas's name. His greatcoat, which the women had been allowed to keep until the hearing. Half a dozen other items — and of course there was Thomas's horse Dandelion.

Not a word of admission about what Thomas's fate had been, in their company. The silence alone was chilling.

Irby and Farris had written out their statements, but both, and Jane as well, were expected to testify at the hearing.

Early, before the first case was to be heard — this was a quarter session, after all, since the district court met only in April and September, so several cases were on the docket — Ben walked alone to the courthouse. On the way, he stopped to look in on the prisoners. The men were still sleeping, but the women were awake, if quiet. Sally looked up, met his gaze through the barred window, then shook her head a little and turned away.

In the courthouse, the clerk, Green, beckoned him to one of the side rooms, where three men assembled. "These are our quarter session judges," Green said, "Hugh Logan, William Montgomery, and Nathan Huston. And this is Stephen Langford's cousin, lately come from Virginia himself — and also lately admitted to the bar."

Greetings and handshakes were exchanged all around, and the men expressed their sorrow over Thomas's death and assured Ben that they would do their best to see the truth borne out at the hearing.

Ben smiled and thanked them. He wasn't sure whether such a warm welcome was due to his kinship to Stephen and the deceased Thomas, or by virtue of his own status as a man of law, but he'd accept it gladly.

After a few minutes' conversation about mostly inconsequential matters, Ben excused himself to go find a seat in the courtroom. Though he knew nothing of the other cases, he was curious to see how things were done here.

All proved to be smaller matters, and by the time they were completed, nearly all the town turned out to hear the details of the murder that had been done and whether these ragged travelers had been arrested for good reason. Stephen and his wife Lucy came and took seats on the bench reserved for next of kin, along with Stephen and Thomas's sister Mary, who had traveled down from where she had been staying with her husband's brother and family, since her widowhood nearly two years before. Ben tucked in next to Mary. Her brother-in-law Thomas Todd, also a judge and serving now as prosecuting attorney, sat directly in front of them all and nearest the bar.

The suspects were brought in and seated at the very front, on the other side from the Langfords. The five witnesses — John Farris and his daughter-in-law Jane, David Irby, Captain Ballenger, and Thomas Welsh, from the posse, were all seated in front of Ben.

With Joseph Welsh, the sheriff, accompanying, the prisoners were made to rise and file across the front before the bar. "You are charged with feloniously, and of your malice aforethought, murdering and robbing a

151

certain Thomas Langford on Wednesday, the twelfth day of December 1798, on the road leading from Kentucky to Virginia through the Wilderness. What say you to these charges?"

The voice of the big man, who called himself Micajah Roberts, rang out. "We did not do any such thing."

The others echoed his words in various ways.

With a sharp nod from one of the judges, the sheriff made the five sit back down, and they commenced with reading the written statements from the witnesses. Ballenger's told how he'd first heard of the murder on the 19th or 20th, and at the request of James Blain, the attorney general of the Commonwealth of Kentucky, organized the posse and set out to find those who were suspected of being the murderers. They'd stopped at the house of John Blain — and Ben recalled this well — where they heard that travelers fitting the description they sought had passed nearby, and roughly the route they'd taken in pursing and overtaking them. The statement went on to list the things they'd found in the party's possession that had belonged to Thomas.

Ben bit back a smile as no mention was made of the jaunt down the road to find sign of his own would-be attackers.

Next they read David Irby's statement of how he and Thomas had traveled together for five days, and how carefully Thomas had recorded their shared expenditures, and specifics of some of them, before parting and agreeing to meet in Frankfort. How Irby learned in Kentucky that Thomas had been murdered on the way, and so he turned back on the Road in order to find out more, and coming to the place Thomas had been buried, he, John Farris, and the man in charge of the burial exhumed the body and confirmed that it was, indeed, Thomas Langford.

Beside Ben, Mary gave a little groan, and Stephen's wife Lucy shook her head.

Next came the statements of John Farris, describing how Thomas had arrived that Tuesday evening, and upon hearing the young man's name, Farris recalled his acquaintance with him, from Thomas's youth in Pittsylvania County. He also noted how he'd opportunity to examine the particulars of Thomas's clothing — no doubt, Ben thought, because of the novelty of new, expensive dress from the East. A few days later, having heard of the murder and inquiring as to the circumstances, he became convinced the person murdered was his own houseguest. He went to the coroner of Lincoln County, where the poor victim had already been buried after the coroner's inquest, and in company with David Irby and Abraham Anthony, who had done the burying, raised the body and inspected it. His face might have been enough to convince him, but a missing tooth in the front part of the jaw proved most definitive.

Ben nodded. He knew well that missing tooth, and precisely how Thomas had lost it.

Jane's statement gave more details on things belonging to Thomas that were found in the Robertses' possession. She also testified to how cheerful all appeared together, and how Thomas seemed to be a little intoxicated, and of the last mild disagreement between himself and the Roberts men, where he mentioned the worth of his saddlebags.

Welsh's statement echoed Ballenger's. After his was read, the judges called upon the witnesses to add whatever they would. Both Irby and Farris described the wounds they witnessed on the body — how the skull was split, no doubt by a tomahawk, and indeed part of what helped the drovers realize there must have been violence done on that part of the Road, when their cattle spooked, was the presence of bits of bone and gore on the trail. Hearing Mary's and Lucy's sharp intakes of breath, Ben kept himself to a mere swallow against the sourness of his stomach. He knew most of these details but had endeavored to not dwell on them more than necessary.

Now, however, there was no escaping it. And if anywhere indeed it was necessary, it would be here.

They described further mutilation of the body, so that beyond complexion and hair color, it truly was the loss of the tooth that proved the key to identifying the body.

In the silence that lay heavy over the courtroom, Ben glanced at the prisoners. The five simply sat there, all perfectly still except for Sally, whose occasional tremor gave away the state of her nerves.

"Bring the accused back to the bar," Judge Huston said. The sheriff did so, and when the five stood there once more, the judge went on, "Do you still deny your involvement in these events?"

Both men nodded vigorously.

"Have you anything to offer in your defense?"

Neither one moved. Huston sighed, exchanged a look with the other two judges, and motioned for them to be seated again while the three of them conferred.

A few minutes later, Huston spoke. "It is the decision of the court that the accused be tried at the District Court in Danville, come April, and that they be jailed until that time."

There would be no visiting by Rachel — at least not until the prisoners were moved to Danville and settled there.

The court was dismissed, and the sheriff prodded his charges to their feet. Sally shuffled along between the other two women, head down, looking neither right nor left.

"Such pitiful creatures," Mary commented.

"Could they not be induced to bathe and comb out their hair, at least?" Lucy said. "Imagine, choosing to live so."

"Actually, it appears that they've done both, at least once since we apprehended them," Ben said, trying to keep his voice mild.

Both Lucy and Mary stood, mouth agape. Ben gave them a thin smile. "And perhaps such a life was not all their choice."

If only Sally could somehow be separated from the others . . .

Mary turned to her brother-in-law. "Has Stephen spoken to you about serving as prosecuting attorney for the trial as well?"

"No, but if he has no one else he'd rather have in that capacity, I would be honored to do so."

Of course it would be better for Ben to not serve in that role, for several reasons, and he held his silence, waiting until Stephen should comment on the matter.

Stephen rubbed his clean-shaven chin. "I'd no one else in mind, nay. So if you do not feel it would be too much a conflict of interest —"

Judge Todd nodded, and the two shook hands, then Todd turned to Ben. "I would, of course, welcome whatever help you are able to give."

"Of course," Ben murmured, but he'd so many conflicting thoughts in his mind at the moment, he'd need solitude and silence to sort them out before he committed himself to anything in particular.

CHAPTER EIGHT

Word carried down from Stanford of the hearing, and how on the next day, the murder suspects were moved to Danville for trial in April, but Rachel heard nothing from Ben. She tried not to fret, but her heart sank more by the day.

A letter came from Reverend Rice, with a vaguely worded response about a wife's duty being with her husband and fervent prayers offered on her behalf and Wiley's, in the expectation that the Holy Ghost would bring a renewal of repentance, if Wiley's baptism and faith were true. In great frustration, Rachel folded the missive and tucked it away among others.

It was near the middle of January, on an afternoon with a snowstorm howling across the wilderness, when a greatcoated figure stepped inside the post, borne on a gust of wind. In the middle of recording an entry in the accounts book, behind the counter,

Rachel cast the visitor but a glance, catching a gleam beneath the wide-brimmed hat and the moment of hesitation before he stamped the snow from his boots. Something in the man's movements seemed familiar, but such was the case with so many who passed through.

She finished writing the entry and looked up again as the man pulled off his hat and offered a half smile over the edge of a frost-covered muffler. A little jolt went through her. *Ben!*

With the recognition came a rush of warmth, and she hastened to tuck her quill into its bracket and cap the ink while he pulled off mittens and unfastened the greatcoat.

Dan reached him first, popping out from behind a shelf where he'd been busy with inventory. "Ben Langford! Good to see you."

They shook hands, and Ben reached up to unwrap the muffler. "I hope you don't mind, I took the liberty of tethering my horse in your stable."

"Oh nay, you're more than welcome! Will you stay the night as well, or have you other lodgings?"

He cast a quick glance at Rachel, who held back a little, feeling suddenly shy. "I would not presume . . ."

"It's no presumption," she blurted. "We'd be saddened if you didn't stay."

His smile flashed again, full and warm, and Rachel realized why he looked so altered. He'd gone from clean shaven to growing out his beard.

Was it lack of opportunity, or was he choosing to look more like the men of the frontier? Regardless, she thought the difference quite pleasing.

Not that her opinion mattered one whit.

He shook out the muffler and looked back at Dan, somber once more. "My deepest thanks. I'd be very happy to accept your hospitality a second time."

Dan grinned. "Wonderful! Rachel can help see to whatever you need, aye?" He angled a look her way, and she nodded, feeling her cheeks reddening.

Her brother disappeared again into the shelves. She turned to Ben. "I'm so sorry —"

"I am sorry —" he began.

They both stopped, laughing.

"You go first," Rachel said.

"No, please — you," Ben said.

She took a breath, finding herself noting again the slight changes a month had wrought in him. "I said so already, but I'm so sorry about your cousin."

He gave a slow nod that was half a bow. "And I am sorry I haven't yet responded to your last letter. There is" — he drew a deep breath — "much to tell you."

It was a quiet afternoon, as such happened there at the station on a winter's day, so Rachel not only saw him seated at the fire with coffee and a sweet roll, but she was able to sit down as well.

"Am I keeping you from your work?" he asked, before a hearty bite of the bread.

She shook her head, smiling a little as his eyes closed and an appreciative hum escaped him.

He chewed and swallowed, his mouth curving sheepishly. "My apologies. Today's ride seemed especially long."

"None needed," she murmured, and while he devoured the rest of the roll, poured herself a cup of coffee and added cream and sugar from an earthenware service on the mantel.

In very short order, he sat back, curling both hands around his mug. "You will doubtless want to know first about Sally." He blew out a breath. "I am not even sure where to begin."

Rachel waited, sipping her coffee.

"I did relate your message when we met.

161

She was moved most deeply. She also seemed cautiously willing to cooperate with the inquiry into Thomas's murder — and who knows how many others — at least at first. Later, however, she avowed it impossible to speak against the men, that they watch her too closely. The older of the women as well."

Ben's face appeared more drawn and grave as he spoke. Rachel could not imagine that involving himself in his cousin's murder would be anything but taxing, and the strain showed itself clearly. "Are Micajah and Wiley guilty, do you think?"

"I cannot say this in a court of law, of course, or anywhere it might be set down as record, but it does appear very likely that they committed at least this murder. Probably more." Ben sighed. "So likely that I fear for Sally, whether she'll escape conviction as an accessory." He scooted forward in his chair, elbows on knees. "It's clear she's unhappy. That she fears both men, and would wish to be free of the situation if she could. But persuading her to have enough courage to speak out . . ."

Rachel sat hunched, cup in one hand and the other folded across her mouth. *Lord God, what can we do here? How do I best pray for her?*

"Not that I blame her dread," Ben added. "There is a most unwholesome feeling around the two of them, indeed over the entire party. I actually first encountered the men myself just short of Crab Orchard."

A sound of surprise and dismay escaped Rachel, and he shot her a rueful smile. "No doubt I should not have attempted to make the journey alone, but I had need of haste if I intended to catch the posse before they set out. Only the grace of God and my very fast and surefooted horse saved me from disaster."

Rachel could only shake her head, wide eyed.

"That said, I can attest that they are . . ."

"Intimidating?" Rachel supplied.

He nodded. "Exactly so. Even for someone who does not fear anything lightly."

She supposed he was speaking of himself but didn't want to pry further. "It would be ungraceful of me to say that I never felt completely at ease with Wiley or Micajah, but —" She winced, remembering the wedding and a handful of times she'd had to do business with them at her father's post. "So, what now? Word reached us already about the hearing, and the trial being set in Danville."

He spread one hand, palm upward. "For

now, we simply wait." He looked at her as if considering something. "I'm not sure your going to visit her would serve anything, but perhaps we can arrange it, once the weather clears."

"Oh, could we? And maybe — just maybe, I can help persuade Sally —"

She stopped, thinking of Reverend Rice's letter.

"Did you hear back from her family?" Ben asked, as if he knew the bend of her thoughts.

"Aye." Rachel told him the gist of it. "You're welcome to read it, later."

Ben nodded, fingering the edges of his beard. "Perhaps . . . perhaps it would help if I wrote to him myself. I cannot see how he'd fail to aid her in whatever way possible, once he fully understood the gravity of the situation."

"I would hope. I didn't give him many specifics in my letter, but I wasn't sure how much he'd have heard before now."

"Apparently not enough."

The strength of feeling in Ben's voice startled Rachel. "I would think," she said slowly, "that you'd be most concerned for seeing Wiley and Micajah answer for their crimes, not . . . not so much helping Sally in the situation."

164

He shook his head. "I confess, I feel very torn between the two. But no woman deserves to live as she's been forced to, when it was through little choice of her own." His gaze came up, sharply. "She said to us that she did not know he was bad when she married him."

A pang echoed through Rachel's breast at the words. "No. None of us did."

Ben's eyes held hers, full of understanding and sympathy.

Once again, Ben stretched before the hearth on a pallet made from a straw-filled tick and several wool blankets. Surprisingly warm and snug, and yet — he could not sleep.

Rachel had given him the letter from Sally's father. He alternated between mentally composing a reply and wondering whether he should travel to Knox County and speak to the man himself. This was January. The trial would not take place until April. Theoretically, he had plenty of time.

He also needed to sit down and compose a letter to Uncle Ben. The older man had written, expressing shock and sorrow over Thomas's sad fate and Ben's part in it all. It was no more or less than Ben expected.

His uncle's letter did not, interestingly enough, include an appeal for Ben to come home and leave all the legal proceedings to others. Not that he would have heeded it.

The fire gave a crackle and a hiss. Ben turned over on his side and settled the blankets more firmly over himself, but his eyes simply would not shut, and he watched the flames while his thoughts swirled.

A sound behind him brought his head up. Rachel tiptoed out of her room, swathed in a dressing gown with her hair in a thick braid trailing out from under a ruffled cap and tucked inside the robe. She shut her door, and seeing him looking at her, hesitated before padding across the floor.

"I couldn't sleep," she said apologetically, "and thought I'd make tea. Would you like some?"

Ben scooted to a sitting position. "I would, thank you."

She moved to the kitchen and filled a kettle with water then brought it to the fire and hung it there to heat.

"I wasn't asleep yet either," Ben said, as she crossed back to get cups and a closed tin.

She set those items on a platter with a silver sugar bowl and carried them to the hearth. "I was hoping to not disturb you."

"Not at all."

He made himself more comfortable as she

reached for a chair. She sank into it with a long sigh, staring into the fire. "I cannot stop thinking about Sally," she whispered after a few moments.

"Little wonder, that," Ben said.

Her eyes shimmered in the firelight. Tears, which he also well understood. "I keep thinking . . . perhaps there is aught I could do to help her in all this. Certainly I must try."

Her words struck an answering echo in his heart. All those years he'd endeavored to keep Thomas from trouble — no, just from outright ruin. That he'd bring as little shame as possible upon Uncle Ben.

And now, this. After a month, he still could scarce believe it. What had Thomas been thinking, to part ways from David Irby in such wild, untamed country, where he knew practically no one and nothing about the customs of folk here? Ben himself had found it foreign enough, although not entirely uncomfortable.

Irby could hazard no guesses either, at least none that Ben could in good conscience offer his uncle. Thomas had ever been drawn to too much drink, and cards, billiards, or games of chance, where he somehow had a knack for losing varying sums of money. Irby said he'd left off most

167

of those on their journey, except for small change, and apart from harmless flirting with comely females along the way, seemed uninterested in dallying with women. So unless Thomas had planned to indulge in gambling or drink, without Irby there to say him nay, it made no sense why he'd insist on not traveling farther with the older man.

If only Ben hadn't lingered behind as long as he did. Of course, he'd little enough choice in that . . . but in retrospect, the business Uncle Ben had tasked him with was of little importance compared to Thomas's life.

"I understand your brother's reluctance to let you go," Ben said at last. "The Road is still an uncertain place, and he hardly knows me well enough for me to serve as escort. Even were it not improper for other reasons."

Rachel's gaze flashed toward him again, and she swiped at her face with the back of her hand. "I understand it as well. Still 'tisn't fair."

The kettle steamed, and she knelt on the hearth to set tea leaves into the cups and then pour the water over them. "Sugar?" she asked Ben.

"No, thank you." He accepted a cup from her, curving his hands around it. She settled back into her chair with her own. The aroma of the tea while it steeped was nearly as comforting as he was sure the tea itself would be. "Hyson?" he asked.

A glimmer of a smile appeared at the corner of her mouth then disappeared. "Aye. It's my favorite for evenings when I can't sleep."

"I can see why."

He breathed in the fragrant aroma again then looked up at her. Dark wisps framed her face beneath the proper cap. Dark lashes fanned across her cheekbones as she cradled her own cup, eyes closed. The wrapper rendered her figure shapeless, hunched as she was in the chair.

"Life is full of unfairness," he found himself saying.

Her eyes snapped open. She straightened a little, lips compressing, and blew out a breath through her nose. "I do realize that. But why should she suffer for her husband's crimes, if she had naught to do with it?" Her gaze dropped back to her tea. "I cannot believe she had anything do to with such unspeakable things."

"I tend to agree," he said slowly.

Her eyes came to his again, deep wells of distress in the firelight. His own heart throbbed in response.

Thomas, Thomas, how could you have left

us in such a predicament?

And, God, for the love of all that's holy, the young woman in question is the daughter of a minister. Would You leave Your own at the mercy of men like these?

He shifted, folding one leg and bringing the other knee up, then tasted the tea. It was, as he suspected, very good.

Rachel sighed again. "I should not burden you with this. It was your cousin, after all, who died so horribly."

It was true, yet . . . "And still God saw fit to have us meet, and share this connection." Another sip — oh, it was good — while he gazed, narrow eyed, into the fire. "What if . . . what if I offered to serve as defense for Sally at least, when they come to trial in April? Would that ease your mind at least a little?"

Rachel gaped at him. "Why would you agree to such a thing, under these circumstances?"

"Well." He wrapped both hands around the cup. "They already have a prosecuting attorney — Thomas Todd, the brother-in-law of Thomas's older sister Mary."

"Too many Thomases," Rachel muttered, mouth twitching, then buried her nose in her cup.

Ben laughed. "And Benjamins, and

Marys, and — Rachels too."

That wrung a brief chuckle from her. "So very true."

"I've no idea if they'd even allow me to serve as defense, officially or otherwise, with Judge Todd as prosecution, but I can at least ask."

Tears filled Rachel's eyes again.

"And," he went on, "I've no idea if it would even make a difference, but I'll try."

"I . . . thank you."

She unbent one arm as if to extend her hand then curled the fingers again as if reconsidering the gesture. But Ben reached over and covered her hand with his. "You are most welcome. As much as I desire to see justice done, it would be wrong not to speak for the innocent."

Her fingers uncurled and her hand shifted to lightly clasp his. "There is no justice if the innocent are not also tended."

"Precisely."

He stared for a moment at their joined hands then lifted his gaze to her eyes, wide and fathomless. The firelight touched the planes of her face and lent — was that startlement? — to her expression.

She was easily the loveliest thing he'd seen out here on the frontier.

"Will you be returning home to Tennessee

anytime soon, or are you planning to stay on here, with your brother and sister-in-law?" He raised his cup to sip his tea without releasing her hand.

She drank as well, glancing away into the fire. "I'm here for as long as Anne needs me, I reckon." She blinked. "Another reason why I shouldn't go traipsing off to see Sally. The baby has been a little fretful, although others say he'll grow out of it."

Ben smiled. "I've little enough experience with babies, so I'm afraid I can't address that."

Rachel's lips curved as she sipped her tea again. "Well, it stands to reason, we do grow out of it eventually. At least," and she grinned, "most folk do. There are some who stay fretful all their lives."

He had to chuckle at that. "Very true." Their hands slipped apart, and feeling keenly the sudden separation, he scrubbed his fingers through his hair. "There is a matter I need your help with on the morrow."

"Oh?"

"If I could get your assistance selecting clothing of a style worn more customarily in this part of the country than my own . . . ?"

Her smile blossomed once more, with but

an edge of teasing. "I can most certainly do that."

"I heard y'all talking after I thought we'd all gone to bed last night," Daniel drawled over breakfast the next morning.

Rachel felt her cheeks burning and spared him but a glance.

Ben she would not look at, at all.

"What was so important that you needed to discuss so late?" her brother pressed, a grin lurking behind his beard.

Anne smirked as well, but her gaze was likewise searching.

"Sally," Rachel answered shortly, and bit into her bacon with studied relish.

Still she felt the weight of his eyes.

"It's too dangerous to let you go," Daniel said.

"The Harpes are locked up now."

His good humor dissolved into a scowl. "You know as well as I do that they're by no means the only ones preying on travelers."

She huffed, her desperation rising. "We could wait until a larger group comes up the road and accompany them."

"At this time of year? Highly unlikely. And where would you lodge?"

Ben's gaze flicked between them. Swallowing a bite of food, he patted his mouth with a napkin and shifted in his chair. "She would be more than welcome at my cousin Stephen's house in Stanford, and the ordinary where I'm staying in Danville has plenty of room."

Daniel shot him a dark glance. "You can speak for your cousin?"

"With reasonable certainty, yes."

He sat back, still looking unhappy.

"If that doesn't suit," Ben said, turning to Rachel, "I'd be happy to take Sally a letter."

She forced herself to take a deep breath and pushed down her frustration. "I suppose I'll have to content myself with that. But when the weather warms, brother —" She threw Daniel her own challenging glare.

He remained completely unmoved by it. Not that she blamed him, but she could not find words enough to explain the need that pressed upon her heart to go see Sally for herself, to embrace her old friend and whisper the things she was longing to say face-to-face and not merely in a letter.

But a letter would have to do.

174

CHAPTER NINE

February 7, 1799

The hours wore away into the dead of night, illuminated by the lanterns of the midwife and her assistant, the silence broken by Betsey's heaving breaths and occasional soft moans, interspersed by the whispered direction and encouragement of the midwife.

Sally had only been present at one other birth, and that was at her mama's last time before Sally was married. Even through the strangeness of witnessing her own mother's travail and delivery, Sally had felt a joy and anticipation infuse the occasion. But there was no joy here. Only the sorrow of a child born in jail to an uncertain future, to a father who Sally knew was as guilty of the charges against him as the day was long — and a mother who hadn't even the protection of that father's name or legal bond.

While Susan paced the cell at Betsey's side between pains, letting the other woman lean

175

on her during, Sally sat curled in the corner, wrapped not only in her own tattered blanket but another besides that some kind soul had offered. She watched, offered occasional prayers on Betsey's behalf, and tried hard not to think about how she'd be travailing herself, very soon.

She also tried hard not to think about Wiley and Micajah, just over on the other side of the building. That was possibly the one good thing about being in jail — being out from under the men's demands for the past several weeks.

If only she could be free of them forever.

The cadence of Betsey's breathing changed, and her whimpering changed to a deeper groan. "Nearly time now," the midwife said, and bustled about, laying out supplies from her basket.

Sally curled more tightly in on herself. Her own babe kicked and squirmed.

Stay inside, little one, as long as you can. . . .

Before long, they had Betsey seated on a birthing stool, and with Susan on one side and the midwife's assistant on the other, the midwife crouched before her. Betsey struggled and strained, and then to the sighs and coos of the other women, her babe emerged with what sounded for all the world like a cry of protest.

In short order, they had Betsey cleaned up and tucked into her bed, the babe at her breast. "A fine, healthy boy," the midwife pronounced, and if sadness edged her voice, rather than the usual joy and excitement Sally had always heard after the births of her sisters and brothers, no one could blame her.

"I'm going to call him Joseph," Betsey said.

What sort of future could this child hope for, in such circumstances, with such a father as Micajah?

What could any of them hope for?

Susan's child, a girl, arrived early in the morning, one day short of a month later. Two months now they'd all lain at the Danville jail. Still a little more than a month to go before the trial. The closer they got, the more restless Sally felt.

The wait was driving them all half mad, though they were treated well enough and the jailer had even provided both Betsey and Susan with hyson tea, sugar, and ginger during their lying-in. Betsey's baby was a little fretful, but not bad as babies went — and Sally had some experience there, with her younger brothers and sisters. He was so tiny, and since they'd nothing else to do with their time, Betsey cuddled and rocked him, swaddling him against her chest near every minute.

Sally expected Susan to be an indifferent mother by comparison, but she wasn't. Susan tended her babe with an intentness and capability that amazed Sally.

Suspicion stole through her. Could it be this wasn't the first babe that Susan had borne?

About the third day, while watching Susan change her little one's clout, Sally sidled closer. She put a fingertip in the middle of the baby's palm and was rewarded by tiny fingers curling around it. Such a beautiful child, with abundant black curls and big, dark eyes. "Lovey fits her," Sally murmured.

Susan dimpled and for a moment looked almost — pretty.

What must the harsh, rawboned woman have looked like back when — well, when she was younger? Before Micajah?

And just how long ago was that?

"Of course," Sally added, aside to Betsey, "Little Joe is a sweet baby too."

It had been an unaccountable relief to her that the boy had a matching full head of dark curls, rather than the fiery hair of Wiley.

Not that such a thing altered the fact that there was good reason he might have.

178

Betsey also flashed a smile as she paced back and forth in their cell.

"Not long now before your time," Susan said, eyeing Sally.

She leaned forward without comment, stroking Lovey's ever-so-soft hair and the tiny, wrinkled forehead.

"Did you" — she pushed the words out before she could lose her nerve — "did you have any others?" A quick glance at Betsey. "Either of you?"

The women exchanged a long look. Betsey drew a deep breath and let it out slowly, but did not reply. Susan finished tying Lovey's clout and swaddled her again in the child-sized blanket someone had given her, then moved her bodice aside and put Lovey to her breast.

Sally sat back and waited.

"None that we were allowed to keep," Susan said at last, very low.

There was another exchanged glance. Sally suddenly could not breathe.

Oh little one . . . stay inside.

March 16, 1799
"They've escaped."

Ben looked up from the letter he was writing and blinked at the clerk of court. It was already too early, and unable to sleep, he'd risen before dawn to finish the letter.

"The Robertses. Or Harpes. Or whatever they're actually called. Micajah and Wiley. They've broken out of jail."

"What?" Ben was up from his chair without thought, snatching his coat from the settee nearby.

A crowd had gathered around the jail, goggling at the gaping hole where once a barred window had stood.

"How did they do it?" Ben asked the clerk. The man spread his hands. "No one knows."

Ben edged closer to examine the damage then without consulting anyone, walked around to the other side of the jail. Someone was already there, door open, speaking with the women. With a nod to the guard, Ben slipped inside as well.

"We heard a terrific noise in the middle of the night, is all," Susan was saying as she cuddled her newborn against her shoulder, her own eyes wide with a look of alarm, or innocence, that could not be completely unfeigned — though doubtless the woman was doing her best.

Ben released a breath. He should not judge before she even stood trial.

"So they broke out and left y'all behind?" The three women exchanged glances that ranged from perplexed to miserable. " 'Pears so," Susan said.

He studied her. Was that cheer, relief, or simply resignation that lightened her tone? It was nearly impossible to tell. Betsey, now, just stared off to the side, her month-old child fussing in her arms, while Sally sat on her cot, leaning against the wall.

"I'll be asking to speak with each of you later," Ben said.

"I want to go."

Daniel slammed his hand down on the table. "If it was too dangerous two months ago, it's even more so now."

Rachel pressed her lips together and held his gaze. "I want to be there for the trial."

Chewing a bite of bacon, he shook his head, a slow wag at first and then more emphatically. "What in the world are you thinking? With the Harpe boys on the loose again, Pa would have my hide — and with good reason — if I let you travel right now."

"Sally needs someone there," Rachel said stubbornly. "Someone who — who remembers who she was, before. Who can help her remember."

Daniel favored her with a baleful stare. Throat closing up and her eyes stinging, Rachel rose from the table and carried her plate back to the sideboard.

"Where are you going?"

"Downstairs to begin work." She tried not to snap but couldn't quite keep the tightness from her voice.

"Dan, I can spare her if there's any way —"

Anne's soft entreaty floated across the room after her, as Rachel made for the door. It was childish of her to go in such a way, but the heaviness would not be denied this morning, and she could not contain the tears.

She pounded down the stairs and dashed into the storage room, to a back corner where she tucked herself on a short stool. Bending, she buried her face in her hands. *Lord God, maybe Dan is right and I'm being frivolous about this, but please make a way for me to see Sally. You tell us to visit those in prison. And You know how much she needs someone.*

Ben's latest letter said that she'd softened a little since Micajah and Wiley had escaped. The trial would go on as scheduled, beginning with Susan, as the oldest of the women. He'd no way of telling which way things would go, but he remained hopeful that some way would present itself for extricating at least Sally from her circumstances.

Please, Lord. Let it be that she's delivered from all this. Even if I cannot be there.

Peace settled over Rachel, and she dried her face and went on to get the post's day started.

Late that afternoon, a small wagon train pulled into their station and set up camp for the night, not a noteworthy event in and of itself. Travelers visited the post, as always, and at one point she saw Daniel in deep conversation with one of the men, over to the side, but she thought nothing of it. Business remained brisk, and after that morning, she was glad to stay occupied.

With the days lengthening, she and Daniel had agreed to keep the post open a little later, but it was just after sunset, with a spring shower freshening the breeze, when a lone rider stopped and dismounted. Dressed as nearly every other man in a hunting coat and black felt hat, she nearly did not recognize him, but — she knew that horse.

Her breath caught in her throat. Ben — here? Today of all days?

She hesitated but a moment then left the counter and ran outside.

He turned as she emerged onto the porch, and even in the dusk she could see the gladness lighting his blue eyes.

They met at the steps, and without

thought, she put her hands out, and he took them. "I didn't expect you so soon," she said.

His teeth flashed in a brief grin against his beard, which had grown in thick and even now. "Well, I was hoping to speak with your brother. Is he about?"

"Oh, he's — I'm not entirely sure." Cheeks warming, Rachel pulled her hands away. Foolish to behave so in the impulse of a moment. What was it about Ben that drew such a thing from her?

His smile remained steady, his blue gaze so earnest her face was like to catch fire if she stood here gaping at him any longer. She swung away. "Do you — are you — planning to stay the night again?"

"I did not want to presume."

She risked another glance. "We are most happy to have you, of course."

His mouth curved again.

They located Dan in short order, and Rachel left the men to discuss whatever it was Ben needed to. Passing strange it was, though, when Rachel was always the one he sought out first. But she supposed she didn't know him well enough to judge what he might have in mind.

It was full dark, and she'd informed the last patrons that they could return first thing in the morning for any additional items they might need, when Dan and Ben came through the doors. Dan saw the last of their customers out then locked the door and crossed to Rachel, where she'd begun settling the day's accounts.

"Just a moment." She finished totaling the page of sales amounts, wrote the figure at the bottom of the column, then looked up.

Dan wore a look somewhere between a glower and expectation. "Can you be ready to leave with the wagon train in the morning?"

The quill dropped from Rachel's fingers. "What?"

Ben's expression gave nothing away, but her brother heaved a sigh. "I spoke this afternoon with the wagon master, and he said his family could accommodate you all the way to Danville. I didn't want to make a decision based only on that — although it was more favorable than I'd hoped for, to let you go. But then Ben showed up and offered to personally watch over you — in the company of the wagon train." Dan's eyes narrowed. " 'Twouldn't be proper for you to be in each other's company without the accompaniment of others."

Rachel became aware her mouth was hanging open and closed it. "Well, of

185

course."

Ben's eyes were sparkling now, and even Dan's look was no longer a glower.

"Tomorrow morning? Truly?" She couldn't keep the squeal from her voice.

"I can walk," Rachel insisted.

Ben had not expected their first disagreement to be over such a trifling thing as him offering to let Rachel ride Ivy while he walked beside.

"The other women walk," she went on, "and most of the children too. It would be disgraceful for me, perfectly well and able to use my own feet, to ride when someone more infirm is made to walk."

She'd done so the day before, but Ben thought that was simply so she could visit with the other women in the party. It was nearly beyond his comprehension that any female would actually refuse the favor of easier transport under such circumstances — but then, this was Rachel, made of far sterner stuff than some of his aunts and female cousins, and neither with child nor unwell as Sally had been when they'd found the Harpes.

"And see," she said, lifting her skirts just enough to extend a moccasined foot, "I'm wearing the right shoes for walking."

Moccasins. Yes, those would be the most sensible, and not the boots that he himself wore.

"Very well," he said at last, and Ivy's reins in hand, turned toward the train, just moving out from where they'd camped on the northwest side of Hazel Patch.

The last place Thomas had been seen alive.

"You won't ride, yourself?" Rachel said.

"No. I'd rather walk alongside you, if you've no objection."

She sputtered a little in surprise, her cheeks coloring becomingly. Ben smiled.

"Well, of course not," she answered after a moment, and fell into step beside him as the procession set out.

Despite her pertness, Rachel didn't immediately chatter at him, which Ben appreciated. Not that conversation with her thus far had suffered from any lack of depth or intelligence. And he should welcome some sort of talk to distract him from the weight of passing once again through this stretch of country.

Oh Thomas, how I have failed you.

Men fell largely into two types, Rachel had observed. First, those so enamored of the sound of their own voice they would hardly shut up, like the wagon master who spent much of the previous day talking with Ben about everything from the weather to the road itself and what it had been like before they'd improved it enough for wagons, rather than travel on foot or by horse. Although, Rachel owned she'd rather walk than be jostled about on a cart or wagon.

And then there were men so taciturn that a body could hardly get a word out of them. Ben seemed to fall into neither category, however — ready enough to converse, and not the mere blathering of some, but content enough to be quiet when the moment called for it.

Now seemed such a moment. She remembered well enough the significance of Hazel Patch to him, and if the memory of his cheerful and naive young cousin brought a pang to her own heart, what must he be feeling?

The weather was fair enough, and the timbered hillsides lovely with dogwoods and redbud blooming, and the forest floor scattered with trillium and Dutchman's breeches. But to know that even now, danger lurked . . . and not some nameless, faceless shadow, but real men she'd met and shared fellowship with, such as it was.

She glanced up at Ben, whose gaze roved,

skimming the country around them, and whose expression seemed to reflect her own thoughts. But was it because of his cousin, or something else entirely?

"What troubles you?" she asked.

His eyes came back to hers, startled. He shook his head slightly, then, "How — ?"

She waited for him to say more, but when he didn't, she said, "I can see it in your face."

He continued to study her, in turn. The silence left her feeling a little foolish, except she had a father, and brothers, and more experience conversing with men than she supposed any young woman ought. And Ben did indeed bear the telltale tightness of mouth, and at the corners of his eyes.

At last he shook his head again and looked away. He blew out a heavy breath. "Just over the Rock Castle River," he said softly, "we'll pass the place where Thomas met his end."

No words came to her this time. Without thought, she reached over and brushed his forearm. He shifted, but only to catch her hand in his and squeeze it in a way that was at once firm and warm and — familiar.

Then he released her, and they kept walking as if nothing had just happened between them.

"Ahh." The word escaped her like a sigh.

189

"I thought that might be it." She hesitated then said, "Will you tell me when we reach the spot?"

He gave a single nod, quick and hard.

The scenery here was beautiful, with rugged cliffs that gave the river its name. The party forded without difficulty — here Rachel did allow Ben to set her on Ivy, for the river crossing and no longer — and then a little farther down the road, Ben's hand brushed hers again.

"It was here." He pointed to a gully just below them, thick with trees and mossy boulders.

Without a word, Rachel twined her fingers with his, and this time neither of them let go for a while.

April 8, 1799

Sally paced the floor, stopping to stretch this way and that. The nagging ache which had begun early that morning came and went, no better but no worse either at the moment.

Betsey stood peering out the window, dandling her babe, while Susan half-reclined on her cot, nursing Lovey, but Sally could feel the older woman's eyes upon her.

"Here comes our lawyer man, Mr. Langford," Betsey sang out suddenly. "And he's got a lady with him."

Sally huffed. Mr. Langford's kindness was not to be faulted — in fact, were she young and innocent again, rather than heavy with child and made ugly by her misfortunes, she might try to catch his eye herself — but she was in no mood for talk today. Certainly not to meet —

Mr. Langford's voice outside was answered by that of their guard, and then the lock rattled and the door was pulled open. Mr. Langford stepped in, hat in hand as his gaze swept the room before settling on Sally, then he reached behind him and drew the woman forward. The lay of her hair, the angle of her jaw, all seemed familiar.

"Rachel!" The name burst from her lips.

The dark eyes of her old friend went wide. "Sally! Is it you, truly?"

And then she was in Rachel's arms, sobbing without reason.

" 'Tis all right," Rachel soothed. "I'm here."

Rachel held Sally's slight form, not quite as bony as she'd appeared during that brief glimpse months ago, but still thin — except for the hard roundness of her belly.

If only they could protect her from all the consequences of that ill-fated choice, nearly

191

two years ago now. But in this moment, all she could do was offer an embrace and tears of her own.

"Is there someplace we might go to talk more privately?" she whispered to Ben.

He nodded and stepped aside to speak to the guard.

Sally drew herself up, breath still heaving a little, and swiped at her face. "Might I — introduce you? Rachel, this is Susan and Betsey."

The women nodded, wary, as Rachel offered a smile and dipped her head in greeting. "Nice to meet you," she murmured. "I'm an old friend of Sally's. Was at her wedding."

The words sounded inane even to her own ears.

And heaven help her, inconsequential though it was in the moment, she looked around and saw the slightest glimpse of blue peeking out from behind the one called Susan. Obviously the woman still had possession of Rachel's gift to Sally.

But it mattered not. There were other cloaks.

The guard bade them outside, and Rachel led Sally with an arm about her shoulders.

Ben took them to the nearby courthouse and through a back door into a dim hallway and a small room to the side. Rachel pulled one chair close to another and settling Sally in one, perched in the other, still clinging to her friend's hands. "I would ask if you're well, but . . ."

"Well enough," Sally said, her eyes touching Rachel's then falling away, full of tears. "I — I can't believe you're here."

She squeezed Sally's hands. "It took me longer than I wished, but I couldn't not come." A sob shook her again, and Rachel pressed her forehead to Sally's. "Tell us what we can do to help you."

Sally shook her head, slowly at first, then more emphatically. "We're being cared for well enough —"

"I mean otherwise, Sally. Ben has told me how reluctant you are even to speak against Wiley and Micajah. Is there nothing else we might do?"

It was somehow the wrong thing to have said. Sally's expression hardened for a moment in an alarming reflection of the women she'd been keeping company with.

"I am sorry. I've not even asked what happened since you and Wiley married. How is it that you find yourself here?"

Her eyes still lowered, the frown deepened. "I wouldn't even know where to start."

"Well, to begin with — who are Susan and Betsey and how do they figure into all this?"

Gaze averted now, Sally said, her voice flat, "They were there, living with Wiley and Micajah already, when Wiley and I first married. Susan got to fussing about me being a legal wife and her not, so in September, Micajah took her off to Blount County to make things official." She was silent for a moment. "But — things being legal or not didn't matter to either of those men."

Rachel clamped her mouth and kept any shock she might have expressed — wanted to express — unspoken.

"And then — well, you probably know how wild they got, there in Knox County. Horse racing, drinking, and causing a ruckus . . . then came word that the livestock they'd been selling was stolen." Another silence. "That, I can't speak to. But I know they stole the horses that got Tiel after them. They came home in a tear, made us pack, and we took off into the wilderness." She blew out a breath, looked past them as if gazing off into the distance. "And that's when things got even worse."

Rachel waited, her heart thudding painfully in her chest, and Ben was likewise quiet, but Sally seemed to come suddenly back to herself and glanced at both of them in turn.

"I dare not tell you," she whispered, finally.

Later, Ben sat with Rachel before the hearth of the ordinary where he'd secured her lodging, both of them sipping coffee served out of porcelain cups. Rachel bent over hers in that posture Ben was beginning to know well, and surreptitiously reached up every so often to dry her cheeks with the handkerchief he'd given her.

"I warned you," he murmured, torn between watching her and averting his eyes. He could not blame her the emotion, nor the shock, but it was hard to see her so and not wish to offer comfort with at least a hand on hers — and here, in such a public place, it would be unseemly.

"You did," she answered, and shot him a watery glance.

Hang it all, anyway. He blew out a breath, and hitching his chair closer, reached out and took her hand. Her fingers closed about his. "I am most regretful at how this has turned out so far," he said.

Rachel squeezed her eyes shut, head tucked.

"We'll see what happens with the trial,

however," he went on. "Perhaps she'll reconsider."

Her grip tightened briefly. "Perhaps," she whispered, and brought her cup to her lips.

"We can pray so."

Her dark gaze came to his, searching, as if surprised, then cleared. "Aye, we can. And we will."

Ripples of pain became waves, slow and strong, washing over her and pulling her under like a river current in the deeps. Sally fought to keep her breathing steady in the darkness, so not to disturb the other women, but as the night wore away, she could not keep the catch from her throat.

"Sally? Are you in labor, girl?"

Susan's voice grated across the silence.

"M—maybe," she responded, half a squeak.

"Get up and pace the floor a spell. It helps."

The woman's unexpected kindness, though brisk, brought a burn to Sally's eyes. She rolled carefully off her cot, wrapped a blanket around herself, and set to the task.

Susan was right. It did help.

Betsey and baby Joe slept on, but Susan crept to the door, whispered something to the guard, then after scooping little Lovey up against her shoulder, returned to watch Sally.

It wasn't long before the midwife and her assistant arrived, and by this time Sally was having to stop and lean on the wall, while a low groan tore itself from her throat. The midwife's hands were unexpectedly gentle and comforting as well, soothing across her shoulders and back. "Don't fight the pains," the woman said. "Just go with it."

As if Sally had any choice. Her body was determined to do whatever it was God made it to when the babe she was growing had enough of being inside. Gone were her thoughts of making it stop. She only wanted it to all be finished.

And long about midnight, or a little after, Sally was astonished to find herself delivered of a tiny girl. As the midwife placed her, still wet and sticky from Sally's own body, into Sally's arms, a powerful wave of a different sort altogether swept through her.

"Oh sweet baby," Sally whispered, trembling, and kissed the tiny head adorned with curls that glinted golden red in the lamplight.

"What'll you call her?" Susan asked.

The midwife draped them both with a blanket, and Sally stared into the wide, dark eyes in the scrunched little face. "Eady," she said. "My mama's name."

And would her mother ever hold this one?

CHAPTER TEN

Monday, April 15, 1799

All of Danville and much of the surrounding county turned out for the trial. Rachel was grateful she'd come early enough to find lodging before the influx of people attending the district court session came, needing to find a place to lay their heads.

She and Ben sat in the row directly behind the women. The court had decided to appoint someone else to serve as defense, but Ben remained as counsel, at least unofficially.

They knew already that Susan's plea would be heard today, but that they'd recommend the women's trials be rescheduled for later in the week, because Susan had taken sick just before the Sabbath and still could hardly stand.

They called her to the bar, and she rose, clutching her month-old child, though Rachel had offered to hold the babe. The charges were read for Thomas Langford's murder, and when asked how she pled, she answered, in a low, scratchy voice, "Not guilty." She followed the words with a fit of coughing.

A murmur washed across the room. The two judges peered at her while the clerk made his notes off to the side. "It has been requested that the trial of Susanna Roberts be delayed, and for reasons evident to the court, we will set her trial for two days hence, on Wednesday, April 17. As we have a full docket on that day already, the trial for the other two women will be set for Thursday, April 18."

All three were led back to their cell. Ben and Rachel followed. Sally was allowed to linger outside the jail for a few moments, and after a moment's hesitation she gave baby Eady over into Rachel's arms.

Rachel stroked the downy curls and cheeks while the tiny lashes fluttered and big, dark eyes gazed up at her. "What an extraordinarily beautiful child she is," she murmured.

Sally's still-weary countenance lifted in a genuine smile. "Isn't she? I still can't believe she's mine."

For a moment, Rachel glimpsed her old friend as she had been. The golden hair was brushed and braided, Sally's face scrubbed clean, her garments neat if threadbare, and joy in her child lit her eyes — but there was still nothing of the exuberance that had been the old Sally.

Then the shadow fell again.

Rachel leaned toward her. "Just a few more days," she whispered.

Sally hesitated then nodded.

"A few more days, and Lord willing, you'll be free."

Her friend would not meet her eyes. "Maybe."

"At the least," Rachel pressed, "you'll have an answer, either way."

A slight nod was her only reply.

"Missus Roberts, you need to go inside now," the guard said, but not unkindly.

Rachel handed the babe back into her mother's arms and quickly, before Sally could protest, surrounded both with her embrace. "I am still praying," she whispered into Sally's ear then released her.

Tears shone in Sally's eyes, and with a tight nod, lips compressed, she ducked back through the door.

Two days later, about halfway through the afternoon, Susan's trial recommenced. As the affidavits were read and the evidence reviewed, which Ben told her had been presented at the hearing back in January,

Rachel felt sick to her stomach. The details of poor Thomas's death, as observed from his wounds and the Harpes' possession of his horse and other belongings — Rachel refused to think of them as anything else, despite what they had called themselves. Ben had brought her to the clerk of court and she'd verified to them that their name was Harpe and not Roberts, but because they'd been indicted under the name Roberts, the trial went forward with that.

In the presence of the two judges and twelve jurymen, Susan was called to the witness stand. She stated that she'd no part in the murders and was completely powerless in the situation to stop the men from doing what harm they intended.

The prosecution argued that Susan had been well able to go tell someone that her husband had done wrong, even if she was uninvolved in the murder itself. The defense argued that under threat of retribution, she might have been and likely was unwilling to risk such a thing. In the end, though, the jury handed down the verdict of "guilty."

Cheering broke out as Susan sat, her back as rigid as ever. One of the judges pounded his gavel and called for order then stated that sentencing would not take place until after the other two women's trials were accomplished.

As it was the last trial of the day, Susan was led back to her cell, and Rachel and Ben rose with the rest of the assembly. A frown knitted Ben's brows, reflecting Rachel's own worry. "Now what will happen? What does this mean for Sally?"

He shook his head. "Let me step aside for a few moments to speak with the prosecution, then the two of us can go for coffee and discuss it further."

So she waited while he slipped through the crowd and joined the growing knot of men at the bar. Her gaze strayed across the crowd milling through the courtroom and trickling out the doors, lingering on those who had become more or less familiar in the week she'd spent here, but her attention kept being drawn back to Ben, standing at the front, his expression intent and earnest as he talked with the others. For today, he was back in his fine, fashionable coat and breeches, with a white cloth knotted about his neck.

He'd kept the beard, though, well combed and trimmed. The lamplight struck golden gleams from the brown strands of his hair, both on the top of his head and along his jaw. He was possibly the handsomest man she'd ever seen.

Rachel released a breath and turned away. Such an observation was wholly unfitting in the moment. Even if things had shifted between them somehow, after journeying together and offering each other silent comfort at odd moments, it was neither the time nor the place to admire anything but the way he'd extended kindness to both her and Sally. Not only had he shown remarkable consideration for her during their journey, but he'd more than delivered on his promise, so far, to do everything he could for her old friend.

She cast him another glance. A man both fair of appearance and kind. Some fortunate female would enjoy both someday. Rachel hoped fervently that she'd properly appreciate it, whoever she was.

Ben returned to her side, and with a smile that was guarded yet still drew a strange flutter from her insides, nodded toward the door and guided her in that direction.

The crease remained between his brows as they walked. "What is it?" she asked.

He glanced down at her and offered his arm. She took it, trying not to notice the firmness of muscle beneath her fingertips, nor the way the blue of his eyes sent yet another frisson through her insides.

"Depending upon how the trial goes

tomorrow for the others, I plan to recommend a retrial for Susan. But we'll see. They'll be choosing a different jury in the morning since the original members were committed only through today." He shot her a tight smile. "So do not worry overmuch for Sally. She's younger, and likely the jury will find her more an object of pity than anything else."

"As they seem to have done so far."

"Yes. The community is quite upset over Thomas's murder and other killings they suspect are also the work of the Harpes, but for the most part they see the women as hapless victims in this situation. And that certainly works to their advantage."

Rachel made a sound of assent. There were too many angles to this situation, and it wearied her to contemplate them all. Ben, however, seemed to grasp them well enough.

Back at the ordinary where they were lodging, he called for a coffee service and drew her to the hearth where they had sat so often already. Rachel took a chair, and Ben settled himself opposite her, hands on his thighs, staring into the fire with eyes narrowed before shaking his head and refocusing on her. "Forgive me. So much to consider in this case."

She smiled a little. "I certainly understand that."

So she wasn't the only one feeling overwhelmed in the midst of everything.

"It's very good of you," she went on, more to make conversation than anything, "to be here in your cousin Stephen's stead."

He smiled briefly. "Stephen hardly knew his youngest brother. He was grown and gone before Thomas was out of skirts. I suppose I was more his brother in that respect, the way I felt I should look after him."

"And why is that?" Rachel asked.

Ben sniffed. "Gratitude for my aunt and uncle taking me in after my parents died, I expect. I never thought overmuch about it."

Coffee was brought in, and the dusky-skinned maidservant bobbed in response to Ben's thanks.

He was unfailingly kind even to the Negros.

Rachel bit her lip, turning away from where that thought led, and took the cup that Ben poured. He settled back with his own and eyed her over the rim as he drank, then lowered his cup. "Regardless, yes, Stephen very much wished to be here. I am sorry he and his family took ill and could not come, but more so that they were unable to extend you the hospitality I had promised your brother."

Rachel felt her cheeks warming — why did that always happen at the most inopportune times? "Oh — it was no trouble to camp with the others for one more night." She angled him a small smile. "As long as it didn't discomfit you?"

He snorted. "No. I bore much worse while on the hunt back in December, I assure you."

Their eyes met, but when Rachel's face heated further, she turned away, sipping her coffee. Of course he wouldn't find such an experience enjoyable, so she'd not admit it was their amiable lingering at the campfire each night that she'd treasured.

And again, she couldn't let herself dwell on such things, when Sally's future hung in the balance over the next few days.

The trial for Elizabeth Walker was the first on the docket the next morning, and Ben could find nothing noteworthy in the proceedings, which led quickly enough to an acquittal. Sally's followed immediately after, once Betsey had been taken back to the cell and Sally brought out.

Ben could feel Rachel's anxiety from where she sat beside him as if it were his own. And indeed, his own gut seemed tied in knots. Such an exercise in folly, and yet not, this putting women to trial for Thomas's awful death — women who doubtlessly witnessed it but Ben was sure had not participated or colluded in it. Whether, however, they were culpable merely by their reluctance to speak against the men was another thing entirely.

Sally too was acquitted, however, and stood at the bar, jouncing her newborn at her shoulder and swaying a little as the verdict was read. Beside him, Rachel sighed and put both hands over her face.

The defense then rose and requested a retrial for Susan. That was granted, and set for the next day.

As Sally was led out — arrangements had to be made for hers and Betsey's actual release — Rachel turned to him.

"Now we see what they do with Susan's case tomorrow," he said, before she could even ask.

That evening, the ordinary was full of talk about the trials, what could be done for the women, how Susan had avowed, along with the other women, that if given the chance, she only wanted to return to Knoxville and begin a new life.

He and Rachel had no doubt that it was true, at least from Sally's lips. The desperation on her face when she'd said it to Rachel and Ben after her acquittal — the tears of obvious relief — were convincing enough. Of the other two, it remained to be seen. Ben had heard stories while in law school of folk who, accustomed to the roughness of a particular life of lowness, were unable or unwilling to choose otherwise when offered the opportunity.

And these women, and their history, were very much an unknown, even now.

He was unsurprised however when a speedy acquittal came for Susan the next day. The courtroom broke out in excitement, with the wail of Susan's baby rising above all else at the sudden tumult. The woman's gaunt face was wreathed in smiles as she patted the child to soothe her, while nodding her thanks to the jury and judges.

This part was over, and perhaps the Harpe women truly would have a new start. Now it remained to recapture the men.

The craving to be part of that chase rose up in him with a hot bitterness that Ben could rarely recall feeling before, if ever — and that likely would never sleep until Thomas's murder was well and truly answered for.

As the women were being outfitted for their

209

journey south — clothing, blankets, food, and even an old mare equipped with wicker panniers for carrying the babies — Rachel was likewise packing to return home.

She and Ben would be part of those following behind the women, partly for their protection and partly to see that they did indeed intend to follow through on what they said. They wouldn't travel right with the women, despite how Rachel had argued for that, but would trail a bit behind. Rachel was undecided on whether she'd only go as far as Daniel and Anne's, or whether she could find escort all the way to Knoxville and home, if Anne decided they no longer needed her for a while.

Early in the morning, the women were led to the edge of town and directed back down the Road toward Cumberland Gap, still the best route south into Tennessee. Mounted on a chestnut gelding that Ben told her had been Thomas's — Stephen had apparently sent it up from Stanford for her use — Rachel sat waiting with the others as Sally and her companions started off into the mist, then they slowly set off as well.

They took an easy pace, almost a dull one, so as to stay just out of sight if not hearing of the women. Rachel glanced over at Ben, who seemed uncharacteristically subdued.

Should she inquire after his state of mind, or would that be prying, even after their apparent closeness these past several weeks?

Finally she could bear it no longer. "And what are your thoughts this morning? You've been very quiet."

He stirred as if caught woolgathering, and gave her a quick smile. "I apologize for my distraction."

"I imagine you must have much on your mind," she said.

He smiled again, but thinly. "It is so, I admit."

Her lips curved, but she turned her face away. How weary he must be of all of this — she certainly was, even after the happy tears she'd shared with Sally the night before over the prospect of returning home, especially with the arrival of a letter from her father, expressing his shock and sorrow over the bad straits Wiley and Micajah had gotten themselves into, and the hope and joy of embracing their first grandchild. Rachel was so ready to see Sally back to her family, and to possibly return to her own, although —

No, she'd not let her thoughts go there. She'd discharged the thing she'd come here to do. And Ben, in all his generosity, had helped her accomplish it, truly had assisted

Sally every way he could and then some, and now — now he could devote himself to pursuing Wiley and Micajah.

"Thank you again for all your kindness with Sally," she said.

"You are — most welcome."

She noted the wording — not *my pleasure* or *it was nothing,* because, well, they both knew it was not nothing, nor had it been enjoyable. "Once we reach Dan and Anne's, then, will you rejoin the hunt?"

He nodded tightly, his expression grim.

Her heart sank a little further. "I'm sorry you've been kept from it so long."

His silence stretched, and feeling his eyes upon her, she turned her head and met his gaze. The blue eyes were somber, but not cold. "Rachel. I'm truly glad to have been of service to you — and Sally."

The look held her, until her heart pounded and her throat thickened. "This cannot have been easy for you," she managed to get out.

He drew a deep breath in, then let it out slowly. "It has arguably been the hardest thing I've ever faced, short of losing my own parents. But your friendship has done much to help me bear it."

All she could find presence of mind for was a tilt of the head, not even quite a nod. "For me as well — although my burden in

212

this has been far different from yours."

His expression softened, and with a short nod of his own, he shifted in the saddle and then refocused on her. "I wonder . . . when all this is finished, and justice is finally served for Thomas . . . might I call on you?"

"Well, of course," she began, without thought — then the formality of his words struck her with such force she had to clutch the saddlebow to keep herself upright. "Wait — surely you don't mean — why would you want to?"

He smiled then, with such sweetness she could not breathe. Mercy, the unfairness of such a thing wielded by so beautiful a man as Benjamin Langford.

"And don't you dare tell me it's because of my uncommon beauty, or any other such rubbish, because then I might just set heel to this fine horse you've loaned me and make the ride straight to Dan and Anne's without your help, or anyone else's."

The words simply fell from her lips, and she caught her breath in horror that she'd actually spoken them, but Ben doubled over in the saddle with a long, gusty laugh. "My word, Miss Taylor," he choked out, "you are a remarkable woman indeed."

Her face burned, but she muttered, "I'm sorry. I just hear too much of that rot from fellows at the post, freshly back from a long hunt and half out of their heads with the loneliness of it."

Ben laughed again, wiping his eyes. "No . . . I will be most careful then, to . . . not tell you such things. Although," and he slanted her a glance, half imploring, half teasing, "I assure you it would not be untrue."

The heat in her cheeks swept her entire body. She opened her mouth to reply and could not.

"I own, however, that it would be most frivolous of me to cite that reason only. But if you would find such attention unwelcome . . ."

"I would not," she murmured, a little too quickly and sharply for decorum, she was sure.

The smile played about his mouth again. "Well then. Let it suffice to say for now, I have so appreciated your friendship, I am reluctant to see it end."

Blast that betraying flush across her cheeks. "I — also — am reluctant for that."

Again that brilliant smile, and such a warmth in his gaze that she could not quite meet his eyes.

They were both silent for a long time after that.

■ ■ ■ ■

That evening, they stopped and camped when Sally and her companions did, just past Stanford. Ben had warned Stephen that they might not have the leisure to stop — though he heartily wished they did, because in addition to the burning need to find Thomas's killers and haul them back before a court, this discovery of Rachel's openness to his attentions begged to be explored.

It had been a risk, for sure, to speak of calling on her — and he was careful to clarify that apprehending the Harpes was paramount — but the sudden, sweet shyness on her part was wholly adorable.

Did she think herself so unworthy of his attentions? He supposed it could be so, but social standing as he'd known it in Virginia seemed not to matter here. In fact, so many things he'd been taught to regard as important were of no consequence in this country, and the freedom of it quite took his breath away. He wasn't sure he ever wanted to return — at least not to stay. And a woman like Rachel was certainly sturdy enough of mind and heart to weather a life on the frontier. While distressed by the destitution of the Harpe women, Rachel had not shrunk from extending graciousness to her old friend, no matter the circumstances of her present situation.

Quite unlike the fluttering disapproval of his cousins and in-laws. Ben wasn't sure he could live with that anymore, even if he wished to.

He was also not unaware of the risk involved in seeking justice for Thomas, nor that he'd nothing to offer Rachel until all that was settled. He'd not wanted to send her back to her family, however, without letting her know of his interest, regardless of how long it might be before he could truly act upon it.

And Lord help him, he'd spoken the truth — he did not want their friendship to end.

It was almost disappointing, the way their comfortable conversation had turned to quick glances and shy smiles, throughout the day and into the evening. She seemed more open around the fire that night, however, edging closer to him as the other men gathered and talked.

They cast Rachel plenty of admiring glances, and speculative looks Ben's way. He was only too glad to have Rachel near and let them draw what conclusions they may, if it protected her.

Otherwise, she handled the difficulty of

216

the trip — the ride, the necessity of sleeping out in the open and eating at the fireside — with perfect calm and cheerfulness. He couldn't imagine any of his aunts or cousins doing the same.

They rose early the next morning and were off again in a light drizzle, still trailing the Harpe women. They'd let a bit of distance fall between the two parties, and some of the men complained about having to ride so slowly. Ben could not blame them, but they were still mostly within hearing, and the tracks were still fresh.

They passed through Crab Orchard and again, stopped for the night between towns. As darkness fell, the fire from the women's camp was visible through the trees, and Ben caught Rachel's gaze straying often toward it as they sat beside their own.

"I know I should likely just walk down there and talk to them," she said at last, looking up to find his eyes on her. "But I feel a terrible reluctance, and I don't know why."

Without thought, he reached out his hand, and she took it. "I understand the reluctance. Even in the absence of the men — even after the acquittal — there is something about Susan especially."

Rachel's head dipped. "Exactly."

He squeezed her fingers. "Keep praying."

"I am."

"Wake up, Sunny. It's time to go."

The whisper pulled Sally from the depths of a slumber she'd only just returned to while nursing Eady back to sleep.

"Sunny. Come on."

"What — it's — but it's still dark."

Susan loomed over her, silhouetted against the stars, beyond the tree branches. The barest hint of color tinged the eastern sky.

"We need to get a move on if we're to slip that party trailing us."

Sally sat straight up, Eady stirring in her arms but not awakening yet. "But —" She blinked and looked around. Betsey was already up, slinging the packs and panniers over the back of the mare. Reluctantly, out of habit more than anything, she snuggled Eady into the blanket on the ground, and rose, stretching. "Why are we leaving ahead of our escort? They're following us for our protection."

Susan snorted and turned away. "Just get your stuff together."

Suspicion soured her gut and dragged at her limbs as she shoved things into her saddlebag — baby gowns, clouts, her own old and tattered gown — then bundled

Eady more carefully for tucking into the pannier.

She couldn't wait to get home — to see Pa's and Mama's faces as they saw little Eady for the first time, to feel their arms around her again —

"Hurry up," Betsey hissed.

Sally fumbled a little, getting Eady loaded on the mare, then hurried back to roll up her blanket. "Why such a rush?"

Even in the dark, she could see Betsey's scowl and finger over her lips.

Taking the mare's bridle, Susan led off — not toward the road, as expected, but straight into the forest, with the lightening sky at her back.

"Wait — what —"

"Shh," was the only reply.

Sally stumbled in her effort to run a little faster and catch up to Susan. "But — this ain't right —"

The older woman stopped and swung toward her so fast, even the old mare bobbed her head in alarm. Susan put a hand up to her nose to soothe her, then glared at Sally. "Surely you didn't think we were really going back to Knoxville."

"I — but — aye." Sally swallowed. "I surely did."

Susan's pitying laugh was barely above a

219

breath, but cut to the marrow, nevertheless. "You poor lamb. And just what do you think Big and Little will do when they find us? Hmm? You honestly believe they'd let us away that easily?"

Sally's mouth worked, but her throat, dry as dust, would produce no sound.

Susan bent close again. "I tried once, years ago. Big liked to have beat me — and more — to within an inch of my life. He's amenable enough if he gets his way, but you've seen it, some. The minute you cross him, watch out. You know already that he killed a man years ago just for saying he was concerned about our welfare. Little thought he was eyein' Betsey a bit too warmly, but nah, it warn't that. Big was being rougher than he otherwise might, and the fellow called him on it."

The world tilted around Sally, and she could not breathe.

Susan straightened. "While that man lives, Sunny, we belong to him. *You* belong to him — you and Little. You said it didn't make no never mind what you were before, and as I told you then, you best not forget it. No matter what a jury or your little friend and that fine bit of a lawyer-man might say. I don't like all the killin' myself, but while Big's runnin' free, we got an obligation to find him."

Sally's lungs burned, and the earth had not yet stopped shifting — but wait, nay, that was just Susan and the mare moving past her, with —

With her baby and all her belongings.

Part of her demanded she run ahead, stop Susan again, take Eady, and run back to the men escorting them, Rachel and Ben among them, and beg them to shelter her. But Susan was already well down the hill, and —

"You belong to him — you and Little."

He will kill you, or worse.

"God," she whimpered. "Sweet, merciful God. Help me."

But like the meek lamb she'd truly become, she turned and followed numbly after Susan and Betsey, away into the wilderness to where, she knew not.

CHAPTER ELEVEN

"They're gone. Tracks lead off into the forest, but the trail is hours old."

Rachel stood beside the road, stooped with grief, hands over her face. "But we should follow after. Keep after them and —"

"And what?" their trail leader said, his face stern but not unkind. "If those women are bent upon finding their men again, naught we can do will stop them. They could already be gone with them."

"Then they could lead us to Wiley and Micajah, and you could catch them — arrest them again! It's the perfect opportunity —"

His eyes turned pitying. "We ain't really set up for a woman to go along on a posse, miss."

"But . . ." Rachel stamped and turned a slow circle, tipping her face to the forest canopy above. *Sally . . . oh Sally. What happened?*

Lord God, will You not intervene again? She has a child now, for the love of all that's holy. A babe! Oh Lord . . .

She didn't realize she was sobbing until someone's hands tugged at her, pulling her close as strong arms almost gingerly surrounded her. "It's all right, Rachel," Ben's voice soothed, above her head and rumbling against her ear. "It may not be, just now, but I swear we will go after them. You simply have to let us get you safely to your brother's post, first."

She rolled her face against the roughness of his hunting coat, still unable to stem the flow of tears.

"Rachel." His embrace shifted, his mouth against her hair and his voice but a breath now. "You know I'll not rest until those men come to justice. Perhaps there will yet be opportunity to rescue Sally from the situation — if she still wishes it."

"No-o . . ." The cry tore itself from her throat, a thin wail. "That — babe —"

The arms tightened, his body swaying as if she were the child. "I know," he whispered. "Just keep praying."

And so he held her until she could find a measure of calm. Even then, she stood, face pressed to his coat, which smelled of woodsmoke and horse and something teasingly spicy. The scent was comforting beyond words — and she didn't even care in the moment that she'd made a spectacle of herself.

Oh . . . Sally. Oh Lord. Protect her in all this. And guide us — or these men — in finding her. In finding Wiley and Micajah and seeing justice done. Please, Lord.

She kept repeating the words as through a haze they finished packing up and she let herself be mounted on the gelding — Thomas's no longer, she had to remind herself — and started off down the road.

"You'll sleep in your own bed at Dan and Anne's tonight," Ben murmured.

As if it mattered to her. If only she had not the limitations of being female and could go with them in pursuit of the Harpes. If only she had one more chance to speak to Sally face-to-face and persuade her not to follow the others. They must have forced her to, somehow. It was the only explanation.

She was finally beginning to feel like herself again about the time they rode up to her brother's trading post, about mid-afternoon — far sooner than they intended because of being able to ride faster on this leg of the journey.

At the rear of the post building, in the tiny stable yard, Ben dismounted and helped her down, and the other men dispersed to find lodging elsewhere. They led the horses inside the stable, where Rachel helped unsaddle and tend the animals.

Neither of them spoke, beyond simple things regarding where to find or put items — Ben seemed to know his way about well enough, she hardly needed to direct him anymore — but as soon as both Ivy and Dandelion were tucked into stalls, Ben turned to Rachel, and gently taking the saddlebags from her hands, set them aside and pulled her into his embrace again.

He'd removed his coat at some point during the afternoon as the air had grown warmer, and she found herself savoring the strength of his arms beneath his shirtsleeves and the beat of his heart beneath his waistcoat . . . as well as the woodsy scent mingled with something that must be uniquely his own, drawn out by the exertion of the day.

But of course, now the tears were flowing again. "I suppose you must leave right away," she said, sniffling.

He pulled back to brush the wetness off her cheeks, and an emotion crossed his face that in the shadows, she could not read.

"Not until morning," he murmured. "And then, yes, the other men and I will go back and track Sally and her companions."

Another sob shook her, and, hands cupping her shoulders, he pressed his lips to her forehead. She found herself leaning in, and once again he gathered her to him.

"Oh Ben —" But the words came out strangled, and her fists knotted, one against his shoulder and the other in the front of his waistcoat.

"Shh, shh," he soothed, and at last she simply threw both arms around him and let the weeping come.

After, she did feel somewhat abashed at seeing the wet stain on Ben's fine waistcoat. One hand framed the side of her face, his thumb sweeping across her cheek, and he tilted her head to make her look at him again. "It will dry," he said, the tiniest smile playing about his lips.

She nodded, and he hesitated, the smile fading. He looked as if he wished to say something but then only nodded as well and said, "We should let your brother and sister-in-law know that we've returned."

He bedded down that night on the pallet in front of the hearth but tossed and turned with the tide of his own thoughts. And on

226

this occasion, Rachel did not rise to partake of late-night tea with him — likely not a bad thing.

Truth be told, this needed to be the last time he slept at their hearth. The strength of his own feelings, taking her into his arms to comfort her that morning in the forest, and then doing so again in the shadows of the stable, had proved far more overwhelming than he ever guessed possible. How did this young frontier woman so enliven all his senses — her scent, the softness of her form against his, the tug of her weeping on his protective instincts?

For heaven's sake, in the moment he'd very nearly forgotten himself and kissed her, when it was neither the time nor the place.

". . . not until Thomas's murderers are brought to justice . . ."

He didn't want to leave her thinking him indifferent to her, but neither would he take advantage of her vulnerability of heart in the wake of Sally's disappearance. And when his own life was uncertain, was it fair to engage Rachel's emotions, only to leave her doubly grieved, if he also fell victim to the Harpes' brutality? Just the thought of the details surrounding the murders they'd begun linking to the pair curdled Ben's insides.

227

Yet, risk or not, Ben had to do this. For his uncle . . . for his cousins . . . for Thomas himself. He'd considered himself as having less to hazard in the pursuit of Thomas's murderers than the others, but now with the complication of a particular young woman —

He vented a sigh. *Lord God, grant me strength and wisdom here. If it be Your will, also grant me protection, but more than anything, grant that I help bring these evil men to justice. Protect the innocents under their influence.*

And — if it be possible — I would be most grateful to be able to return hale and sound to Rachel, and — and perhaps see if You intend more from this connection between us than simply mutual support and comfort during the worst of this trial.

Although I am not unmindful of the value of that, if this is all it be.

He fell asleep shortly after, the prayer spent.

The mood around the table the next morning remained cordial but grave. Both Daniel and Anne seemed distracted, and only the baby, so much bigger and more aware now than when Ben first had met them, was untouched by it all, grinning and chortling at Ben's silly faces. Rachel

228

watched his antics with a smile tinged with sadness.

"We'll find her, I promise," Ben murmured, when she finally met his eyes.

She gave a quick nod, firmed her mouth, and rose to gather dishes too quickly.

It was all he could do to not rise and follow after and catch her into his arms again. Instead, he turned to her brother and sister-in-law. "Thank you for all your hospitality. I hope I shall not have cause to trouble you again, except to bring good news."

Dan's gaze flicked to Rachel and back. "You are always welcome here."

His wife echoed the sentiment, but from the corner of his eyes, Ben had seen Rachel's slight hesitation before pressing into motion once more, tidying what appeared an already-spotless living space.

Unable to delay any further, he finished his coffee and pushed back his chair then carried his own dishes to the tub of hot, soapy water Rachel had prepared. Still she did not turn, so he fetched his saddlebags and bundle of bedding — far less than he'd slept on last night — and with a last word of farewell to his hosts, went through the door and down the steps.

If only this leaving did not feel so final, and his gut so hollowed.

In the stable, he set aside his baggage and, with a pat to Dandelion, led Ivy out to the breezeway to groom and saddle her. He'd be leaving the gelding for Rachel's use, if she wished, or for them to sell, if the price was right, although at some point Rachel would likely need conveyance to return home to Knoxville, and riding Dandelion was far more comfortable than in a wagon.

He was nearly finished brushing Ivy when a gowned shadow, small bundle in her arms, appeared in the open stable doorway.

Rachel.

His heart stuttered.

She came toward him, cheeks flushed and eyes reddened, her gaze darting toward him and away. "Anne packed you a little something. She handed it to me after you'd gone and told me to make sure you got it."

Ben accepted the bundle and set it on top of his saddlebag, but his attention never wavered from Rachel, whose hands knotted in her apron as he turned back to her.

"I — did you mean it when you said you hoped never to come back?"

The tremor in her voice wrung at him. "I said, except to bring good news. Not that I never intended to return at all." A breath. "Did you think that was what I meant?"

She lifted watery eyes to his. "I — wasn't

sure. I know you have a task to complete, which by all rights comes first — but I think of all the horrible things those men have done —"

A step, and he'd gathered her in his arms. Despite the distress of the moment, it felt as though she belonged there.

"Yes," he said, "finding the Harpes is the most pressing matter in my mind, but I assure you, Rachel, I want very much to return to you. Just — under circumstances that would let me have something of substance to offer you if — if you decide you would be amenable to more than me merely 'calling upon you.' "

She pulled back just enough to look up at him, her hand coming up to rest on his bearded cheek. The eyes searching his were full of wonder. "I can hardly believe a man such as yourself would truly be interested in me, the mere daughter of a merchant."

"Is that your hesitation?" He narrowed his eyes at her in mock severity for but a moment, then smiled. "But out here, does any of that truly matter?"

Her expression remained somber. "Sometimes." Her fingertips stirred briefly against his cheekbone.

He reached up and brushed his knuckles against her jawline, in return. "You are an amazing woman, Rachel Taylor, and any man — anyone at all, of any station, would be honored to have you accept his suit."

Her lips parted, the brown eyes widening a fraction and darkening . . . and all his resolve crumbled.

He leaned down to kiss her, intending it to be very light, no more than testing the softness of her mouth, but she met him halfway, rising on her toes. The catch of her breath and the scent of her skin proved too heady, and he found himself lingering, wholly enchanted.

They broke at last, her cheeks rosy and eyes shining.

"You go catch the Harpes," she whispered, "but then I want you back. Safely, if you please."

"Yes, ma'am," he murmured, and folded her in for another kiss.

Sally could not take another step. Were it not for her fear for little Eady, she'd not have gone this far, but in this moment, the weariness dug so deep into her soul, into her very bones and spirit, that Susan standing over her, hands on her hips, did not matter.

And her insides were beginning to hurt,

likely from the walking so soon after giving birth.

One of the babies was crying, a thin wail that tugged at her. Sally thought it might be Eady. But she could only huddle there on a rock, forehead to her knees.

"Have a little mercy, Sue," Betsey said. "She just had that baby a week ago."

Susan hated being called that. But to Sally's faint surprise, her only response was a long sigh. "Fine then. We'll make better time with her riding the old mare. Hardly much to her, anyway, and she can nurse her babe while we go."

The two women were there on either side of her then, Betsey's hands and voice oddly gentle and comforting, and even Susan less rough than she was wont. And somehow the glad prospect of riding did give her enough strength to get back up and climb on the mare.

One of them shoved Eady into her arms and helped her tie the baby close. Out of habit, as the crying faded to whimpers, she opened her bodice and put the tiny thing to breast.

As the horse started into motion beneath them, a strange relief flooded her, and she closed her eyes and released a sigh.

Lord . . . oh Lord . . . protect us . . . cover us

under the shadow of Your wings. . . .

She was under a shadow, of a certain. Whether it was the Shadow of God or not, remained to be seen.

The rest of the day wore away. Eady slept, between brief times awake to nurse. Long about evening, they stopped near a creek to camp, and while Betsey and Sally set everything out, Susan led the mare away to a nearby settlement. Sally was too weary to even ask why, or inquire as to where they were. She simply rolled herself in her blanket with Eady tucked up against her breast, and fell into a deep sleep.

When Susan nudged her awake, just before dawn again, the horse was nowhere in sight, and there was a canoe drawn up onto the bank. Without a word, they packed their belongings into the conveyance, stepped in, and pushed off into the water.

Betsey paddled in front, and Susan in back, while Sally curled up as small as she could in the middle. It was the most comfortable way of traveling yet.

If only she didn't know with awful certainty that at some point or another, they'd meet up with Wiley and Micajah again.

Susan and Betsey chatted quietly, wanting to be as unobtrusive as possible on their journey downriver.

Lord . . . oh Lord . . .

She should give up on trying to pray. It was clear the Lord had no deliverance for her in all this. But the words kept echoing through her head, a plea that found no other articulation but just that single form of address.

One day blurred into the next. Sally took the occasional turn paddling, just to spell Betsey and Susan a bit, but for the most part she huddled there in the middle, soothing Eady when she cried, feeling the heaviness pressing upon her more with every mile down the river.

God . . . oh God, I thought You promised to protect Your children. I thought . . . that I was one of those. Maybe I'm not anymore.

The echo of her father's voice, so long unheard, rippled through her memory. *"I am the good shepherd. . . . My sheep hear my voice, and I know them."*

And then another scripture, rising from the imprint of the family Bible, the pages crackling beneath her fingertips: *"For he hath said, I will never leave thee, nor forsake thee. So that we may boldly say, the Lord is my helper, and I will not fear what man shall do unto me."*

Sally blinked. How long had it been since she'd thought about the Holy Word of God, let alone heard it?

Lord, is it true? You really will never leave me or forsake me? Even now? Even — in this?

She peered into the sleeping face of the baby in her arms.

"Thou hast covered me in my mother's womb . . . I am fearfully and wonderfully made."

Surely such a tiny, precious thing could only be the work of God, even in Sally's circumstances. And Sally wanted so much better for Eady than she had gotten.

Sometime during the second or third day on the river, she stirred, curious as never before about the women whose fortunes she'd shared these past almost two years. "Did you know Big and Little were going to escape?" she asked Susan.

At first, the rawboned woman gave no sign of hearing the question. "I knew they'd planned to," she answered finally.

"Is it true they bought off the guard?"

Susan's almost-black eyes leveled on her then, a hard look.

"How was it that you and Betsey came to be with them in the first place?"

This time the older woman's expression held something of the exasperation that Mama's used to when Sally pestered her

236

with too many questions, in the middle of Mama trying to work and think about other things.

"We was — very young, Betsey and I," Susan said at last, slowly. "It was the summer before I turned thirteen. Betsey was about eleven. The war was in its last days — the British hadn't surrendered at Yorktown yet and signing all the treaties wasn't for two or three more years after that, but Big and Little was wild Tory boys who stole us and two other girls from our homes." She pressed her lips firm and drew a long breath through her nose. "We thought it a lark, at first. Big and Little's daddies had fought together, and Big's daddy was at Kings Mountain, where they'd seen the killing for themselves, Big and Little had —"

"Wait, daddies? They're not brothers?"

Susan smiled a little. "Nah, at least — I don't think so. Their dads were brothers, but Little's died earlier in the war, and Big's stepped up to take care of him as well." She hesitated, her voice softer. "He was dad to all of us, really."

A sudden suspicion grew within Sally. "Old Man Roberts?"

The older woman's smile widened. "One and the same."

It had never occurred to Sally to ask —

when the grim, hulking man stood as witness for Micajah and Susan's wedding and signed the marriage bond, and Susan had first given her name as Roberts, it was easy to just assume and accept that Old Man Roberts was her father, and Betsey her sister.

But suddenly — now that she knew the truth — other details appeared in a different light. The older man's sternness with Big and Little, while still tolerating their presence, and his gruff gentleness toward Susan, Betsey, and Sally. And the presence of a tall, strapping lad with wild black hair, whose skin was not quite as dark as Micajah's, but bore him a startling resemblance. "Is Burt — ?"

Susan sighed a little. "My boy, and Big's. He was my first."

Oh Susan. "How many were there?"

The older woman was quiet so long, Sally wasn't sure she'd answer, but finally she did, softly. "Him, and another what didn't live."

Sally let the flow of the river fill the silence for a bit. But still the questions bubbled away, inside her. "So what happened to your own father?"

"He — Betsey, look sharp there — log ahead. He and Betsey's dad tried to get us back. Got one of the other girls — another run off on her own — but Betsey and I, we stayed."

"But — why?" The words were out before Sally could stop them.

"Because." To her shock, a flush crept from Susan's neck, upward across her face. "By the time our dads found us, the damage was done. No one else would have taken us. What else were we to do?"

"Your dad *said* that?"

"Nah. But I knew it was the truth." She was silent for a moment. "I never spoke to him again. And he was killed in some skirmish not long after."

Sally swallowed past the thickness in her throat.

"Besides." Susan's voice went tart again. "It ain't like I was pretty, like you or Betsey. Though, I own I was a mite prettier then." She shook her head. "Not anymore though. God made me tall and ugly — and tough." Her gaze skipped across Sally, hard and scornful. "To help take care o' the likes of you."

Sally stared at her. At the moment, Susan appeared about the bravest woman Sally had ever known.

"How can you even bring God into it like that?"

The curl returned to the older woman's

239

mouth. "Why, what's wrong with it? That it don't square with your idea of Him, Miz Baptist Preacher's Daughter?"

"Shh," Betsey said. "Y'all are loud."

Sally felt herself flushing and looked away. "So what happened then? Where did y'all go after the war was over?"

"West," Susan answered without hesitation. "We stayed with the Cherokee awhile. That was . . . interesting. They's some good people, most of 'em. And unlike white folk, they sure didn't care how me and Betsey came to be Big and Little's women."

Sally had been aware for some time now that it was no wonder Wiley had known so well how to sweet-talk her into giving him her all. It still stung, although these days, she felt mostly numb to it.

"We was in Nickajack, in fact, when word came that the white settlers were going to attack. But we got out before it happened. Not long after that, Big and Little decided they wanted to try their hand at living in white society. More and more, the Cherokee are being pushed out anyway." Her gaze refocused on Sally, sharp and half amused. "That was about the time Little met you and decided he just had to have you to wife."

Betsey snorted and cast a sour glance

240

back. Sally flushed even more at that.

And here she sat, in the middle of a canoe on the Green River — she'd finally asked Susan where they were — headed for the Barren and then, at least the other women hoped, they'd find Wiley and Micajah.

Their third day out on the river, they pulled up the canoe at some rough-looking settlement, one of dozens strung out along their way, and during a quick visit to a trading post for a few provisions, heard talk of a pair of murders. The most recent was some hapless older man, out fishing, gutted and his body stuffed with stones before being sunk in the river — just like a man down in Tennessee, last year. But the one before that was even more terrible — a young boy, his bloodied body flung into a sinkhole even as his father was being asked to join a posse to find the murderous Harpes.

Doubtless, folk agreed, it was these same dread criminals who were at fault, having broken out of jail the previous month and now making their presence known in west-central Kentucky. But where would it end?

Sally exchanged a glance with Susan and Betsey, and they finished their purchases and hurried back to the canoe.

None of them drew an easy breath until they'd pushed off once more, she knew. And by the fierceness of Susan's expression, Sally also knew that the older woman liked it no better than she — or Betsey.

"We could still go back," she found herself saying. "There's still time."

Shutting her eyes briefly, Susan shook her head, and Betsey just looked drawn and mournful.

CHAPTER TWELVE

Barely two weeks out on the trail, and there were all the leads in the world — and yet none at all.

Ben found it absolutely maddening.

At least a dozen or more different bands of mounted men, by his reckoning, combed the Kentucky wilderness. From one perspective, it could be only a matter of time before the Harpes were caught and brought in — but from the other, Ben had seen firsthand just how dense and tangled were the forests and canebrakes, not to mention numberless caves tucked up into the hills, and all the different ways the fugitives could slip away.

How could they ever know where these men were, except by the trail of woe they left?

They sat at the moment, men from three different search parties, in a tavern on the Little Barren River, where a man living alone on the banks of a nearby creek had gone to greet who he thought were new settlers, but discovered the Harpes instead, and fell prey to their predations.

A handful of the men Ben rode with months ago were here, Ballenger and his brother among them. A grizzled older man was present, Henry Skaggs, who Ben had been told was among the earliest settlers almost thirty years before, along with Colonel Daniel Trabue, who had lost his son, a boy of only twelve, to the Harpes. "Didn't find his body for two weeks," Trabue gruffly said. "We thought he'd done been kidnapped, but when we ran across a place where the Harpes had kilt a calf to make themselves new moccasins, there weren't no sign of any footprints but theirs." He sucked his teeth a moment. "I was at a log rolling when Skaggs here was with the posse come seeking men to go with them. They'd found the Harpes, had a run-in with 'em on the trail where the Harpes were surprised but ready to shoot. Skaggs suggested they go back to his house, get his dogs and track them by scent, and then they tracked them up to a terrible thick canebrake. He felt they should go after them but needed more men. But the log rollers didn't think they was needed." Trabue sucked a deep breath

244

through his nose, mouth compressed. "They know now they shoulda done their duty in turning out. Law's too sparse out here yet to leave it to them."

Men all around the table tucked their heads, peered closely into their cups.

"So, you said the Harpes didn't even take the sack of seed beans the boy had gone to fetch home?"

"Aye." Trabue cleared his throat. "They took the sack of flour I'd sent him for, but not the beans. And — he was cut in pieces." He shook his head slowly. "These men — it's like they ain't even men. Ain't got the heart God gave ordinary human beings. They're just in it for the fun of shedding blood."

Shaking of heads and muttering greeted that statement. Ben held his silence, gripping the cup in both hands. The brew was decent, but he'd no taste for it at the moment.

Trabue lifted his anguished gaze to Ben's. "You lost a cousin in all this, yourself, and they tell me you're a man of law, to boot. What's your thought about it all?"

"I would agree with your assessment," Ben said. "There's no sense or reason, but only a certain unwholesome air about these men." He cleared his throat. "I encountered them myself, back in December, on the road to Crab Orchard, not long after my cousin was found murdered. Only by the grace of God and a fast horse did I escape."

He let a half smile lift the corner of his mouth at the oft-repeated phrase, and brought the tankard to his lips just by way of breaking the moment.

The wording reminded him, though, of Rachel. Of course, nearly everything reminded him of her.

Lord God, please let this business be done quickly. Please . . . for Uncle Ben, and so I can return to Rachel.

He'd not even time to dash her off a letter.

"Well," Trabue said with an answering smile, also somewhat wry, "we're glad to have you and your fast horse join us."

Rachel smoothed the newspaper out on the counter. *May 9.* It still amazed her how they could receive the Frankfort *Palladium* just two days after it was printed.

"BY THE GOVERNOR," the article read, "A PROCLAMATION."

Whereas it has been represented to me that MICAJAH HARP, alias ROBERTS, and WILEY HARP, alias ROBERTS, who

246

were confined in the jail of Danville district under a charge of murder, did on the 16th day of March last, break out of the said jail; — and whereas the ordinary methods of pursuit have been found ineffectual for apprehending and restoring to confinement the said fugitives, I have judged it necessary to the safety and welfare of the community and to the maintenance of justice, to issue this my proclamation and do hereby offer and promise a reward of THREE HUNDRED DOLLARS to any person who shall apprehend and deliver into the custody of the jailer of the Danville district the said MICAJAH HARP alias ROBERTS and a like reward of THREE HUNDRED DOLLARS for apprehending and delivering as aforesaid the said WILEY HARP alias ROBERTS, to be paid out of the public treasury agreeably to law.

"Well," Rachel muttered, "at least they're recognizing their true names now."
She kept reading.

In testimony whereof I have hereunto set my hand and have caused the seal of the Commonwealth to be affixed.
Done at Frankfort on the 22nd day of April in the year of our Lord 1799, and of

the Commonwealth the seventh.

(L.S.)

By the Governor   JAMES GARRARD

Harry Toulmin, Secretary.

MICAJAH HARP alias ROBERTS is about six feet high — of a robust make, and is about 30 or 32 years of age. He has an ill-looking, downcast countenance, and his hair is black and short, but comes very much down his forehead. He is built very straight and is full fleshed in the face. When he went away he had on a striped nankeen coat, dark blue woolen stockings, — leggins of drab cloth and trousers of the same as the coat.

WILEY HARP alias ROBERTS is very meagre in his face, has short black hair —

Rachel straightened. " 'Tisn't black, but red! At least, when he's washed on a regular basis."

— but not quite so curly as his brother's; he looks older, though really younger, and has likewise a downcast countenance. He had on a coat of the same stuff as his brother's, and had a drab surtout coat over the close-bodied one. His stockings were dark blue woolen ones, and his leggins of drab cloth.

248

She puzzled over the similarity of dress. It was known now that they'd murdered and robbed a peddler on their way up the Road, before encountering Thomas Langford. Perhaps they'd cadged the clothing from there.

Regardless, the description was otherwise fair enough. Downcast countenance, indeed. What Sally had ever seen in Wiley —

In a flash, she remembered the shine of his gaze as they stood before her daddy, saying their vows. At least in the moment, perhaps he did at least believe himself in love with her.

Unfortunately the memory brought with it the recollection of meeting Micajah's eyes, and the shiver that had coursed through her then returned, redoubled. To know what that man had been capable of, indeed was just months away from committing —

And then there was Hugh White, and the unbelievable coincidence of his connection with the Langfords — which then led to the wrenching sorrow of Thomas's fate, and a flutter of longing for the grave, elegant cousin.

Whom she still could not quite believe had kissed her so thoroughly before riding away that morning.

Remembering the press of his mouth on hers, she touched the edge of her bottom lip with her fingertips. She'd never realized just how strong those feelings could be — and what was it about the peculiar mix of the man's own winsomeness and sweet intoxication of his embrace that made her forget herself in the moment? Because it already seemed a strange kind of madness took hold when his gaze turned to her and he smiled — and then to add a touch or a kiss —

She blew out a long breath and looked again at the newspaper. If what Sally had felt was anything like this, Rachel could not fault her for the desire to follow her heart. Not at all.

The snippet of a scripture floated through her thoughts, *There be three things which are too wonderful for me, yea, four which I know not: the way of an eagle in the air; the way of a serpent upon a rock; the way of a ship in the midst of the sea; and the way of a man with a maid.*

Even the Bible attested that it was a strange and mysterious thing, not to be explained.

But Sally's blithe and tender heart had been shattered. And what did she, Rachel, know about Benjamin Langford, besides the word of Hugh White? What if he too turned out — God forbid — to be a terrible man?

Or even if not terrible, less than what Rachel needed in a husband?

What if someday Ben decided Rachel really was beneath him, despite his protestations to the contrary?

'Twould be better for her to harden her heart now, or at least pull back far enough to exercise extreme caution, before her own heart wound up as Sally's.

If only she didn't feel half shattered already at the mere prospect of never being kissed again by Benjamin Langford, or held in those strong arms.

Later in May, 1799
Sally lost track of the days as they continued paddling down the Green River, through flats and hollows full of canebrakes and more wild, forested hills, the stream ever widening until they reached what the other women and folk along the way proclaimed the mighty Ohio.

Sally had never seen anything like it, so wide and deep — and muddy.

Betsey and Susan were at the paddles, and with their usual skill navigated the current, evading large limbs and in one case a whole tree with apparent ease.

They were headed for a place over on the Illinois side called Cave-in-the-Rock. None of them had ever seen it, but Susan insisted they'd know it, and by word of Old Man Roberts, that was where they'd rendezvous with Big and Little.

Sally's gut grew tighter and more sour by the day.

Most of a day on the Ohio, and they rounded a bend to see it come into view: a lovely arched opening in the rock face overlooking the river, with a sandy strip before it and a couple of small watercraft pulled up on the shore. The women angled the canoe toward the bank.

"Halloo the cave!" Betsey called.

A figure appeared, mostly concealed in the shadows beyond the opening.

They ran the canoe aground, and Susan hopped out, swooping little Lovey into her arms with a hissed command to stay put, then she walked up the sandy strand toward the cave. Sally's heart was pounding, but after a quiet exchange, the man emerged — not Big or Little, either one — and came back to the canoe with Susan. "This is Captain Mason," she said. "He's in charge, hereabouts."

A little younger than Old Man Roberts, leaner and rather handsome, the man nodded, searching their faces, assessing. "Your men aren't here, but you are all welcome to stay for as long as you need. We don't harm women here."

Grateful to be ashore, Sally let herself be handed out of the canoe, and taking up Eady and one of her bundles, followed with the other women up to the cave.

The interior was cool and spacious, with a sandy floor and high, arching ceiling that opened farther near the back than even the wide entrance hinted at. Several people were already in residence in various corners of the cave, but Captain Mason led them farther and pointed to an area. "You may set up camp here, if you wish." His gaze was still questioning, but kind.

Only a day or two passed before Susan and Betsey decided to go paddling back up the Ohio to wait for Big and Little. Sally felt all too content to stay put, despite being among strangers.

These at least were folk who would not question where they'd come from — and she felt oddly safe among them, despite their fearsome reputation, which she knew already, as river pirates.

Rachel hugged Anne, lingering in the comfort of her sister-in-law's embrace while

Dan stood by holding little Jesse, big enough now to bounce up and down in his daddy's arms.

"You're welcome back any time, you know," Anne murmured.

"I'll be back," Rachel said, past a lump in her throat that would not ease. "I just need to see Daddy and Mama."

Anne gave her a last squeeze. "I understand." She let go and stepped back, her smile tremulous. The two of them had truly become dear to each other in the past months.

Next Dan engulfed her in his arms and kissed her on the head. "Stay out of trouble, little sis."

She smiled though her eyes were stinging. "I'll try."

Up she went into the saddle on Dandelion, astraddle as she always did with her full skirts bunched about her knees and ankles, an old pair of Dan's trousers underneath for comfort and added modesty.

Anne stepped forward. "Are you sure you don't have a message for me to give Ben if he shows up?"

Rachel forced a thin smile and shook her head.

Her plump sister-in-law laid a hand on her knee. "Rachel . . ."

She blinked and glanced away then met Anne's eyes again. Blue, though a different shade from Ben's.

"It hasn't been long enough this time for his lack of writing you to signify," Anne pressed.

Rachel sighed. "Just tell him I went home."

A nod and a dimple, and she stepped back. Rachel lifted the reins on the fine gelding.

Another reminder of Ben.

God . . . keep him safe, regardless of what happens.

"Ready?" Jed Wheeler called, and shook out his own reins.

His oldest son, Isaac, a little taller and more filled out than when she'd made the journey up with them a year ago, nodded crisply and flashed a businesslike smile from his seat next to Jed, but Rachel could see the open envy in the lad's eyes at her mount. Dan had insisted she take the horse, saying that Ben had told him just before leaving that he intended it as a gift to Rachel whether or not he returned from hunting the Harpes. If it was a weakness of heart that she could not refuse this one thing, then so be it.

■ ■ ■ ■

Hot, tired, mud-spattered, they gathered once again at an inn, somewhere in the more western section of Kentucky. Captain Ballenger looked very hangdog as he shook his head and explained the situation. "We ain't doing any good here, boys. Those blasted Harpes are just too slick, and there are too many conflicting rumors. Besides, Colonel Young has his troop from Mercer County already working on sweeping all the outlaws out of this corner of Kentucky and across the Ohio, like they did up by Frankfort. I can't put off going home and seeing to my farm any longer."

A rumble followed his words, some agreeing that they too needed to tend their homes, while others voiced the willingness to go on.

Ben knew a little of what it must have cost Ballenger and others like Trabue to bow out of the pursuit. Unlike the older man, however, he had no firm obligations to send him home before this was resolved.

Nothing but the memory of Rachel, soft and sweet in his arms, which seared every time she came to mind.

"And you, Langford?"

"I'd like to join Colonel Young and the others, if possible," he said.

And so it was that Ben found himself riding with as fiery a band of men as he'd ever encountered on the proper side of the law.

They rode fast and hard, for sure, half of them appearing as if they were part Indian and had spent the better part of a decade in the wild — and perhaps they had — and others more like Ben, with some eastern ways and dress about them, but looking more acclimated to the wilderness than he.

Colonel Young led them with a single-minded focus, determined to flush not just the Harpes out of hiding but drive any other criminals from the state as well. But it soon became apparent to Ben that Ballenger was right — rumors of the Harpes and their doings abounded — and the handful of fresh murders since their escape almost two months ago were more than enough to fuel whispers of three times that many.

Who knew at this point what was truth and what was not? It made Ben's head ache just to contemplate it.

He wasn't the only one with the thought on his mind. More and more of the men grumbled, though Young made a grand production out of pursuing the Harpes and others. And with all the commotion they made doing so, there was less and less chance all the time that Ben would be able to even catch sight of Sally, let alone do anything useful toward apprehending those worthless men.

Justice for Thomas and his promise to Rachel, both left utterly undone.

God, why am I even here? Is there yet any good I can do in all this?

Deep in his gut was a nagging hollowness that told him he dared not let up, dared not rest.

Among the men just out for fire and glory were good ones, however. Ben learned names and faces and places of residence. One such distinguished himself from many others, even among those who seemed more part of the wilderness than not, a tall and lean fellow by the name of Bledsoe, with long dark hair braided back, an intentness to his expression, and eyes so pale they were nearly gray, eerily piercing one moment and laughing the next. He shared many the jest with a tall blond youth who Ben learned was Bledsoe's brother-in-law.

Bledsoe, as Ben also learned, was also one of myriad Thomases.

Again the memory of that particular topic of discussion flitted through his head, reminding him of Rachel.

258

Bledsoe had been a scout and post rider, but for the past few years tended a piece of land up by Elizabethtown, not far from his wife's family. They'd a pair of young children with another due sometime the coming winter.

When asked his thoughts about their chances of actually apprehending the Harpes, Bledsoe looked graver than ever and finally shook his head. "I understand the need for more men, but — with this mob? Nay. If it's so that they spent time with the Cherokee, then they'll be too canny to be caught. They'll go to ground, or fly out of reach until they think it's safe."

"That's been much my mind of it as well."

"But," Bledsoe added, "I allow we should probably let Young have a crack at it first."

Ben scrubbed at his bearded chin with his fingertips, grimacing when a rough fingernail caught on skin and hair. He should trim that tonight before falling into his bedroll, exhausted. Time was when he kept both hands and face immaculately groomed . . . no longer, out here. "My concern is that the Harpes will, as you say, lie low and then come back, worse than ever."

"Mine too," Bledsoe said. His gaze, cool and assessing, met Ben's. "You lost a cousin to them last winter, didn't you? It'd be an honor to ride with you again, if the worst does happen and there's need for us all to keep on the hunt."

"It'd be an honor for me as well," Ben said, and meant it.

It was balm indeed, Rachel found, to be caught up in a bear hug from her father, and even to endure her mother's clinging and kisses. "We've so worried about you!" Mama exclaimed, and embraced her for the third time since Rachel had dismounted.

She endured the fussing and petting, and the inevitable questions and speculative looks about Dandelion and how she'd acquired him. All the shock and horror of the past months had taken its toll on her, and there was a definite peace to being home again.

She didn't even mind the chattering of her younger siblings, for once. The noise reminded her that each was still here, alive and breathing.

Once everyone had settled from her homecoming, the first thing she did was get right back on Dandelion — younger brother accompanying of course, and a pistol snugly in her own pocket — and ride to see Sally's family.

Reverend Rice received her with a sort of

stiff formality at first, but then Sally's mama broke down weeping on Rachel's neck before she could get hardly a word out. At last, the woman regained control, and they ushered her inside and sat her down for a cup of tea.

Grief rimmed their faces, made them appear years older since she'd last seen them. "How are you faring these days?" she asked, just to start out.

"We are well enough," Reverend Rice said, but woodenly, and Missus Rice dabbed at her eyes.

"Please," she said, "how did Sally look, when last you saw her?"

Rachel thought hard. 'Twould be more unhelpful to be completely honest about the destitute state Sally had found herself in, but they needed something from her. "She has the sweetest little baby girl. Red curls. And Sally named her Eady."

"Oh-h," Missus Rice half squealed, and brought her handkerchief up to cover her face. Her husband likewise bowed his head, shoulders shaking.

If Rachel had harbored any lingering resentment toward Sally's parents for their perceived indifference, it was fled clean away now. For all the stoic nature of his first letter, this had been well nigh on devastating to them both.

"It is a hard situation, and desperate, to be sure," Rachel said. "But I'm praying that God will yet deliver her."

Still overcome, neither parent could reply for several long moments.

"Thank you," Reverend Rice managed at last, "for helping her in all this. May we yet indeed have confidence in our Lord to bring her home. What we have heard — what has been written us — is unthinkable." He flashed her a watery glance. "I hope you know we'd never have countenanced her marriage to Wiley — no matter what had transpired between them — had we the slightest inkling that this would all happen, after."

Rachel nodded.

He gave a gusty sigh. "I confess I had many misgivings at the time, but there seemed to be no other impediment to their union."

"Hugh White and I both felt uneasy at different moments but could not say why, and I brushed the feelings aside, thinking it simply envy for a friend being wed before me." Rachel laughed a little, brokenly. "If only we'd known . . ."

"We can blame ourselves all we like," Missus Rice murmured, her voice raspy, "but none of it will mend the situation." She pressed the back of her hand under one closed eye. "Only God Himself can do that. And, as you say, He yet might do so."

"We will all keep praying," Rachel said. "This is no ordinary misadventure of a husband. There is evil at work here, plain and simple."

They both stared at her, as if stricken anew, but then Reverend Rice slowly nodded. "Then we best can fight it by taking up the armor of God and submitting ourselves to His holy will."

"This is no jest, Micajah Harpe. You and yours cannot stay here. Pack your things and leave, this instant."

Captain Samuel Mason, infamous leader of the river pirates in residence at Cave-in-the-Rock, stood with hands planted on his hips, staring down the younger and more substantial Big, who still half-collapsed against Little in shared peals of laughter over their latest "prank."

Several paces down the rocky strand, others were busy removing the broken and bloodied forms of a horse and naked man, which Big and Little had sent together over the top of the cliff above.

Sally, Susan, and Betsey stood clinging to

263

their squirming, squeaking babes, and each other. *Oh Lord, have mercy on us. . . .*

Mason's gaze swung between the huddled women and children, and the men, who had once again committed the unthinkably cruel, and then found humor in it.

What kind of monster had she wed, two years past? It was a question she should give up even asking.

"I am in earnest here," Mason said, his voice dropping. "We'll not have this sort of thing happening in our company."

Big drew himself up, sobering, and Little beside him. Neither was inconsequential, and Mason had at least six decades to his credit, though still hale and hearty.

Susan was the one who moved first. "Come on," she said, soft but clear. "We'll pack."

Sally's heart dropped to her feet. This was the first place she'd found any measure of safety after Susan had turned them from the Road, over south of Crab Orchard. Though subjected to the usual trials of marriage once more — if one could call it that, since Little still shared her liberally with Big — being among this band had proved more or less a calming influence on the two of them. At least until today.

And now — to be thrust out because their

shenanigans had proved too much. It was only bound to get worse — again.

Chapter Thirteen

Ben stepped inside the cabin in Bledsoe's wake and for a moment wasn't sure whether to laugh at the chaos ensuing within, or retreat again to the porch. The house fairly overflowed with children, more than he knew Bledsoe and his wife had produced on their own.

Kate Bledsoe was a pert little thing with a crown of dark gold, braided and wrapped about her head, and warm brown eyes a shade or two lighter than Rachel's. Despite the brightness of her welcoming smile, the comparison still drew a pang.

But, Lord willing, he'd see Rachel again in a few days.

The two of them, Thomas and Kate Bledsoe, were openly affectionate with their greeting, although not uncomfortably so, and Ben found himself drawn in and introduced to the assortment of "young'uns" as Bledsoe called them. Most were younger sisters and a brother to Kate, with only two — as Ben already knew — their own off-spring, one with light blond hair and equally light blue eyes, and the other with brown hair and eyes. Ben unexpectedly found it fascinating to study the differing combinations of the parents' features and coloring.

Kate sat them down at the table with coffee and a plate of some sort of sweet that Ben could swear she'd just finished baking — as if she knew they'd be there. Or perhaps it was just to feed the passel of young'uns she'd taken on for the day.

"Mama's not been well of late," she told Bledsoe, with an apologetic half smile. "But I'm sure 'Mima and Pa can take them all back come evening." The full sun of her grin flashed for a moment. "You're home sooner than we reckoned. Not that I'm complaining."

He caught her in a one-armed embrace as she bustled past him, and this time Ben did have to avert his eyes. It was too easy — and stirred too deep a longing — to imagine doing the same with Rachel someday.

Please, Lord.

The frustration welled in him anew at the fruitlessness of their chase these past few weeks, but he shoved it down and buried it under a bite of pie and slurp of coffee.

267

"Colonel Young accomplished what he intended, I suppose," Bledsoe was explaining to his wife, "in that it looks as if we've clean swept all the outlaws from that quarter of the state." He smiled thinly at her. "But you know I'm ever skeptical."

Kate lowered the coffeepot she held to the tabletop, all humor fled from her face. "Well then," she said slowly, "we stay on guard, rifles to hand."

Bledsoe grinned. "That's my girl."

She glowed under his praise but remained somber. "Honestly, though, Thomas. From what I've been hearing, might be that nothing prevails against these two but old-fashioned prayer — and maybe fasting."

Bledsoe chewed for a moment, appearing to be thinking, then gave a firm nod. "You might be right, at that. But a canny group of men scouring the countryside can't hurt neither."

Though the Bledsoes were kind enough, Ben took his leave very early the next morning. He made Stanford shortly after noon, even at an easy pace — but it helped that Ivy was well conditioned from weeks on the trail.

He stayed the night with Stephen and his family, catching up on news and receiving a packet from Uncle Ben, cash money for the

268

intent of providing for his needs while out on the chase for the Harpes, and a letter asking whether they'd done any good yet.

Nothing from Rachel, however. Not remarkable in and of itself but . . . it troubled him.

He left again the next morning, set Ivy at a brisk pace, and arrived at Taylor's post about midafternoon. Although unsure as to why he felt it the right choice to do so, he tied Ivy out front rather than stable her in back.

It was Anne, baby on her hip, who stood behind the counter and greeted him. Something passed across her face but disappeared with a smile. "Ben! So good to see you."

Dan emerged from the back room with more warmth, but when Ben glanced around, looking for Rachel, they both anticipated his question, and the cloud returned to Anne's expression. "She's gone home to Knox County, Ben. I think the strain and worry over it all were too much, and she said she felt a need to see Mama and Pa again."

An unaccountably unsettled sensation fluttered in his middle. "I can certainly understand that."

But Anne frowned more deeply at him. "Did the two of you have a falling out, by any chance?"

His heart dropped completely. The memory of their parting washed over him, sweet and sharp. "I — no. Not that I know of."

"Well." Her expression cleared somewhat at that. "Maybe she's just feeling — overwhelmed." She peered more closely at him again then glanced at Dan, who stood listening and watching.

"Just what are your intentions regarding my sister, anyhow?" Dan said.

The tone remained mild, and his face nearly impassive, but Ben's throat suddenly dried to dust. "Honorable ones, I assure you."

The corner of Dan's mouth twitched, and the brown eyes sparkled. "Mm-hmm."

"I — we've not known each other for very long — and the circumstances —" Ben had never found himself at such a loss for words before.

Dan folded his arms. "Life is uncertain out here on the frontier. Folk tend to move fast."

Ben held the other man's gaze.

"*. . . if you decide you would be amenable to more than me merely 'calling upon you' . . .*"

Well, she'd yet to decide, that was certain. But Dan had asked only about Ben's intentions.

"I intend to court your sister properly, with the hope that she might indeed become my wife at some point." He cleared his throat. Blast the nervousness that made him need to do so. "Sooner rather than later, I'd prefer, but I'll not press her."

Dan sucked his teeth for a moment. "Fair enough." He swung toward Anne. "Can you bear putting this fellow up for the night? Or," and he turned back to Ben, "would you rather get a head start on your way down to Tennessee?"

Ben stayed, glad enough for the meal and company and the opportunity to speak with the two of them honestly — as well as give Ivy a bit of a rest. The only moment of hesitation came when Anne led him to the room that had been Rachel's and said he might as well sleep in a real bed as on the floor.

That too he would be grateful for, even if he fancied as he fell asleep that Rachel's scent still lingered there — and it was too easy to imagine her soft weight in his arms.

He must remember that she was most definitely not his wife — not yet. They'd not even any formal understanding between them.

May came to a close and June began with

271

thundershowers that cooled the air but left everything damp and sticky. It hadn't been much different up at Dan and Anne's, so Rachel couldn't complain, but the grayness of the day cast a bit of a pall over everything.

There had been no more word of the Harpes, or anything really, since the papers feted Colonel Young's brave expedition to chase all the outlaws from Kentucky. But banishing the Harpes solved nothing, and only put Sally and her little one even further out of reach.

Rachel tied on her apron and crossed from their family's cabin to their trading post. The station had grown larger and busier in the months she was gone, and as she walked, she let her gaze skim the forested hilltops rimming the bustle of wagon, horse, and foot traffic out on the road. Daddy had been here for half an hour already, but she'd gotten delayed at the house. Busy as it was, though, he'd be champing at the bit for her to come help.

She slipped in the back, through a storage room very like Dan and Anne's, and weaved through the tall shelving to the counter. Daddy's voice echoed from near the front, and she rounded a corner to see him deep in discussion with two other men, next to a display of Pennsylvania rifles.

Stepping behind the counter, she glanced again. One of those men was Hugh White. The other had his back to her, clad in hunting frock and black hat, one side cocked with a turkey feather, and the end of a golden-brown tail curling a little below the hat brim, at the man's nape.

Hugh turned and flashed an uncharacteristically wide grin as Daddy kept explaining something to the other man. Rachel hesitated then came out from behind the counter again.

Why was he all the way over here on this side of Knox County?

But it was the vague familiarity of the other man that tugged at her —

He turned, and Rachel's breath seized. "Ben?"

He took off his hat and stray wisps fell around his face as a hesitant smile tugged at his bearded mouth. "Rachel."

The way he said her name sank into her heart like butter into bread fresh from the oven. Her feet dragged to a stop. "What — how — when did you get here?"

The smile wavered again, though his gaze remained steady. "I stayed with Hugh and his family last night."

Hugh — who still looked unbelievably smug. Half a dozen different responses

273

sprang to mind, and she could speak none of them.

She glanced at Daddy. He also appeared entirely too pleased with himself.

A sigh escaped her. Things had seemed so much simpler — a world apart from here — at Dan and Anne's.

But here was Ben, in the flesh, looking at her with an expression that bordered now on desperation.

"You look well," she murmured.

His head dipped. "I am. And yourself?"

"Well enough." She hesitated, included the others in her attention this time. "Daddy, I suppose I need not introduce you . . . ?"

He hooked his thumbs into his waistband. "I know only that this is the young man responsible for providing you with that fine horse."

Rachel felt herself turning crimson. "Aye." She refocused on Ben. "Any success?" she asked, softly.

He shook his head the tiniest bit, gravely. "None that I'm happy with. I rode with Colonel Young — you might have heard about that?"

"Aye. Hailed all up and down Kentucky and Tennessee as a great hero, but —" She let the sentence hang, unfinished.

"My thoughts precisely." Ben's mouth thinned. "The Harpes remain at large, so — Sally has disappeared."

"So what now?" She'd lost count of the times she'd said those words to him, and he was likely sick of hearing it.

He huffed. "Wait until, oh, they come out of hiding, as some of us feel is bound to happen. Then go after them again." He tilted his head toward Daddy. "I'm taking the time to arm myself a bit better than before. And" — a shy smile made its reappearance, as he tucked his head for a moment — "visit you. That is . . . if you don't mind."

The tightness in her breast finally began to ease. "Not at all. I'm . . . glad to see you."

Hugh was grinning ear to ear, the meddlesome man, and Daddy wore his own smirk.

Suddenly all she wanted was to speak with Ben, alone. "Would you — perhaps — want to come on a short walk with me? Daddy, could you spare me for a bit?"

His grin matched Hugh's for a moment. "Don't go far," he rumbled.

"If you could set aside that rifle for me, sir?" Ben said.

"Be glad to." Daddy nodded at Rachel. "Away with you then."

She kept her hands knotted in her apron

as she led him out through the rear entrance. "We'll stay within sight of the house," she explained, feeling foolish about the entire thing. "Still the threat of — well, the Harpes, essentially. There's a lot of folk I don't know round the station these days, and we all trust one another less than we once did."

Replacing his hat, Ben nodded, gaze narrowed as he surveyed their surroundings. "Perfectly understandable."

The cadence of his speech was comfortingly familiar, though she sensed a new hardness about him. "How are you, truly?"

The smile flashed, briefly. "Well enough, as you said. A little weary of it all, however, I confess."

They set off at an angle, so to pass the house and walk among the trees beyond.

"I've missed you," she found herself murmuring.

"And I" — he heaved a great sigh — "have missed you. Tremendously." He stopped and swung toward her. "Rachel —"

"A little farther, please." She could feel the flush starting back up her cheeks. "My younger siblings have uncanny sharp hearing."

He grinned and fell into step beside her again.

They'd gone but a little farther when he said, "I must first ask, have I done anything to offend you?"

"What — offend? Nay!" She did stop then, beneath a spreading oak, turning to face him. "Why would you think so?"

He only searched her face, gravely, until she blushed again and dropped her head. "Your sister-in-law was — concerned," he said, finally.

"Oh." She grimaced and muttered, "Meddling sisters."

"Your brother asked, as well, what my intentions were. I assured him they were honorable, but — I wish to know, Rachel. You told me you'd welcome my calling on you, but if you've changed your mind —"

"I haven't," she said, then, "It's only that . . . oh, I don't know how to say it."

She felt his gaze upon her still. "I've all day. Longer if need be," he said.

Why, oh why, did he have to be so wonderfully patient? This was not helping her resolve. . . .

He went on, "Your brother said people out here often make quick decisions on things such as marriage because life on the frontier is so uncertain. I've come to better understand that, truth be told, but —"

"Sally decided quickly, and look what happened," Rachel said softly.

"Ahh." Ben released a heavy sigh, and at the edge of her vision, his feet shifted. "I hope you know —" He sighed again, cleared his throat. "I — understand."

She angled a look at him then, found him peering at his feet.

With a sudden jolt, she realized — he was wearing moccasins. And leggings. Last she'd seen him, he had on very proper breeches and cavalry boots, even with his hunting frock. But now — she let her gaze travel upward, noting the checked shirt over the buckskin covering his thighs, the open neck showing a gleam of sweat, that gold-glinted beard and the lengthening hair.

He looked almost a complete frontiersman, lacking only a few accoutrements, where just months ago he was the very picture of an eastern dandy.

His glance flicked upward, the blue eyes meeting hers — and holding.

"Ben." It was all she could manage. In this moment, she wanted nothing more than to fling herself into his arms and discover whether his kiss was as strangely wondrous as it had been at Dan and Anne's.

But was it worth the risk?

He'd ridden all the way to Knoxville for her, one voice in her head argued.

He was a good friend of Hugh's, and might have only come to visit him anyway, another countered.

But he'd brought her the news — which was no news, but still — of the hunt for the Harpes, which included concern for Sally's welfare.

"I know we've been drawn together through awful circumstances," he said.

"Circumstances that still have no resolution," she murmured. "And I'm already so indebted to you."

"I am as vested in this pursuit as you," he retorted, but quietly. "And, Rachel, I swear —" His chest rose and fell. "After being apart from you for the past six weeks, and seeing you again, I'm certain there's no other woman I could ever want."

A lump rose in her throat, and her vision blurred. "Ben Langford," she whispered. *Which is likely what Wiley told Sally.* But 'twould be unfair to say that aloud.

He stepped closer. "When we kissed before, well, I thought — it seemed as though — you were also certain. What changed?"

Her breath caught, but she still couldn't reply.

Taking her hand, he brushed his thumb across her knuckles and reached up to trace the back of his other hand against her cheek. His eyes, clear and vivid as the sky above them, begged her attention. "Are you afraid, sweet Rachel?"

She nodded sharply.

"Of what?" he breathed.

She swallowed hard. "Of — of you. Of — losing you, if not to the Harpes, then — at some other time." It sounded foolish even as she said it, and further words failed her.

He blew out another long breath, and shifted back a little. "I told your brother I'd not press you. If you simply need time —"

"Aye," she said, too quickly. But time was — good.

"Very well." His hands and gaze fell away, eyes narrowing upon something in the distance. She almost whimpered with the sudden loss of his touch. "I'll be at Hugh's for a few more days at least, unless word comes of something happening." His eyes flickered back to hers. "How do Sally's parents fare with it all?"

"They are — holding up as well as could be expected, I suppose." She hesitated. "This has well-nigh devastated them. The church seems to have rallied around them, though, as they should."

He nodded, glancing aside again. "Shall I walk you back to the post?"

"I believe I can find my way," she said dryly, but it drew no answering smile from him, only a single nod.

He stared at the ground for a moment then looked up briefly. "Be well, Rachel," he murmured, and turning, walked away.

She folded both arms around her middle. It took everything she had to stay put and not run after him to apologize.

If she needed time, he'd give it to her. Perhaps not willingly, but he'd given his word, hang it all.

A burn rose from his gut into his chest and throat, nearly choking him, strangling breath and rational thoughts. How unwise was it, anyway, to consider courting a woman he knew only because of criminal proceedings — worse, because of his own cousin's murder and her association with the guilty parties?

Ridiculous for him to even contemplate it.

Except that it was far beyond any of that, and utterly useless to tell his heart to disengage.

He strode back to the trading post, where Mr. Taylor and Hugh still stood talking. Their conversation fell silent, however, when he walked in, and both men gaped, no doubt at seeing him alone.

"Where's Rachel?" Mr. Taylor asked, straightening, alarm tightening his features.

"She'll be along directly." He realized suddenly how it must look, him returning without her. "She's — not terribly wishful of my company at this moment."

The man came to his feet without a word, his dark eyes so hard it sent a chill down Ben's spine. Even Hugh looked at him askance, one brow raised.

"I — she's well, I assure you. She simply declined to walk back with me. Perhaps I presumed too much feeling on her part from our friendship these past months, but — I've done nothing dishonorable, I swear."

"I'll let my daughter's explanation be the judge of that," Mr. Taylor said.

"Good Lord, Ben," Hugh exclaimed, "what did you do?"

For a minute, all he could do was stand there, his own jaw slack.

"I'll go find Rachel," Hugh said, and whisked out the door.

Ben dragged a breath into his aching lungs. In this moment, he thought he'd rather be facing the Harpes.

"Mr. Taylor, I — I love Rachel. It must seem sudden, I realize, but it's the truth."

The older man leaned back against the counter, arms folded across his chest.

"Good to know I hadn't misread the intent of your interest. So you're telling me Rachel doesn't feel the same?"

"She assured me weeks ago that she welcomed my suit. But now — well, she said she needs time. That — Sally married so quickly, and because that turned to such disaster —" Ben shook his head. He was faring no better at explaining than Rachel had.

"Hmm." Mr. Taylor rubbed his bearded jaw. "Do you know how many young bucks my girl's had to fend off over the years?"

Ben gave a short laugh. "I can imagine, sir. But I'd no thought at first of pursuing her in that way. I was merely extending friendship. Trying simply to make the best of a wretched situation, between my cousin's murder and her distress over Sally's situation." He lifted a hand and let it drop in a gesture of frustration. "Perhaps she was only flattered by my attentions when I spoke of more, but . . ."

He floundered to silence. There was no coolness in the way she'd returned his kisses in the stable there at Dan and Anne's, but — come to think of it, even then she'd seemed conflicted. And perhaps he had misread her response. . . .

Either way, though, he couldn't say *that* to

her father.

"If she didn't let you know straight out that she *wasn't* interested," Mr. Taylor said, "then that's remarkable in and of itself. For her to say you were welcome to — how was it you said?"

He coughed another broken laugh. "I asked her if she'd mind my calling upon her, after the Harpes were caught and I was no longer obligated to see justice done for my cousin and the others."

"And she said . . . ?"

"That she'd be glad of it." He hesitated. "Of course, that was when we thought we'd have the Harpes back in jail by now."

Mr. Taylor let out a long breath. "Aye, and more's the pity." He shook his head. "Almost beyond believing, what we've heard and read."

"It is."

"Rachel's taken it hard, this whole thing with Sally. She stood up for her there at that wedding, did she tell you?"

Ben nodded. Just the thought of Rachel in the presence of those men — and Hugh had signed their wedding bond —

"I promised her I'd do everything I could for Sally. They wouldn't let me serve as anything but counsel for the defense, but she was acquitted easily enough. And then

284

the women took off into the wilderness —"

"Did they ever find out where they'd gone?"

"Some of our party tracked them to the Green River, where they traded their horse for a canoe and slipped away downriver. They could be anywhere now."

Hugh reappeared through the back door — alone. "Rachel's gone back to the house for now," he said to Mr. Taylor. "She bids me tell you she'll speak with you later, but assures me there's no fault of Ben's in the matter."

He shot Ben a pitying look.

The older man had returned to rubbing his jaw thoughtfully. "Rachel refusing to even face a suitor. Now there's an interesting turn."

"How unfair of you, to argue for him!"

Rachel stood almost toe-to-toe with Daddy, who regarded her with maddening calm. "The man cares for you, plain and simple. If you don't care for him in return, then be honest and tell him so. Don't leave him hanging."

"I —" Rachel stomped her foot and whirled away, covering her eyes with one hand. "I can't."

"Why not?"

She couldn't even begin to explain to him all the reasons.

"If you're worried about him turning out to be a rascal, sweetheart, I can tell you . . . he ain't like the Harpes, by a long shot."

She did not move. "I know that."

"And if — honey, we've stood back and watched you with one lovesick fool after another. Ain't never seen you run away from any. Are you just spooked because you let this one past your defenses, but when faced with really trusting him . . . ?"

Rachel sucked in a breath that was too much like a sob. "I don't know if I can bear losing him, Daddy. The Harpes aren't anything close to finished yet, are they? No? Well then, even you agree. And he's determined to hunt them until justice is served or —" She fought down the weeping. "What if they kill him too?"

Daddy took her by the shoulders, turned her around. "C'mere, sweetheart."

She sagged against him, forehead to his chest. This — this was what she missed with Ben —

"We can't live our lives running scared. God gave you a family who loves you — and just maybe a man of your own in this Langford fellow. Nay, don't be squawking just yet," he said to her protest. "Stranger things have happened, you know."

"Aye, but God gave Sally a family who loves her too, and — look what happened."

He kissed the top of her head. "Bear in mind, her folks were none too pleased with Wiley Harpe, willing though they were to believe he'd made a true profession of faith and was the right man for her." He chuckled. "You have to admit, it's plenty ironic that I'm the one telling you to give Ben Langford a fair shake here."

Sniffling, she nodded and pushed herself upright.

"Do I have your permission to invite the man to supper some night?" Daddy's smile was teasing.

The supper invitation never happened, however. Daddy sent an inquiry over to the Whites, only to hear back that Ben had, after a brief visit with the Rices, departed for Virginia.

That was a safer route than striking off into the wilderness to hunt the Harpes on his own — which she'd feared he might consider doing. But the regret that he'd gone without a farewell — that she'd not properly greeted him after so many weeks apart — struck her more deeply than she expected.

CHAPTER FOURTEEN

Standing before his uncle, Ben closed his eyes and let the sorrow wash over him.

It wasn't that his family's greeting was lacking. But after the openmouthed stares and expressions of shock, he knew he'd never be part of this world again.

Even if Rachel ultimately did not trust her entire heart to him.

From the large upholstered chair behind his desk, Uncle Ben fussed over the failure to apprehend the Harpes, then lapsed into reminiscing about the wildness of the mountains of Virginia, not so many years ago, and even to this day. What cut most deeply was how the older man had aged — what appeared a decade or more — in the months Ben had been absent. Then, tears in his eyes, he waved a hand. "And look at you, dressed as a savage yourself."

"No, many of them dress more finely," Ben said, but his uncle missed the dry humor entirely.

"Well, there you have it. Go shave, have your hair cut, and wear something appropriate to your station."

Ben released a long sigh. "I am thinking of settling out there," he said.

His uncle narrowed a look upon him, lips thinned. "I should have expected that."

"I'm also thinking of marrying soon — once the Harpes are brought to justice, of course."

"Ahh-h." His uncle sat up, shuffled a few papers on his desk, and glared at Ben again, but it lacked the heat of a few moments ago. "You'll leave many a girl's heart broken, here in Virginia."

"I never gave any of them cause to hope. Not with Thomas to look after."

He regretted the words as soon as they escaped his mouth.

The older man stilled then sighed as well. "I suppose you are right. I am sorry, my boy."

Ben's eyes burned. His uncle had never, to his memory, apologized. "I am more sorry that I could not look after him as well as I should have, out on the frontier."

"Yes. Well. See to apprehending those scoundrels, at least."

■ ■ ■ ■

June whiled away into July, unrelentingly hot and sticky. Two months and more it had been since they'd had word of the Harpes. Folk had begun to let their guard down. Talk was that the notorious pair had doubtless either gone farther north, across the Ohio, or floated on down toward the Mississippi. Perhaps they'd find their ilk in the wild town of New Orleans, and if so, good riddance. Let the authorities there deal with whatever mischief they caused.

Lord God, continue to watch over Sally. Protect her and little Eady . . . and the other babies as well.

It was Rachel's almost continuous prayer.

And protect Ben and keep him well — wherever he is.

No more word had come from him. Rachel supposed it was to be expected, but she missed his articulate letters as well as his presence.

Independence Day came and went with its usual celebrations, a feu de joie that to be honest was little different from the everyday commotion of Knoxville. In the past, Rachel had found it exciting, but this time it all just wearied her.

How did folk who lived in Knoxville proper bear it on a daily basis? Even removed as they were, but positioned on a main thoroughfare, the constant activity of Campbell's Station had begun to wear on her as well.

Although, perhaps it was only the tension of waiting for word of the Harpes. Rachel wasn't sure she could bear that even one more day.

But bear it, she did. Day after day, until nearly half the month slipped by, and all of them were wilting in the July heat. The cooler weather of September could not come soon enough.

She remained busy at the post, and while working on accounts and wishing for a walk down by the creek, just to dip her feet in for some relief, she overheard a snippet of news from one of the men out on the porch. "— murder, out along the Road in Roane County."

Every hair on her head and arms rose with the chill.

It was the Harpes, she knew it. Even as the men on the porch soothed each other with, "Nah, it couldn't be," she knew.

July 29, 1799
"I knew that couldn't be the end of it," Ben

muttered, setting down the delicate porcelain coffee cup and scanning the words of the newspaper article with more intensity.

"What is it?" Hugh leaned from his chair at the breakfast table, to one side of Ben, and at the other, Hugh's wife Eliza likewise sat a little straighter.

Ben handed him the paper. "Boy of Chesley Coffey, up over on Black Oak Ridge, found murdered. After that farmer over in Roane County."

Hugh paled. "That's right up where the Harpes lived when Sally wed Wiley."

Eliza's cup clattered in her saucer. Hugh exchanged a long look with her then turned to Ben. "I know you'll be going, but I can't leave Eliza, so close to her time."

"Understandably." He lifted the coffee cup again and drained it. "I should prepare to leave right away."

Eliza put out a hand. "Will you be stopping to see Rachel first?"

Rising from his chair, Ben hesitated. A pang still rippled through his middle at the thought of her. Even though he'd been back in Knoxville for the past week, he'd not ventured over to Campbell's Station to see her.

Eliza's earnest gaze was full of sympathy. "You should, Ben. Regardless of your last parting."

He made no reply, and apparently Hugh felt the need to chime in. "Don't give up on her quite yet."

"I'm not giving up," Ben murmured. "Only — ordering my priorities." When they still looked pointedly at him, he went on, "I cannot properly court her until the Harpes are brought finally to justice."

And Sally good and well rescued, but he'd not add that.

"Still," Eliza persisted. "Hear that from me as a woman, as well as the wife of your friend. Don't discount her need to be reminded that she's likewise one of your priorities." Her lips curved, the gray eyes sparkling.

He gave a reluctant nod. "Thank you both for your hospitality."

"You are always welcome," Hugh said. "And our prayers go with you."

By the time he'd packed his things, including the beautiful rifle he'd purchased from Rachel's father, and saddled Ivy, his mind was made up.

Mist clung under the trees and in the soft folds of the land, leading down to the river as Rachel walked across from their cabin to the trading post, carrying a basket over one arm. 'Twas a pretty sight, the way the sunlight pierced and lit it, lending a dream-like quality to the early morning. It had the effect of slightly muffling the sounds of the station awakening as well.

From just down the road, a lone rider appeared like a shadow, the horse's smooth single-foot gait carrying him in what appeared a rippling glide. It was a familiar-enough sight, as the trait was favored among horsemen all up and down the frontier, but of course ever since Ben, the glimpse of such a horse in action never failed to tug at her heart and memory.

They still kept Dandelion too, and she and Daddy both enjoyed rides on him whenever possible.

As he neared, face turned her direction but indistinguishable under the brim of his hat, the rider reined his mount to a stop at the edge of the road. The horse sidestepped, eager to keep moving, and pulled at the bit, but the man astride kept his attention fixed on Rachel.

A chill swept her, not an ill sensation but rather — a knowing, and a surge of longing. *Ben.*

She turned, facing him, clasping the basket in both hands, tilting her head in hopes of a better glimpse of his face. Neither of them moved for a long moment.

Then her feet were carrying her toward him, and he dismounted and met her halfway.

They stopped a little more than arms' length from each other.

Rachel swallowed. "You're going after them, aren't you?"

He nodded.

Tears were rolling down her cheeks before she could stop them. Oh, how she regretted these last weeks, and the way his last visit had ended.

She reached out a hand, blindly, and he took it. Whether it was he who closed the remaining distance between them, or both of them, she never knew, but his arms around her were a comfort too sweet for words.

And she didn't even care that they stood out in full view of anyone.

"I will find them, I swear it," he murmured. "And if the Lord wills, come back to you after."

She tipped her head to look up at him. "I'll be praying for that, every moment."

He didn't even hesitate, but kissed her, warm and strong and confident, until both of them were breathless. Even then, he drew back only a bit, the brim of his hat shielding them both from the morning sun. "Twice now you've kissed me goodbye," he whispered. "Promise me that next time you'll kiss me hello as well."

Her broken laugh came out in a shudder, like a sob. She curled one hand around the back of his neck and tugged him toward her. "I promise," she breathed, as his lips settled against hers once more.

Three murders in the span of a week, two of which were almost certainly the Harpes. The last one bore the now-signature slashed gut filled with stones and the body sunk in the river.

Ben should not have been riding alone, much less to a place where they were known to have connections — however tenuous those were, or however long since anyone had even seen the Harpe women.

But somehow he couldn't deny the impulse to go visit Reverend and Missus Rice and their family.

Nothing seemed amiss when he approached the cabin. The expected sounds of children playing echoed from behind the house, and a cow and horse lounged in adjacent pens. "Halloo the house!" he called as he rode into the yard — the custom not so different from rural parts of Pitt County,

296

Virginia — but definitely more needful on the frontier if one wished not to be shot on sight.

And something about this visit felt very wrong, despite the warmth the Rices had extended him when he'd been here last month.

A movement showed at one of the windows, then Reverend Rice himself opened the door and stepped out onto the porch. Ben noted that he was careful to shut the door behind him.

"Mr. Langford. We'd not expected you today."

A chill touched Ben's shoulders. This was certainly not the welcome of last time. "How do you do, Reverend Rice? I was in the neighborhood and thought to look in on you and the family."

The preacher came to the top of the steps, and even to Ben's eye his smile appeared forced. "We are very well, thank you. And yourself?"

"I am well," Ben said.

A baby's cry came from inside the house, and Reverend Rice flinched but did not otherwise react. But such a thing should not have been unusual for their home, full of youngsters as it was.

And then a second cry — two at once.

Reverend Rice looked pained.

The door opened again, and Ben should have been unsurprised when Sally appeared in the doorway. She frowned at Ben for a long moment then said, "You might as well come in, Mr. Langford. It's just Betsey and Susan and I — and the babies too, of course."

He tethered Ivy, scanned the yard for signs of the Harpe men, then stepped inside.

The interior of the cabin was hot, but the other women huddled close. On a blanket spread on the floor, one of the babies lay, kicking and cooing, while Susan had picked hers up and sat preparing to nurse the child. Sally's mother held the third while an older girl — presumably a sister — leaned over her shoulder.

"What are you doing here, Mr. Langford?" Sally asked, a note of alarm in her voice.

"I was coming to look in on your parents, and to let them know —" He looked around the room, not missing the obvious joy of Missus Rice in Sally's baby — even Reverend Rice's expression was one of tenderness as he watched his wife and grandchild. Ben cleared his throat. "I simply wished to make my farewells before I leave Knoxville."

The women all exchanged glances, seeming to grasp the implication well enough.

"And how fares Rachel?" Sally asked softly.

"Rachel seems to be well. Concerned for you."

Sally's eyes darted about. "She shouldn't be." The words were blithe, spoken with a forced cheer. "I am well, as you can see, and so is little Eady."

Ben was weighing a response when she rounded on him, her voice dropping. "Thank you for your concern, Mr. Langford. You should go now. It ain't safe for you here."

And God help him, but the fear gripped his throat at her words. To be caught alone if Micajah and Wiley returned —

He made himself keep calm. "How is it you came to be here?"

She flashed a brittle smile. "Big and Little know the value of family. They were kind enough to let us stop so Daddy and Mama could see the babies."

He tried to hold her gaze, but she was watching her mother with little Eady again. Suppressing a sigh, he gave them all a nod. "Missus Rice. Miss Rice. Susan, Betsey. It has been good to see you. Reverend Rice." He reached out and shook hands with the preacher, whose relief shone in his features. "Thank you for your time."

"Keep us in your prayers, son."

"Already done." He hesitated at the door. "Sally? It isn't too late."

But she shook her head and turned away. "Is so," he thought he heard her mutter.

With another nod to the room at large, he took his leave, neck and shoulders prickling as he fetched Ivy — but there was nothing amiss in sight.

The Harpe women at the home of Reverend Rice. Who would believe such a thing?

And would they be here long enough for Ben to arrange pursuit, or even an ambush?

They were back, and Sally could not still the trembling in her middle.

She knew it was only a temporary reprieve at best, Big and Little agreeing to let them visit Daddy and Mama. It was a gift, truly, one she'd never dreamed they'd allow, that she'd gotten to set little Eady in Mama's arms and share her happy tears.

And they'd been welcomed with open arms, more's the wonder. Oh, there were plenty of searching looks and inquiries after her health, as well as anxious glances outdoors, but neither Daddy nor Mama seemed anything but beside themselves with joy to see her and the baby.

They'd even treated Susan and Betsey like

family, and cooed over their little ones as well.

But of course, it had to come to an end. Big and Little came riding into the stable yard, bold as you please, bawling for them to come out and pack up. And so began the process of bringing the rest of the horses out, packing all their provisions and belongings on them, and the women mounting up as well.

Sally was more than grateful to be riding, but — still.

She tried not to look around. It was hours since Mr. Langford had been here, and it wouldn't do to make either of the men suspicious by appearing that she expected someone else to be there.

They were nearly ready now. Sally stood by her horse and turned to look for Little so he could help her mount. To her shock, Daddy stood talking to him, almost nose to nose.

She could only catch bits of the conversation. "— said you were serious about the kingdom way . . . baptized . . . profession of faith. What happened, Wiley?"

A mocking half smile curled Little's mouth. "Just keep praying for me, Preacher."

Daddy didn't budge. "And you, repent

before it's too late. Or be sure your sin will find you out."

Wiley laughed and strolled toward Sally. Avoiding his eyes, she let him hand her up. When she was settled in the saddle, Mama came near and handed little Eady up so Sally could bundle her against her breast.

"Take care of them, son," Daddy said, and this time his voice did shake.

"Oh, I will," Wiley said, still grinning, and went to his own horse. Daddy stepped up beside Sally and reached for her hand. His hazel eyes burned into hers. "You come home at any time, you hear me? *Any* time."

She squeezed his hand, and then her horse was moving. Though tears blurred her eyes, she turned in the saddle and watched them until the trees hid them from sight.

The clop of horses' hooves, the creak of the saddles, and birds in the trees were all that filled the silence, until one of the men — she was sure it was Little — burst out in high-pitched mockery, " 'Repent before it's too late.' "

And both Big and Little guffawed. Sally closed her eyes and let the tears fall.

At least Susan and Betsey did not laugh.

CHAPTER FIFTEEN

July 30
Robert Brassel was the man's name, and he'd narrowly escaped being murdered by the Harpes, the day before.

His brother James had not been so fortunate.

"They was alone when my brother and I encountered them on the road away from Knoxville," the man said. "Like any travelers, they stopped and asked what was the news. We told them of the recent killings, and they expressed shock and outrage like any good men might. But then — while we were talking, one said suddenly, 'Why, you are the Harpes!' and lifted his rifle to shoot. I jumped off my horse and ran away — yelled at James to do the same — and somehow, ducking through the rhody bushes, I outran Little and got away, though he shot at me. Didn't stop running till I'd gotten ten miles up the Road and ran into a party traveling south. They'd only one gun between 'em all for protection, but they agreed to let me ride back with 'em. And then — we found James —"

He drew a deep breath, then another.

Ben let him take all the time he needed. Too well he knew that overwhelming grief, fresh after news of the loss.

"James, he was beat up bad, and his throat cut. We bundled his body and brought it back so I could help his family bury him, but then —" Brassel caught his breath again, gaze bouncing between the tabletop and the faces of the men sitting around him. "There they come — the Harpes — again. Only this time, they had their women and children and baggage with 'em." He grimaced. "One of Dale's men suggested we just ride on past if they gave no sign of fighting, and of course they all agreed." Brassel swallowed heavily, looking sick. "So we did. Just rode on past, us on one side of the path, the Harpes on the other. The men, they looked awful at us, rifles across their saddlebows, but nobody said nothin'. And those I was with, they kept on saying nothin', in case the Harpes would hear and thinkin' it a threat, turn back on us."

A mutter rose from the men sitting there.

"Dale and his men said later, what could

we all do with only one gun? But I swear, I never met such a lily-livered bunch."

"Well. We'd all be glad to ride out after them." William Wood nodded toward Ben. "Langford here, his cousin was the first known victim of the Harpes. So he's plenty motivated himself."

Brassel looked at Ben with new interest, the pain and understanding so clear in his eyes that it fair took Ben's breath away. He nodded slowly. "Well then, I'd be honored to have you ride with me," Brassel said quietly.

July 31
"Look." The farmer Tully's voice rose, almost frantic. "I helped y'all by carrying messages back and forth from your old man to your women, weeks ago. Even though the law and the papers was saying terrible things about you. What more can I do? I got a wife and children —"

There was a softly snarled word from Big, then the flash of sun on a blade as he raised his arm and it fell.

Sally, already trying not to look as she fumbled to latch a crying Eady on to nurse while still a-horseback, flinched and squeezed her eyes shut.

The babe whimpered even as she set to

suckling.

God . . . oh God, I cry out to You in violence. . . .

She remembered the farmer, his kind, pitying face as he gave Susan a message and took one in return.

Big and Little were dragging the man away, out of sight. They returned shortly enough, laughing quietly as they swung up onto their horses. "We sleep at Old Man Roberts's tonight!" Big sang out as they set off.

As if that would be aught to boast about. The only thing noteworthy was that they had good horses and could make easily fifty miles a day.

Ben's party made good time up the trace from Knoxville — not on the usual road, toward Cumberland Gap, but farther west, through timbered hills that were the wildest Ben had seen yet. They turned almost due west at the lower spur of Cumberland Mountain and pressed on toward the Tennessee-Kentucky state line.

Attempting to trace their progress on a map was frustrating as always, but by his calculations they had passed over into Kentucky when a commotion on a farm along the way drew their attention. Their party turned aside and found that John Tully, the man of the family in residence there, had disappeared the day before, and the neighbors turned out to help search for him. Missus Tully was in great distress, but trying valiantly to put on a brave face in the presence of their eight young children.

Ben and the others joined the search, and it wasn't long before, alerted by the smell, they found the man's body near the road, hidden under a log.

As the neighbors stepped up to help with funeral preparations and consoling the grieving now-widow, Ben's party agreed it was needful for them to assume this murder had also been done by the Harpes, and to press on in pursuit of them.

One of Tully's neighbors and one of Ben's party continued to the northwest, heading for Daniel Trabue's home and store some forty miles away. If the Harpes were bent on revenge — which seemed likely, once Tully's dubious connection to the Harpes had been revealed, from just a few months before — then it followed that Trabue might become a target, for his part in pursuing them after his son's murder in April.

"Old Man Roberts's house is just up the way as well," the neighbor, Nathaniel Stockton, commented. "Mebbe they're headed there."

"And how many men will Roberts have?" someone asked. "Do we dare even try to corner them there? Better to try to catch them alone, wouldn't it?"

Ben gritted his teeth with the frustration of it all. He'd no more wish to throw himself before a rifle ball — or tomahawk blade — than anyone else, but this was ridiculous.

He could tell by Brassel's face that the other man was of a similar mind. But it was true — what could the handful of them do if the Harpes' manpower were doubled or tripled?

"Perhaps we could watch and wait, catch them as they leave," Ben suggested.

They all looked at one another, no one saying a word. The weariness of the chase lay heavy on them already, and it felt like they'd hardly begun.

August

Murder should not happen on such a beautiful morning.

Little Eady strapped to her chest, Sally strolled the old buffalo trace as if there were no screams or wicked laughter filtering through the forest behind her. It was before dawn and mosquitoes swarmed thick around her face, but she merely brushed them away and kept walking.

Better them than to have to watch the bloodshed behind her.

It was a whole family this time — Big said for the sake of horses and provisions, although the women were already well mounted and they'd lacked for naught of late. There was no justification for what they were doing, or had done, these past weeks.

Sally had nearly lost count. A father and son who graciously shared their camp on an unexpected stop on the way up to see Old Man Roberts — who ironically enough, sent them on their way far sooner than Sally would have expected.

Maybe he too had lost patience with Big and Little's shenanigans.

From there, they'd ridden farther west and a little south. Running across a young Negro boy on the way to the mill with a sack of grain balanced across the withers of his horse, Big and Little indulged their hellish sense of fun on the lad, but then spooked by sounds of pursuit on the trace behind them, left the lad's broken body behind without taking the horse or grain.

And this — this was almost worse than anything else.

I will never leave thee or forsake thee.

Could it be true? Was the Lord with her, even in this?

Lord, show me. Help me. Save me, Lord, if I'm truly still Yours.

I cannot bear much more of this.

It was a typical August late afternoon where a haze thickened the air, and the sun shone blood red as it sank toward the west. Lanterns hung in the trees all about, and women fanned themselves as everyone gathered in the open, lighted area.

This was no ordinary Bible meeting, however, comprised of church members from Baptist, Methodist, and Presbyterian persuasion. Reverends Ramsay and Carrick of the Presbyterians had joined together with Reverend Rice and called for all, far and wide, to gather for prayer.

It had started with Reverend Rice calling for his own congregation to pray — for the Harpes to be stopped and Sally and the other women to be rescued. Rachel could see the desperation in his face, but the church members were of a good will to intercede for such a cause, and Rachel as well.

It was, in fact, the only thing that felt even remotely useful these days.

■ ■ ■ ■

Ben tied Ivy, nearly as sweaty and lathered as the half-dozen others he rode with, and stepped inside the dim closeness of the tavern. Like the others, he asked for ale, grateful of something stronger than water to quench his thirst.

The tavernkeep handed him an earthenware tankard, brimming to the top with foamy amber, and Ben pushed a coin across the rough countertop. "My thanks. Does the post travel through this part of the country?"

The man shook his head and frowned. "Tryin' ta get it, but haven't yet. Mebbe next year."

Ben nodded absently and drank deeply, savoring the cool bitterness. He nearly could not remember a time he was not riding some trace, on the pursuit of men who even with their women and babies in tow could seemingly vanish like the mist. Some of the men he rode with had begun to speculate that the Harpes must have otherworldly help in escaping the search parties, because even when half the countryside had turned out to chase after them, the trail always went cold, either blurring with that of other travelers, or disappearing altogether in some watercourse.

He'd gotten somewhat skilled, himself, at reading sign — not just hoofprints of their mounts but other signs of a traveler's passing, such as broken twigs or other vegetation, or spiders' webs swept aside. They needed more, however, if they hoped to actually catch the Harpes. And Ben was past weary of riding to and fro on the same trails and traces, sometimes in circles, and all still for naught.

By the same token, this was a wondrously beautiful land. He could see why so many folk flocked to it. The tales he'd heard of wild animals and men alike were nearly too fantastic to be believed, and while even the Cherokee were more sparse than they once were, Ben and whatever party he rode with for the time frequently encountered Indians and stopped to ask if they'd any news about the Harpes. Their bronzed, stoic faces often went even more rigid, betraying their disdain for either the outlaws or those pursuing them — or, Ben thought, perhaps both.

They also caught glimpses of herds of bison or elk and sometimes hunted from the same, proving that the wilderness was not yet bereft of such richness. Flocks of parrots fluttered through the trees above, their brightly colored plumage like chirping, moving flower gardens.

More than once, Ben thought he could be completely enchanted with this place, were it not for the rigors of the chase.

The men comprising his posse came and went, some riding along for a day or two, some for as long as a week before domestic duty called them back home. The worst happened, however, when word came of another posse encountering the Harpes, only to be overcome and most of them slain. The two who escaped carried yet another variation on what had become a universal narrative of the Harpes' cruelty and unbearably intimidating presence.

Even prayer had become a weariness. *Lord, forgive me for that,* he found himself imploring. There was a ripple of something Ben thought he remembered feeling like peace, then that too was lost to the muddy, rushing river that the course of his own days had become.

Like such a current, however, swift and deep and utterly irresistible, Ben could not stop. From Thomas to James Brassel to John Tully, and then the ruin they'd found of two families — including women and children and slaves, all slain where they'd camped on their way to the Promised Land — there

313

was a continual reminder of why Ben rode these paths.

"What ails that child?" Little growled, hunched over a leg of a turkey they'd roasted over the fire.

The babe had set to wailing even before suppertime, and Sally barely snatched a bite before strolling around the camp, alternately patting Eady's back and putting her to breast, trying to soothe her. "Nothing. She's just a little fretful. Be fine in a bit."

Both Big and Little had warned them never to let the babies cry — especially during the past week, as they'd circled around and traveled back north, shaking off what felt like a dozen or more search parties after the string of killings the men had done all up the Kentucky Trace. She and Betsey and Susan usually walked away from the camp until the little ones were soothed, often even staying the night a ways out so the men's sleep would not be disturbed by their fussing. But this evening, Sally was just plain tired herself. The air hung hot and muggy while they all slapped and itched at the mosquito and chigger bites. Who would not be fretful under such circumstances?

And it certainly couldn't be good for the babies that all three mamas felt the terrible burden of what their daddies had been do-ing. Unnatural it was, though all three of them tried to carry on as if it weren't.

Huffing, Sally sat down on a rock so she could get a better latching on, but poor Eady only whimpered and gurgled, then after suckling a bit, pulled away with another cry.

Big shoved to his feet, glaring at her. "Shut that thing up!"

"She's got a tummy ache," Sally said, and shifted the babe back to her shoulder while she fumbled to put clothing back in place. Eady's cries were only muffled at best, and her tiny toes dug in under Sally's ribs. She gave up on trying to arrange herself and cuddled Eady with both hands again, seek-ing the particular angle that she knew would help the baby's pains. "Shh, there, little one. All will be —"

With a roar, Big loomed close and snatched the tiny girl from her grasp. Eady's wail pitched suddenly, terrifyingly high as in a move nearly too fast for Sally's eye to fol-low, Big swung the baby by her feet and dashed her against a nearby tree trunk.

Sally's lungs seized. Silence fell. No one moved. The babe's lifeless body dangled from Big's hand, and he stared at it as if not realizing what he'd done, before tossing it aside.

As if it were nothing but a bit of rubbish.

He looked across at Sally. "I told you I can't abide no crying babies."

Plunking himself back down next to the cook fire, he grabbed another piece of meat and shoved it in his mouth.

Breath returned, searing. A thin scream rent the air — Sally's or someone else's, she could not say — but Betsey and Susan took her arms and dragged her away into the woods.

God — oh God — oh — God —

They released her and she collapsed to the ground, sobbing.

Of the next hours, Sally could recall little, except that Betsey and Susan stayed with her all night, one on either side, sleeping in bits when they weren't tending their own babies. She herself slept but fitfully, dozing off somewhere halfway to dawn, after Susan covered her with something warm and comforting.

When she awoke in early daylight, it was the same blue cloak Rachel had given her on her wedding day.

Susan watched her in silence as she sat up and fingered the fine woolen weave. Their

316

eyes met, and the older women gave a single nod.

It was no substitute for a child — no consolation for the jagged sorrow shredding her heart — but Sally held the garment to her breast and wept.

As full dawn broke, the women gathered her up, their own sleeping babes bundled against them, and led her back to camp. Both men were up and packing. Wiley refused to acknowledge them but looked a little pale and drawn. Even Micajah seemed more subdued than usual.

Susan sat Sally down and bid her stay, then she and Betsey bustled about and finished packing without her.

Despite the day's heat, Sally clutched her cloak about her. Tried to close her eyes and not think — or feel — but the horror of the place and the men's movement about her would not allow her not to keep watch. Her eye kept being drawn back and back to the tiny heap of cloth over on the other side of the fire pit, though, where flies were already swarming.

Could they not even take the time to bury her poor little one?

She dared not even ask.

It was Susan, again, who led her to her saddled horse, but Wiley who gave her a leg up. He stood for a moment, hand on her knee, looking as if he wanted to speak, but turned away without a word.

Bits of conversation floated to her as they rode. Susan's voice, low but insistent, and Micajah turning in the saddle, glowering at her with a rumbled threat. She was quiet for a moment but then shot back a soft retort, and after a lingering scowl, he turned back around and did not reply.

Yea, though I walk through the valley of the shadow of death . . . thou art with me. . . .

Her eyes burned. She was walking that path, for true.

She lifted her gaze to the blue sky, full of fluffy white clouds. *Oh Lord, did You receive little Eady's spirit? Is she with You, even now?*

Micajah's horse came up lame, and cursing, he dismounted and led them to the edge of a farmstead where Sally was sure they had been before. A man worked a field of corn in the company of two Negroes, and they all straightened, wary, as their party approached. "Ho there!" Micajah called out. "We have a horse that just came up lame. Need to trade for a fresh. Would you be able to help?"

The man shook his head, eyeing them all. Sally noted the length of his beard — so full and long that he'd braided and pinned it to

318

his trousers to keep it out of the way. "And what would y'all be needing another horse for?"

"Oh, we're on our way to join up with those who be huntin' the Harpes," Micajah answered easily. It wasn't the first such time he'd used the ruse. "We be William and John Roberts, and these are our wives, Honey and Tunney." He twitched a nod toward Sally. "That 'un's Sissy, our child."

Well, that was new. Sally sat her horse and didn't move.

Betsey's babe, little Joe, stirred and began to cry. Sally's breasts, already aching, let go with a burning ache that flooded her front with wetness. She folded her arms against herself, beneath the cloak, glad for its cover.

"Sorry, but I can't help," the man said at last. "I ain't got a horse to spare."

Micajah huffed and started to stomp, but Susan flung herself off her horse and ran to him. "Don't you be givin' in to this now," she said, her voice strangely sweet and cajoling. "Come and let your brother the preacher pray over you some more."

Betsey went to his other side, and between the two of them, they led him back to his lame horse. Betsey prevailed on him to mount hers, and she climbed up behind Susan, after they'd put little Joe and Lovey in panniers on the lame horse.

Micajah led off in a lather.

Later that day — or maybe it was the next — at the edge of a blackberry thicket, they'd stopped to rest and pick berries, when a small girl came wandering into sight. Micajah and Wiley dismounted and stooped to talk with the child. Talk turned to teasing, and Sally was the first to turn her horse's reins and flee when the men's intentions became obvious. Susan and Betsey followed hard after, both white faced.

They camped for the evening on a creek bank when here came both men, not with the little girl but a young woman and man. Susan stood up from the fire they'd built, hands on her hips. "What are you two doing?"

"Just havin' a little fun," Big rumbled, and shot her a look that sent shivers through Sally's middle.

The young woman begged and pleaded, the young man likewise, as they made him strip off his clothing and parade around camp, bare as the day he was born. The young woman sobbed quietly. Neither Sally nor the other women could bring themselves to look.

Tiring of that, Big and Little looped one

rope around the young man's neck, another around his feet, and Little splashed across the creek. They commenced to swinging him between them, letting his head drag through the water. More crying, and begging, from both captives. Big and Little went on and on, letting the young man's head stay under a bit longer each time, until finally he was limp and silent.

"Doggone it, Little, you let him die too soon."

At that, the young woman screamed.

God — have mercy!

"Just tomahawk her and be done with it," Big growled.

They knocked her to the ground, and Big held her feet while Little stood on her outstretched arms, tomahawk uplifted.

Sally was the one sobbing now, but she could not move. *Please, sweet Lord, do something here! Not for me, but — for Your name's sake!*

The woman's cries changed in pitch and cadence. She too was praying. "Father — oh Father, help me! Father, come to me!"

Please, Father! Sweet Jesus, have mercy on us sinners. . . .

Betsey and Susan were also weeping.

"Father, save me! Come to me now!"

Sally bolted off through the brush lining

321

the creek. Susan followed, then Betsey, both carrying their babies.

The sound of the woman's frantic prayers followed them. *"Father! Please! Help me!"*

Wiley himself came bursting through the bushes, eyes wild, mouth wide, tomahawk still clutched in his hand, but — unbloodied.

Cursing, and the sound of blows, punctuated with the woman's weakening cries, kept on. Wiley fell to his knees, and dropping the tomahawk, clutched the wooly locks of his hair.

"Father-r-r!"

One more curse, then the commotion of animals being driven through the brush. "Catch your horses! We must fly!"

CHAPTER SIXTEEN

"Colonel John Leiper of the local militia, at your service."

Ben shook hands with the man, who looked as rough as Ben did himself from weeks on the hunt, and lean and weathered to boot, about twice Ben's age. "Good to meet you."

They sat down, each with a tankard. Ben felt the other man sizing him up, just as he did Leiper. "So, I hear you have a connection with these rascals."

"My cousin Thomas Langford was their first known victim, last December. I've been on their trail most of the time since."

"Myself as well, these past couple of months."

"What news of late?"

"What was the last you heard?"

"Well, I came with a party up the Kentucky Trace almost three weeks ago, and it was James Brassel, John Tully, and the two

Trisword families on that stretch. Then I heard of a young Negro boy, and a father and son who were clearing land." Leiper nodded, and Ben went on, "More than a week ago, most of a posse met an ill end, but beyond that, I've not been able to sort between fact and rumor."

Leiper wrapped both hands around his tankard. "I can attest to a few more. About that same time, there was a little girl who'd wandered from her mother and father, out picking berries." He grimaced. "The description of what they'd done does not bear repeating, but she was — dismembered. Naturally her mother is inconsolable." He cleared his throat, glanced aside for a moment. "There was also a young man of the area, a Silver May, who with a young neighbor woman, Helen Levi, was taken — she while at her spinning wheel, of all things — and much tormented until he died. Helen survives, although badly beaten."

"She survives? Truly?"

"Aye. Her family and neighbors keep watch on her, though, day and night. They fear for her soundness of mind." Leiper shook his head a little. "And yesterday a man was murdered coming back from one of the salt licks. Trowbridge his name was."

Ben spread one hand flat on the table.

"God have mercy. This just gets worse and worse."

"It does. Things have been mostly quiet for the past week, though old Jim Slover said he'd had a near run-in with two men who just moved into a nearby cabin, up near Red Banks, and who he thought were likely the Harpes. One tried a shot but his gun only snapped, and Slover took off. He got a couple of men up to help him watch the place, but the women weren't there, and he wasn't even sure it was the same men, so they gave up and left 'em alone. Then there was Trowbridge a day or two later, so — foolish it was, to think they'd gone far." Leiper's eyes narrowed. "I'm determined to see this out, however long it takes. You're more than welcome to come stay out at my cabin and ride with me when next the call goes out."

"I'd be honored," Ben said.

Not for the first time, but he still meant it.

"Does the post serve this town yet?" he asked.

"Madisonville? I think not. Soon, though." Leiper shrugged.

Ben suppressed a sigh. He'd not yet been able to send Rachel — or anyone else — a letter.

325

Lord, have mercy on us indeed. Cover and protect us — and give us clear eyes for the hunt. Let these monsters show their hand soon.

No letters, but that didn't surprise Rachel. She knew the post only ran to the middle and eastern parts of Kentucky. It barely went to Nashborough at this point.

News, however, traveled like wildfire. How much was truth and how much simply wild tales, one could never tell. She spread the paper across the counter. Once in print, either way, folk believed it like gospel truth.

If even half of it was true . . .

Merciful Lord in heaven, protect us all. But especially Ben, and any other men who give their time to catch these wicked men.

She shook her head, remembering that wedding two years past. *And . . . protect and preserve Sally, Lord. She so needs You. As do we all. But You know how heavy my heart is for her.*

The Leiper family was kind and welcoming, and Ben hadn't realized until then how much he missed ordinary family life. After supper they spent a quiet evening, during which Ben engaged in several games of checkers with a serious lad who peppered

Ben with questions and then pestered his father to let him go along the next time the Harpes reared their ugly heads. Leiper just laughed and told him he'd think upon it.

Housed in the narrow, cramped loft of a cabin that looked much like any other in that part of the country, Ben slept reasonably well, after settling the restlessness of his heart in a time of prayer for Rachel, her family and his, and the entire situation.

Oh, how he missed her. But like Leiper, he would see this through.

A leisurely breakfast followed the next morning, and Leiper and his children, the boy and a pair of twin girls about four or five, engaged in the happy task of showing Ben about the farm.

The sun had climbed high and they'd just returned to the house to dip water from the well when a rider galloped into the yard, clattering to a stop. Leiper and Ben both swung toward him, hands on their guns, but the man only pulled off his hat and swept a forearm over his sweating brow.

"Moses Stegall," Leiper greeted him. "What's the trouble, man?"

The big man shook his head, gaze casting wildly about. Both he and his horse panted, and Ben motioned to the boy to dip another pail of water for both.

"My house — burned this morning, with my wife and babe inside. And Bill Love too, who was spendin' the night."

"Dear God," Leiper murmured.

"Silas McBee and William Grissom was there before me, and told me they'd found both Love's and my wife's bodies, half burned. My — my wife — she'd been stabbed — three knives, one of 'em her own butcher knife — still in her —"

Stegall bent, nearly double in the saddle, but accepted the dipper Ben passed him and drank noisily. Wiping his mouth on his sleeve again, he nodded his thanks and hauled in another deep breath. "I know it's the Harpes. I just know it. I ran into them yesterday on my way down t' the salt licks — don't ask me why I didn't let anyone know, I'm sure enough sorry now — and Big said I owed him a dollar. So I told 'im to go ask my wife."

He leaned one forearm on the saddlebow and sat there, hunched, for a moment.

"Do you be organizing a posse?" Leiper asked, with deadly quietness.

"I do." Stegall's gaze went to him and then Ben, in desperation. "McBee and Grissom are also in. Will you come?"

"We'll both come," Leiper said. "Go stable your horse. I have a couple other men I'll

328

go ask as well."

Stegall shook his head. "I'll come along. Can't rest until I see this done, I reckon."

Sally was tired of riding. Tired of running. Tired of hiding.

Tired of living.

She didn't know why they wouldn't just go and leave her behind.

God, please . . .

She didn't even know what to pray anymore.

After a week of hiding out in the woods, where the men were gone more than not, Big and Little hustled them through packing up — how many times this made, she couldn't say — and led them off south and east.

At least, she thought it was south and east.

The sun glared in her eyes as they wound on a trace so narrow it could hardly be called a path — Big and Little were good at finding such things — so she closed her eyes and tipped her head.

Prone to wander, Lord, I feel it, prone to leave the God I love . . .

The tune broke from her throat, just the softest hum, but the words would not be denied for long.

"O that day when freed from sinning,
I shall see Thy lovely face;
Clothèd then in blood washed linen
How I'll sing Thy sovereign grace;
Come, my Lord, no longer tarry,
Take my ransomed soul away . . ."

"Who's singin'?" Micajah growled. "Stop it, right now."

Sally sucked in a breath, her eyes popping open. It was like surfacing from a lovely dream only to find she was trapped in a nightmare.

Wiley cursed. "Worse than the babies crying."

She couldn't stop the tears, nor did she want to. *Oh sweet Eady . . .*

Lord, am I still Yours? Does Your blood cover even this? Oh Lord . . . I'm so sorry for wandering away from You. Maybe — maybe if I'd trusted You sooner — none of this would have happened.

A bit of scripture floated through her memory, *We know that all things work together for good . . .*

Can You still bring good out of any of this?

It was a solid bunch Ben rode with this time, all swearing to hunt the Harpes and bring them to justice at last, whatever the

330

cost, no turning back.

He owned he was ready for that himself, after nine long months of this.

He and Stegall had made the rounds with Leiper the day before, and they'd collected two other backwoodsmen that Leiper said were their most solid choices for holding firm under fire, should the need be, a Matthew Christian and a Neville Lindsay. They set out from Leiper's before dawn the next day and made the trip back northwest some fifteen or twenty miles, arriving about midmorning at McBee's, where another half-dozen men were gathered and introductions made all around. An older man by the name of John Tompkins told how just two evenings before, he'd met a pair of rough-looking but decent-seeming men claiming to be Methodist preachers and had invited them to supper. The bigger man stood and gave what Tompkins swore was a fifteen-minute grace before the meal, and both were as personable and warm as could be throughout. "In fact," Tompkins said, "when they asked me why I had no meat at supper, I told them I'd run out of gunpowder and so hadn't shot any deer in some time — and that big one just pulled out his horn and poured me a teacup full of powder, generous as you please." He shook his head.

"Who could have guessed they'd turn out to be such scoundrels, and yet leave me still living and breathing."

"I'm betting it was them at my house after dark fell and the moon was up," McBee grumbled. "I heard my dogs make a racket, and looking out, saw them bitin' and snarlin' around a pair of men. Figured the men was up to no good, so I didn't call 'em off." He huffed. "I'm guessin' they went to Stegall's after that."

Moses Stegall had recovered somewhat but still looked stricken. "I wish I'd gotten home sooner," he muttered.

McBee reached over and patted his shoulder. "We'll catch 'em, man, I promise."

The chase did nothing to soothe Stegall though, and Ben couldn't blame him. A wife and baby freshly dead — they'd hardly stopped long enough to bury his wife's charred body, and what little they could find that remained of the babe — and the past year and more's labor in smoking ruin.

And then, just before leaving McBee's, while they were still in the process of making sure women and children left behind were properly fortified and defended, word came that yet another two men were found slain on the road to the salt lick, by name of Hutchins and Gilmore. It was readily agreed that the search party would use that as a starting point.

Ben kept watch but let the others track, since they knew the country better than he. Some had begun to look familiar — but then the rolling hills interspersed with hidden rills and caves looked much the same mile after mile.

Still, this was the easiest tracking Ben had witnessed yet. They struck the trail just south of the road leading to the salt lick, but it wasn't long before they nearly lost it again, in what appeared to be the tangle created by a drove of buffalo. Their quarry's intent remained too obvious, however, and before long they'd picked up the trail again. Interestingly, it appeared that the party of Harpes had split in two, parting and following roughly parallel paths for a mile or two before converging again.

And then — the trail was perfectly clear.

At nightfall, they camped on the western bank of the Pond River, ate a quick supper, then tucked in for whatever sleep could be snatched. Many of the men were snoring in minutes. Ben envied them, as he and others tossed, seeking either a better position or more tranquil thoughts.

Somewhere out there, likely on the other

side of the river, were the Harpes. Would tomorrow be the day they finally confronted them?

Ben slept at last, only to be awakened by a short but brisk rain shower sometime after midnight, but that ended quickly and most of them fell back asleep. Dawn found them stirring and saddling up again after the briefest of breakfasts. They forded the river and easily picked up the trail on the other side.

Under the spreading trees, the morning cool lingered even as the sun rose higher. It seemed, though, that the entire country held its breath, waiting, watching —

"Hie there, here's something," Leiper called out from his place in the lead.

Two hunting dogs, lying beside the path with their throats cut.

"Those look like the hounds belonging to Hutchins and Gilmore," Tompkins muttered, and McBee nodded.

"I'd say the Harpes took 'em along, and then, when it looked like the dogs might give 'em away by their barking —" The man chewed his lip, shifting his solid frame in the saddle. "Seeing as how the bodies haven't bloated up in the heat, they haven't been here long." He lifted his head and looked around. "We might want to dis-

334

mount. Send three or four of our best on foot ahead, while the rest bring the horses along, slowly. Stealth is our best weapon here, like Indians."

Leiper, Stegall, Christian, and Lindsay ran ahead on foot, while Ben, McBee, Grissom, and Tompkins all each took an extra horse. Ben chafed to be left behind with the older men, but owned that he might not be as skilled as the backwoodsmen at being quiet.

They'd only gone another mile or so farther, however, before the four came trotting back and remounted. "There's nothing this close," Leiper said, "and we're too slow on foot anyhow."

They settled in, riding single file down the trail again, looking this way and that as they wound up and around a rugged hillside.

Movement caught his eye, over on a hillside opposite them, across a narrow hollow. At the same moment, McBee pointed and cried out, "There they are!" and spurred his horse off the trail.

And surely it was. Not two men, but three — all afoot, Micajah holding a horse, while he and Wiley faced the third man. Both Micajah's and Wiley's heads came up. Wiley took off on foot, while Micajah leaped on his horse and sped away.

Ben and the others were already in pursuit, behind McBee, crashing through the bushes. The third man turned toward the mounted party then suddenly darted to the side and hid behind a tree, which did not quite cover him. McBee drew his horse to a sliding halt, and taking aim with his gun, which he'd loaded the day before with two balls, fired away — just as Stegall cried out, "Don't shoot! It's George Smith, from up the river."

The smoke from McBee's gun was still billowing when the man squealed, hit, and came staggering out from behind the tree. "Squire McBee! I'm so sorry — don't shoot again —"

McBee lowered the gun and swung off his horse. "What are you doing, man? I might have killed you!"

He inspected the man's wounds — both balls had found their mark, in his right thigh and arm, but neither appeared to be life-threatening. Smith was shaking, half laughing, half sobbing. "I'm sorry. I was 'most out of my senses, expectin' to be killed any moment by the Harpes — and then you all rode up and I just couldn't recover soon enough and treed instead of calling out."

"Well." McBee set to reloading his gun. The Harpes were quite out of sight already. "How did you happen upon them?"

"I was just out huntin' and came upon Little Harpe on foot, gun in one hand and kettle in the other, going for water in the creek there. He commenced to asking me about the settlements, but I could tell by the way he talked loud, he must have wanted someone else to hear — and then Big rode up and dismounted." He heaved a breath and peered up at McBee. "I've never been so glad in my life to have someone show up as y'all. Might you do me the favor of helping me back home?"

McBee peered at the forest around them. "If he was on foot, coming for water, their camp must be close. Let us go on in pursuit, and then we'll be back. Will you be fine on your own for a little while?"

Smith nodded, and taking himself over again to a tree, sat down heavily. "Aye, I'll just rest a bit."

Ben, Leiper, and Stegall were already inspecting the ground for the trail, and the party set off again.

Sally woke in the cool dimness of the little cave they'd found, tucked under a rock overhang in the side of a hill, its opening shielded by yet another stone outcropping. Big and Little were already up and about — Little had taken the kettle for fetching water, and Betsey and Susan were about the work of tending little Joe and Lovey. Both were old enough to sit up now — well, Lovey nearly so — and both grinned widely at their mamas and the world at large as swaddling was changed and such.

Sally's breasts had finally ceased their aching — but her heart, not.

In short, an early morning like so many others.

A clattering came from outside the cave, and Big ducked inside, expression fierce and breath coming fast. "Get your things — we have to go."

"What?" Susan burst out. "I thought you said no one would find us here."

"Just shut up and come, woman!"

He went back out — likely to saddle the horses. Susan and Betsey exchanged a glance and were in motion immediately. Sally grabbed her bundle — she'd not properly unpacked the night before — and followed them out.

Little was there as well, the reins of a saddled horse already in hand.

"— should just kill the babies too and be done with it," Big growled. "They'll only slow us down."

"Nay!" Susan cried, shrill.

Little only grimaced. Big turned upon her,

his visage terrible in its fury. "Dinnae ye want to live, woman?"

Susan and Betsey both paled, exchanging another glance. "I —" But she could only shake her head.

A strange calm settled over Sally. "Let me take 'em. I'll keep them safe — give them a chance — give y'all a chance at getting away too."

Big looked murder at her, but unmoved, she tossed her bundle aside and held her arms out to the other women. "Here. Please, let me do this."

Susan gritted her teeth then handed Lovey off to her. Betsey followed suit, and Sally balanced the two, one on each hip, as the women scrambled to mount.

"We'll go thataway," Big said, pointing down the hill, "and you go the other. We'll meet up — oh, over opposite Cave-in-the-Rock again, I reckon."

He cast Sally another glance then mounted up again and led the other women off at an angle down the hill, as fast as the horses would allow.

Little stood still, staring at the ground, making no move to mount.

"Wiley." She spoke his name, but he gave no sign of hearing. "Wiley," she said again, stepping toward him.

He tossed the reins over the horse's head, checked the cinch, then froze. Finally he did look at her, his eyes shadowed, pleading and desperate.

They stared at each other until the crackling of leaves and brush carried to them, from somewhere out of sight around the ridge. Wiley threw himself on the horse, and without a single word, galloped away, in a different direction than what Big had directed.

Sally blew out a long breath she hadn't realized she was holding, and shifting the babies on her hips, carried them inside the cave and set them down. "Don't y'all get yourselves into trouble now. I'll be back."

And so she was standing there outside the cave, waiting, when the other men came, more than half a dozen. The lead was a stocky man, not old but not young either, who gazed at her sternly then looked around, as they all did. "Are the Harpes still here?"

She folded her hands into her ragged skirt. "They've gone. Big Harpe was just here, mounted each of his women on a good horse, then took off." She nodded off down the hill. "That way. Little took off as well."

The man bobbed a nod to her and led away in the direction she'd indicated, the rest of the party following.

"Sally," a voice said, startling her.

She looked up into the bearded face of a younger man who could be any backwoodsman, except — "Mr. Langford?"

"It's me, yes," he said, with a thin smile, barely holding his horse back. "Did they leave you here alone?"

She nodded, her gaze straying to the search party stretching in a rough line across the hillside, picking their way down, then looked back at him. "They left the babies here. I ain't goin' anywhere."

He glanced about then apparently coming to a decision, gave a firm nod of his own and said, "I'll be back for you, I promise," and took off after the others.

Feeling weary beyond her years, yet with an eerie lightness, like she was in someone else's body, Sally grabbed her bundle and trudged back inside the cave. More than half their provisions still lay scattered around. Little Joe sat sucking his fist, grinning at her through the slobber, while Lovey had rolled to her back and tried to grasp her feet through the swaddling.

Dropping her bundle, she took her blue cloak, spread it out over against the wall, and carried the babies to it, one at a time. Then she lay down, and while Joe amused himself with the edge of the cloak, she nursed first Lovey to sleep then shifted to her other side and did the same with Joe. She had little enough milk left, but they seemed satisfied.

She'd nearly drowsed off as well when a clattering of horses' hooves echoed again from outside. Sally carefully disentangled herself from the sleeping babes, and rising, was refastening her clothing when the man leading the party appeared in the opening, pistol in hand and pointed at her. "Where again did you say they've gone? If you've deceived me, woman, I'll shoot you right here and now."

Mr. Langford was right behind him. "Mc-Bee —"

She sighed and brushed off her skirts. "You'd be doing the world — and myself — a favor, I promise you."

Brushing past them both, she emerged into the sunshine. The rest of the search party pulled their horses out of the way, as if she were also armed and would somehow fell them on the spot. But she ignored them all, and tracing the path where Big and the women had gone, walked a few steps down the hill and lifted her arm to point. "There, that way," she said, turning back to meet the older man's gaze.

Only slightly less severe, he glared back then put the pistol away. "Y'all go on — I'll catch up," he said to the others, and except for Mr. Langford, they filed away once more, on the corrected path this time.

The man marched over to where the Harpes' horses were tethered — they'd acquired several by now, some for riding and others as pack animals — and took the one that was still saddled. "Get on. You'll come with us."

"But — the babies, in the cave —"

He glanced toward the opening in the rock, shook his head. "Nothing for it. I'm not letting you out of my sight."

"McBee," Mr. Langford said, in a tone of protest.

The older man rounded on him. "Do you want to stay and be nursemaid, or catch the Harpes? I'm not leaving this one behind. We can come back for the infants."

Chewing his lip, looking furious, Mr. Langford finally nodded. "Come, Sally. I'll give you a leg up."

With another sigh, she climbed on, without question. Better to be in their company than another moment with Big — or Little. But —

Lord, protect the little ones! And let us not be away too long.

343

CHAPTER SEVENTEEN

Blast his need to be up with the heart of the chase, as well as see to Sally's safety. McBee likely could be trusted to guard the woman, but Ben had to be sure. Sally was doing a fair job of keeping up, however, and McBee of catching up, as intent upon the chase as Ben.

Ivy didn't like not being in the lead, Ben had already discovered, and during the ensuing chase, she not only caught up with the others but edged her way near the front of the pack, until only Leiper and Christian were in the lead. Tompkins had a good horse — a Virginia thoroughbred that, if not having the single-foot gait and overall stamina of Ivy, was still renowned for her speed — but held her back, probably for the purpose of saving her strength.

Ahead of them, Leiper pulled his mount to a halt, and hallooed to three mounted figures just ascending the next ridge. "We see you! Stop and give yourselves up!"

Micajah was immediately off again, as Leiper raised his rifle to his shoulder and shot, but to no effect. The women's horses jumped, one shoving against the other, and for a moment they had a hard time of it, controlling the animals. Ben urged Ivy down one hillside, across the stream below in a single leap, and back up again, with both Leiper and Christian keeping pace.

Susan and Betsey glanced this way and that, first in the direction that Micajah had gone and then back at the search party. Apparently they saw the futility of running any farther and didn't even attempt to escape this time. The barest recognition flickered in their eyes as Ben drew up, with the others gathering around the women. "Ladies," he murmured, but neither responded.

Leiper dismounted, yanking at the ramrod in his rifle. "Doggoned thing must be swollen from the rain last night."

"Here, take mine," Tomkins said, offering both gun and powder horn.

"Well, why didn't you shoot?"

The older man shrugged. "Nance here is fast, but she'd shy at the shot and I'd miss anyway."

Leiper fairly growled through clenched teeth, staring longingly in the direction the elder Harpe had gone, then turned back to the women. "Where's Little Harpe?"

"Wasn't with us," Susan said.

"Here." Tompkins dismounted. "Leiper, you take Nance — she's faster'n yours. Lindsay and I will stay back with the women. The rest of you go on ahead."

Leiper was already in the saddle, the borrowed gun in hand and horn slung around his body, and they were off again in a pack.

McBee and Sally were nowhere in sight, but Ben had to trust that the older man would be along in a moment, without harming Sally.

This time the line of them was strung out a little farther — Leiper in the lead, Christian not far behind, then Ben, Stegall, and the others — he couldn't see just who was where, right after.

Five of them gained enough on Harpe that Christian pulled ahead a little and lifted his rifle, then shot. Harpe flinched, and blood appeared on his leg. Stegall was next but missed, then Ben and Grissom in turn, also missing. Tompkins's thoroughbred surged to the fore again, leaving even Ivy behind, but Ben had a clear enough view, while trying along with the others to reload from the saddle, to see when Micajah hauled his own mount to a stop and wheeled to face Leiper.

"Stay back or I'll kill you all!"

Did he think Leiper's gun empty as well?

"Give yourself up, Harpe, now!" Christian roared.

Leiper jumped off the thoroughbred, refreshing the priming of the rifle even in mid-motion, and lifted the gun to his shoulder. Smoke billowed with the shot, and Micajah reeled from the impact. The men beside him cheered, but Micajah lifted his own rifle and leveled it at Leiper, only to have it *snap* — a misfire.

Snarling, he cast the rifle aside and set heels to his mount once more. Leiper hauled himself back into the saddle, and he, Christian, and Ben were once again in close pursuit.

Stegall and Grissom had apparently lingered to reload, because they were far behind. The forest was but a blur of green around Ben as he kept Ivy close on the heels of Christian's mount, while Leiper was just ahead.

The three of them fanned out, trying to flank Micajah, who had his tomahawk out now. "I told you, stay back!"

"Give yourself up!" Leiper shouted in return.

Blood ran down Micajah's front, and it was an obvious struggle for him to stay in the saddle. His tomahawking arm sagged. "Stop your horses! I'll surrender. Only, don't kill me."

Suspicion clogged Ben's throat, but seeing Micajah pull his mount to a halt, the three of them did likewise, dismounting. Micajah sat his horse, leaning against the saddlebow, the tomahawk barely hanging from his fingertips.

Christian and Leiper took the moment to reach for powder and shot, but Ben pulled one of his pistols from his belt. "Get off your horse," he told Micajah.

The big man huffed, then with a "Haw!" set heels to the horse's side. As the animal leaped away, Ben fired, but again missed, and the thoroughbred Nance likewise startled and galloped after. Cursing, Christian mounted and followed, while Leiper stood, hands on knees, also spitting epithets. "Very well," he growled aside to Ben. "It's one or the other of us be killed here."

Christian had the thoroughbred caught already and was bringing her back. They mounted again without reloading and once more gave chase.

Down into a hollow, through a small but tangled canebrake, then bursting out the other side —

Where they found Micajah and his horse

at barely a walk, the man himself drooping in the saddle, hands empty now and clutching only the saddlebow and mane.

Leiper and Christian made no hesitation, but drawing their horses up beside Harpe's, one on either side, they pulled him from the saddle while likewise dismounting. Ben also swung down and hovered to see if he should be of assistance, but as Harpe lay stretched on the ground, unmoving, he took the moment to catch all the horses' reins and tether them to nearby trees.

"Water," Harpe rasped. The wound in his breast went all the way through to his spine and beyond, and by the awkward angle of his legs, appeared to have paralyzed him.

With a huff, Leiper glanced about then yanked off his own moccasin and went down to the stream. Christian knelt near Micajah's head. Ben withdrew his pistol and stood at the ready.

Words failed him, suddenly, and his heart pounded. Here Harpe lay, felled at last — the monster who had ended Thomas's life and that of dozens more — or one such monster, at least. Where the other had gone, only God knew.

A crunching and crackling announced the arrival of the others. Stegall and Grissom emerged through the cane, while here came

McBee splashing across the stream, with Sally yet in tow. The woman's eyes were round as saucers in a face far too full of shadows.

McBee dismounted and knelt before Micajah. "You appear to be dying at last, man, and as much as we'd like to hasten that, we'll give you time to pray and prepare yourself for the next life."

The big man closed his eyes a moment. "Water," he said again.

Leiper was nearly at his side with the brimming moccasin, but Stegall surged forward with a curse and knocked it out of his hand. "Perdition take him already, and welcome! Have you no thought to what you've done, Harpe, so carelessly taking the lives of my wife and son?"

Micajah squinted up at him. "Aye. Though the only life I truly regret taking is that of a child of my own blood."

With a howl, Stegall lifted his rifle and pointed it at Micajah's head, but the fallen man jerked this way and that to avoid the shot, while the others took hold of Stegall and pulled him back. "Not like this, lad," McBee said. "Let him go on his own now."

"*. . . a child of my own blood . . .*"

Ben looked across to Sally, huddling white-faced in the saddle.

Just whose baby had Harpe murdered?

McBee crouched beside Micajah again. "You killed your own child? And how many others?"

Micajah grimaced. "Too — many. I — I wish — to see Susanna, my wife, again, and to do better by her. I've means — if she were here — to tell where, over on the eastern fork of the Pond —"

"Ah, now he's just speaking nonsense," Christian muttered. "There ain't no eastern branch of the Pond River."

Harpe babbled on for a minute or two more, about people and places Ben had never heard of. Perhaps he was merely delirious now.

McBee interrupted him, quietly but firmly. "Come on, man, get a hold of yourself. Call out to the Lord. You've no other chances."

Micajah coughed a laugh and squinted at McBee. "I suppose — you want me to confess — every one of those I killed as well?"

"Just confess it to God, son. That's enough."

With another broken chuckle, he started a litany of names and places that, unsurprising to Ben, didn't even start with Thomas. Ben tried to count them as he went, but as the number climbed past two dozen, his at-

351

tention floundered over the details of the ones for which he'd witnessed the aftermath.

For a few moments, Ben wasn't even sure his mind correctly registered the details of what Harpe was relating.

"And then there was the two men comin' back from the salt licks who we accused of killin' the Stegalls. But we done it. I'd already tomahawked Love in his sleep for makin' so much racket by snoring. And then Missus Stegall's babe was cryin' while she fixed us breakfast the next morning. I told her, we're good with cryin' babies, ain't we, Little? But when she come over and found how we'd gotten him to quiet, her smiles all turned to screamin' and — well, I couldn't abide a screamin' woman neither —"

Stegall shoved forward with another roar, and before anyone could stop him, shot Harpe in the side, straight through the heart.

The big man twitched once, and lay still.

Panting, Stegall glared at the other men, shocked to silence. "There. I couldn't stand it anymore. Y'all can't blame me for it!"

Swiftly then, he whipped out his knife, a wicked, long thing, and before anyone could move, he knelt and, seizing the long, tangled locks, sawed at the dead man's neck.

Ben couldn't bring himself to watch. Two or three men turned away, gagging. Sally peered between her fingers then covered her face completely.

"Lord in heaven, have mercy," McBee muttered, but it was done.

Sally could feel no more shock. No more sorrow.

In this moment, she could feel naught at all.

The mad chase through the forest had seemed well-nigh dreamlike. The man — McBee, someone had called him — had led straight through canebrakes and thickets, and having nearly nothing to lose, Sally clung to her horse and followed hard after.

And then to witness Big being yanked from his horse and dropped to the ground like a rag doll. Even when his body failed him, he hadn't given up, prattling on like one of Sally's younger brothers caught making mischief, casting about for a way out of the inevitable punishment. But just like with her brothers, punishment came anyway, only for Micajah, in such a bloody, violent, sudden manner they all were left breathless.

Except for Stegall, who lifted the dripping head, glancing about as if the others would challenge his right to the trophy, even casting Sally a fierce look that drew a shiver from her. And she'd not shivered in a long time.

He snatched a provisions bag from his saddle and stuffed the head in. "Come on, boys," he growled, and there was naught else to do but get back on their horses and ride back the way they'd come.

And Big's body, they just left there.

Fitting, after what he'd done to little Eady.

Vengeance is mine; I will repay, saith the Lord.

Sally couldn't help but shudder again.

At the crest of a ridge, they met up with Susan and Betsey and two other men. Stegall opened his provisions bag enough to show the bloody thing and prove Micajah's end, and both the other women turned whiter than Sally had ever seen. Betsey slapped one hand across her mouth and turned away, but Susan slowly straightened, shifting her gaze over across into the trees, and gave something like a nod.

Back to the cave camp they went, and at the ringing silence — except for the noise they, the horses and riders, made — Sally flung herself out of the saddle and beat even Susan and Betsey inside to check on their babies.

Two bundled forms still lay curled on the

354

cloak, so quiet that for a moment Sally's heart dropped until little Joe twitched and she could see Lovey's breathing.

How could they both yet be asleep? Or was that yet one more small miracle wrought by the Lord on this day, like the ending at last of Micajah's life?

Susan and Betsey whisked past her, picking the babies up, and Sally lifted the cloak and shook it out then gathered it into a bundle in her arms and stood by while the men filed into the cave, peering everywhere and inspecting everything. Then she slipped outside to stand there, in a pool of sunlight, face tipped to the sky.

Thank You, Lord. Thank You so much.

They made northwest again, with the eventual aim of Red Banks, Henderson County seat, where the most recent of the Harpes' crimes had been committed, to see the women tucked safely in jail once more. They camped for the night at Leiper's then pressed on the next morning, with the local men, Christian, Lindsay, and Leiper himself accompanying.

Even with Ben taking the first watch, many of the others were slow to settle and sat up discussing matters until well into the night. The possible fate of the women.

Whether or not to go after Little Harpe. Whether they might collect on the reward for Big, regardless.

Ben shook his head, hearing that. He cared little for the reward. It wasn't for monetary gain that he'd engaged in the hunt.

While the other men huddled around a small fire, more for comfort than warmth on a night like this, he sat apart, beneath a great oak. From here, he could observe both the men in conversation, and the women a very short distance off, bundled in blankets beneath the stars. He'd eaten but little supper, his gut still hollowed with the brutality of Big Harpe's end — and he'd not been the only one — but for now, hat laid on the ground beside him, he nursed a tin cup of coffee in one hand and a lit pipe in the other.

The matter was done, for the most part. He'd seen Micajah not brought to justice in the way he'd sought, but justice was served, nevertheless. Yet — what of Wiley, who was certainly just as guilty? Ben could not say he'd fully discharged his duty without Little Harpe also being apprehended.

Uncle Ben would agree, he was sure.

The hunt would have to continue. For now, however, the sheer relief of having seen this much accomplished was enough to steal whatever impetus he might have had to do anything but lounge against the trunk of this oak, for the rest of this night and possibly another week or more.

Although it was also uppermost in his mind to see Rachel again. . . .

One of the women rose and walked toward him, her delicate frame wrapped in what Ben knew before he saw it was the blue cloak. Sally. How she'd obtained it back, he'd yet to learn.

There were things he'd not inquire after, with all the others present.

She stopped a few paces away. "May I sit?"

"Of course." He sat a little straighter, his back still tucked against the tree trunk. "May I get you something to eat or drink?"

"I've enough for tonight, thank you."

A length or so away and a little to the side so his view of the other women was unobstructed, she perched on the arch of a tree root and folded herself small, the cloak swathing her completely. He waited for her to speak first.

When at last she did, he nearly could not catch the words. "Thank you for — all else, as well."

He nodded. "I was glad to be there today. Well," he added slowly, "as much as a man can be, under the circumstances." He angled her a look. "Where is your baby, Sally?"

"With the angels," she said, almost absently, peering up at the sky.

Just as he'd suspected.

He sighed. "I am most regretful for your loss."

"And — I for yours," she murmured, sounding close to tears this time.

He could only nod, and sip his coffee.

"It was — it was terrible, all that they did," she continued. "I can't speak for Susan and Betsey, but I'm ready to tell everything this time. Everything."

"And what about Wiley? Any guesses as to where he's gone?"

She shook her head a little then said, "Micajah mentioned them meeting up over across from Cave-in-the-Rock. But —" She took a quick breath. "Is it wrong of me to wish that I never see him again?"

"No." He set the cup on the ground, between his knees. "Something I find myself wondering is, Micajah referred to having slain his own child." He hesitated. "But if that child was yours . . . ?"

She shrugged, not looking at him. "It's as likely little Eady was his as Wiley's."

Ben scrubbed a hand down his face. He felt a strong urge to hie himself off into the bushes and heave up the contents of his stomach. "I am so very sorry. And — Wiley let this happen?"

"Aye," she whispered. "He wasn't so happy about it at first, but — Big threatened him."

Ben cleared his throat. "Still. I would definitely say, under the circumstances, your marriage to him is no longer binding."

Sally caught her breath, noisily, as much a sob as a gasp. "I would find that most welcome."

They sat for a while in silence, then she asked, "Are you — and Rachel — still on good terms?"

He gave a short laugh. "I most earnestly hope so." Feeling her gaze upon him then, he went on, "I hope to marry her. Sooner rather than later, but I'm willing to wait for her to be sure."

"And she isn't?"

The amazement in Sally's voice warmed him, but he dared not let flattery erode his resolve to hold to honor and patience. "She cannot be blamed if having to witness your misfortune has made her shy of trusting anyone for herself."

"Ahh." It was barely a breath, followed by a *tsk*. "That makes me . . . oh, so sad. If anyone deserves happiness, it's Rachel.

She . . . has been a friend to me when I had none." She glanced toward him again. "Yourself as well, and once more, I thank you."

The next day would see them the rest of the way to Red Banks, on the Ohio River. At a well-traveled crossroads a few miles short of their intended destination, however, not far from his home, Moses Stegall insisted on a stop. Choosing an oak tree of some size, he chopped a branch short, sharpened the remaining portion, and there impaled the head of Micajah Harpe.

Once again, to the silent shock of Ben and the others, he swung his horse in a circle and glared at them. "Let that be a warning to any and all. Aye?"

No one could say him nay, and they continued on toward Red Banks.

Among those bringing up the rear of the party, Ben watched the reactions of the women as they rode past.

Betsey, with quick glances, finally turning her face away.

Susan, with a long, unbroken look until she was past.

Sally, a sidelong peek, yet steady, ending in her shoulders rising and falling, and her head coming up.

Would the three of them be acquitted this time? Sally, he was more sure of, but the other two? He had far less confidence regarding them.

And at what point would he feel at liberty to return to Rachel? Regarding the matter of Wiley Harpe on the loose, he and the other men had discussed what Sally shared and debated the merits of another search. Though the man needed to answer for his part in the murders, not to mention the failure to uphold his marriage vows, Ben had to admit it was very unlikely they'd find him. And they all agreed that only time would show whether Micajah had been the driving force behind their crimes, or whether Wiley was equally dangerous on his own.

At the moment, Ben still felt a curious lack of desire to do anything but see to a fair trial for Sally and then hasten to Rachel's side as soon as humanly possible.

And discover if she intended to keep that promise about greeting him this time with a kiss.

But if justice was left undone for Thomas while Wiley Harpe still ran free, was Ben ever truly free of the matter himself?

Once again, it seemed he'd failed Thomas — and Uncle Ben. Yet — he would leave

Rachel waiting no longer than he absolutely must.

CHAPTER EIGHTEEN

The word spread like wildfire all across the frontier. It was so much the topic of conversation among those who came into the post that Rachel became near sick of hearing the details of how Micajah Harpe met his final, gruesome end.

Still she listened, though, because they'd yet to say whether or not Wiley had also been taken.

August trickled away into September, and news changed to how the women had appeared before the Quarter Session of the Henderson County courts, been determined guilty of murder and robbery, and were set to be tried at the next district court session in Logan County, come October.

She knew she couldn't expect Ben just yet, but as the wait stretched on with each additional day, while Micajah's death was endlessly hashed over and the fate of Wiley speculated upon, patience proved more and more elusive.

She kept praying — for Sally, for Ben, for those in charge of seeing justice properly done. Her thoughts even strayed to Wiley. The Lord only knew where he lurked these days, but He surely did know, and that, Rachel supposed, was the important thing.

They'd not even received the first newspaper articles on the matter yet. The worst, though, was not hearing anything from Ben — nor any word on how the pursuers had fared in the chase. In this case, Rachel clung to the hope that no news truly was good news.

Oh, how she regretted the lost time, those weeks he might have spent at her side instead of at Hugh's or — wherever else he was. Her reluctance now seemed silly, or at least the way she'd found herself completely unable to speak openly to Ben because of her own fears and doubts.

And yet — did not the current news still bespeak of those who purported to be one thing, who pulled the wool over the eyes of at least a few unsuspecting and trusting folk, and then proved to be something far different?

"He ain't nothing like the Harpes," Daddy's voice echoed.

Late one afternoon, Rachel could stand it

no longer, and in a lull between customers and accounts, she escaped through the storage room and out the back door. Leaning against the wall of the post building, she closed her eyes against the hot sunlight and fought for several breaths to contain her weeping.

Lord, You've answered where stopping that terrible murder spree was concerned — at least with stopping Micajah. Will You not answer in regard to this as well? Or does it merely serve the continued purifying of my soul and faith to be tried in this way?

"Rachel!" Daddy's bellow could shake the whole building and in this case carried from the storage room, through the closed door beside her.

The door swung open. "Rachel —"

"Right here, Daddy." She wiped her face with a corner of the apron.

He twitched toward her, actually startled for once, then his eyes crinkled, face squinching oddly. "You're needed out front. Come on."

Naturally she was. Suppressing a sigh, she dropped the apron's edge. Never mind how she looked. She didn't care — and there was no one she sought to impress at the moment anyway.

She followed in Daddy's wake, through

the storage room and out into the main area. Then Daddy stepped abruptly aside, and there by the counter was —

Ben.

Rumpled from traveling, wearing the same shirt and leggings she'd seen him in weeks ago, with the day's sweat causing his hair to stick around his face where the hat had pushed it down — but it was he, nevertheless, whole and sound.

Overcome, she ran straight to his outstretched arms — and lifted her face for his kiss, which he gave without hesitation. Daddy laughed, and others hooted and catcalled, but she cared not a whit.

Ben buried his face in her hair and clutched her tighter. Was he also trembling? "We got him, Rachel. I expect you've heard the news already —"

"A thousand times over," she said, with a watery giggle.

He chuckled as well, but unsteadily. "Well — but we got him."

"What about Wiley?" She pulled back just enough to peer up into his blue eyes, and pushed away an errant lock of the gold-brown hair, bleached almost wheaten by the sun.

His mouth firmed for a moment, and he shook his head. "There's some who promised to be on the lookout — Sally actually told us where he might show — but I'm betting he knows now that Micajah is gone and thus might run fast and far." His hand cupping her face, he brushed a thumb across her cheekbone. "And Sally and the others will come to trial in about six weeks. Would you want to go?"

"Of course!"

Daddy cleared his throat, and they both looked at him, propped against the counter with arms folded across his chest. Ben's embrace loosened, but he still clasped her hand.

"I'm not sure I should let you two journey anywhere together until you're properly wed."

A flush swept Rachel, head to toe. Ben angled a look at her and said, without a trace of hesitation, "I'm willing. But only if Rachel says aye."

She could only stand there, mouth open like a fish and heart pounding in her throat. And of course she'd kissed him in front of everyone, and likely obligated herself, but —

More whoops from the onlookers. "Well, what about it, Rachel?" one asked.

Suddenly weary of being on display, she dragged Ben away to the back room. When she stopped and swung to face him, he caught both her hands in his. "My apologies, Rachel. I'd have chosen better timing for a proposal, I swear."

She shook her head, still unable to speak. All she could think of for the moment were the implications of Wiley disappearing but Sally not yet formally released from her marriage to him. "How — how is Sally?"

His expression hardened, pain flashing in his eyes. "As well as can be expected. She —" He sighed. "Among all the other wretched acts Micajah committed — the murder of Sally's baby was one."

The tears choked her again. "Oh no . . ."

"And —" He huffed. "I should not tell you this. It serves no good purpose, except — it may come up in trial, and forewarned is forearmed. And Sally herself confirmed it." He ducked his head for a moment. "There is a very strong possibility that the father of her child was Micajah himself, which makes the circumstance even more heinous."

Rachel recoiled, hands over her mouth. "Oh — poor Sally."

That predatory look, at the wedding. Sally's pleas for prayer. It all made so much sense now.

Her stomach near revolted.

"Did Wiley ever intend to honor his marriage vows, I wonder?"

"With him vanished into the wilderness, perhaps for good — we may never know."

Rachel considered him for a moment as he watched her in return. Standing back. Waiting.

"And you — have you remained well through it all?" she asked.

"Quite, thank you."

"I am so glad to hear that," she whispered, throat closing again.

Ben most certainly was not Wiley. Not in the least. He couldn't be perfect, of course, and doubtless with more time she'd discover all the ways he was simply a man as any other, but — she knew his was a heart she could trust. Humanly speaking, anyway.

"Rachel Taylor," he murmured, "would you indeed do me the honor of becoming my wife?"

Something between a sob and a laugh shook her. "I will," she said, and threw herself back into his arms.

"Oh, how I've missed you," he rumbled, his breath warm against her neck. "But are you sure you can bear being married to a lowly frontier lawyer?"

A definite laugh this time. "Aye."

"Even if we settled in the wilds of Kentucky?"

She burrowed more snugly into his embrace. "Benjamin Langford. I don't know how or when it happened — but nowhere is home without you. So I reckon wherever you choose would be just fine."

Once the question was settled, they did not delay — and Ben was glad of it.

He could recall very little of other weddings he'd attended, but no other bride had ever been as radiantly lovely as Rachel, he was sure, who somehow in less than a week, with the sewing help of her mother and a younger sister, managed to produce a cool summer gown of white muslin.

Not that he cared what she wore. She could have been attired in horse blankets and he'd have found her completely enchanting.

On a fine, hot September morning, Reverend Rice read the ceremony over them. Hugh White stood as witness, with Ben signing his own marriage bond alongside Rachel's father. Much of the community attended — Hugh's wife, Eliza, delivered just weeks before of their first child, and the Rice family, among them. Ben could not remember a more joyous occasion.

But then, Rachel's sparkling dark eyes, laughing mouth, and sweet blushes were all he could seem to give attention to.

A wife of his own. God willing, a family to follow. And, please God as well, someday a place to belong.

At one point in the festivities, the women all surrounded Rachel, giggling and chattering, and Ben turned to Hugh, lingering at his side with a pipe and tankard of ale. "So, I have you to thank for much of this."

"Or blame, depending upon how things go between you both." Hugh grinned. "It has come about far differently than I imagined, but aye, I've long thought the two of you would suit." He nodded toward Rachel. "And she seems very happy."

"I hope to continue making her so," Ben said quietly.

Russellville, Kentucky
The first of the three trials took place Monday, October 28, 1799. The jury was chosen and sworn in, then Susan was led up before the bar, and the charges read. She pled not guilty, as Ben knew she would.

Not everyone believed even the possibility that the women could be innocent. They'd had a long time and many opportunities to escape such a horrendous situation. How could they witness the things that had been done, stay silent, and not be guilty?

It didn't help when Susan claimed, at least for a while, that Micajah would never have committed a single murder if not for Wiley's influence. Both Betsey and Sally quietly contradicted her, though, and soon enough she gave up that argument. Ben had counseled her during the initial questioning to simply admit what she'd seen Micajah do and leave it at that. The man was dead now — no reason not to. But Susan's own hold on reality seemed tenuous at best. Or she was simply incapable of not trying to shift a situation to her own advantage.

He couldn't blame her, really he couldn't. To live for as many years with the man as she had — it appalled him to think of it, more than half her life as "wife" to a Harpe, and involuntarily so for at least the first years.

She could not, in any sense of the word, be completely whole and sound of mind or body after enduring so much.

But innocent of having actually committed those murders or assisting with them in any way? Yes, he could well believe that.

It was still difficult, however, to believe how much tenderness the woman yet held for a man she'd seen perpetrate such horrors. "Big weren't so sound of mind himself," she'd confided once to Ben. "So many times, he'd swear he could feel the ground shaking under his feet, when no one else could. And sometimes he suffered powerful bad headaches."

She and Betsey both owned, however, that after the first accusations in Knoxville more than a year before, Micajah and Wiley had declared war on all mankind, and determined to wreak as much damage as they could.

After hearing all the evidence, the jury deliberated then handed down the verdict of "not guilty."

Ben exchanged a look and quick smile with Rachel. Just two more trials to go.

Betsey's was scheduled for the next day. A different jury was selected and sworn in, and once again the evidence was read.

Washed and well dressed, Betsey could be considered almost a beauty. She was a mystery in and of herself, and Ben should not have been surprised when, at the outset of questioning after Micajah's death, she'd stirred as if waking for the first time, fixed him and the other men with a look, and began with, "I was born Maria Davidson, daughter of John and Clarissa Davidson of North Carolina. My father served as an officer in the war against England and died at the Dan River by the hand of the British.

When I was but a girl, William and Joshua Harper — those were their names then — stole me from my home, and I've served variously as wife to both, as it suited them. But I was never legally married to either."

She was soft spoken, which he'd expected, but astonishingly articulate as well. And when asked why she never left the men, she tipped her head and gave them all the sort of look one would a vexing child. "Do you think we never tried? They threatened to hunt us down and make our lives even more miserable than they already were, until we'd learned that we rightfully belonged to them." She cleared her throat and refolded her hands in her lap. "I called myself Elizabeth, Betsey for short, and Susan and I both took the alias Roberts and called ourselves sisters to make it harder for our families to track us." She hesitated. "Susan had a brother who might have, but there was no one who cared so about me."

Ben had related all this later to Rachel, who was equally astonished by it. She'd become as determined to make a show of support for Betsey and Susan as for Sally, through everything.

And so it was with genuine happiness and relief that they received the reading of Betsey's acquittal as well.

■ ■ ■ ■

The morning of Sally's trial dawned clear and cool, and as the other two women had been moved already to other lodgings, Rachel took it upon herself to go to the jail and help Sally dress and prepare for the event — even as difficult as the prospect was of leaving Ben's side so early. Ben resolved that, however, by rising early as well and now stood outside, chatting with the guards and sharing the sweet rolls he and Rachel had brought from the ordinary.

Rachel had assisted in washing Sally's hair the night before, and this morning made her friend sit while she brushed and dressed the locks that, though still golden, were not quite as lustrous as they'd been at her wedding. The experience of wandering the wilderness, often in very great haste, hadn't allowed Sally to properly care for herself, though by the time Ben had brought Rachel up to Russellville to await the trials, Sally had imposed some order on the tangled mane. But it was a comfort to both of them for Rachel to do this, even if it didn't take long, and Sally had been given a proper cap to cover it all with after.

The people of Russellville, like those of

Danville, had proved amazingly generous in providing all three women with clothing and other needed items. Sally truly lacked for nothing as she faced the prospect of another trial.

"There," Rachel murmured, setting the last of the pins in place and smoothing back a few stray hairs. "You look lovely."

Sally fingered the cap, lying in her lap. "Thank you so much. Should I even bother with this, do you think?"

"That's entirely up to you. It seems to be less the custom here, although a cap is always useful while working about the house to keep one's hair clean."

Rachel held a small looking glass while Sally settled the cap into place and adjusted it. "Makes me appear more respectable, I think." Her blue eyes darted to Rachel's and away. "The more of that the better, don't you agree?"

Rachel made a sound of assent — she hoped it sounded encouraging at least. It was so hard at times to know just how to respond.

In this moment, though, Sally folded her hands into the skirts of her gown and tucked her chin. "I wish — I wish I could undo the whole last two years. Pa says — he says that everyone at home has been so concerned, surely they'll continue to be understanding about it all. That they've all said they're ready to welcome me back and do whatever necessary to help me live a normal life again."

Sally's father had made the journey up to Russellville with Rachel and Ben to attend the trial, in the hopes of bringing Sally back home with him when it was all over.

Sally snorted softly. "As if I could ever feel normal again, after everything."

Rachel let her hand rest on Sally's shoulder for a moment then circled the chair and crouched before her friend, covering her clenched hands with her own. "No one blames you for this, Sally."

Tears stood in her eyes. "I know how people talk. For that matter, I've heard them here. Not everyone thinks us innocent — thinks *me* innocent. There's been talk of hanging us regardless." She sniffed. "Moses Stegall even brought a bunch over, intending to lynch us, but Mr. Stewart who keeps the jail took and hid us in a cave until they got tired of waiting around."

"Well. Shame on Moses Stegall then."

"It's a hard thing having your wife and child burned in their own house," Sally whispered.

"Still. Neither you nor Susan nor Betsey

were there when that happened, were you?"

Sally shook her head then swallowed hard. "But we were there for — others."

Still holding Sally's hands, Rachel sighed and leaned her forehead on Sally's knees for a moment. *Dear Lord, give me wisdom here.*

"I am so sorry you've had to endure all this," she said at last.

Sally's hands uncurled and clasped hers in return.

A knock sounded on the door outside. "It's nearly time," came Ben's voice.

"And we're nearly ready," Rachel called out, with a little smile.

An answering smile curved Sally's mouth, briefly lighting her shadowed eyes. "He's one of the good ones, Ben is."

A giggle escaped Rachel even as a blush swept her face. "He truly is."

Sadness rimmed Sally's expression for a moment. "I confess I'm a little envious of you, in fact."

Rachel could not speak, at that. "Oh Sally," she whispered at last then rose to her feet and tugged Sally's to hers. She reached for the blue cloak, a little worse for wear but carefully cleaned, and settled it around her friend's shoulders. "Come. Let's get this

378

day over with so you can indeed return home."

EPILOGUE

February 1804 (five years later)
"Daddy! Daddy! Daddy!"

Ben stepped inside the cabin and, pulling off his hat, went to one knee to greet the boys, Thomas and Nicholas, ages four and two, respectively. Sliding one hand across her rounded middle, Rachel smiled and turned from the table where she'd just laid out bread and butter.

She never tired of watching Ben gather their children into his arms, or their enthusiasm for his appearance, even if, like now, it was simply a brief visit home for luncheon. One arm about each of them, he grinned at her over their heads, then scooping them both up, levered to his feet and gave both a small toss to better settle them against his side. Tom whooped, but Nick only chortled.

Thus encumbered, Ben sauntered toward her and kissed her warmly, to the renewed giggles of the boys, then he set them down. "Off with you for a moment. I want to kiss your mother some more."

"Eww!" Tom declared, and ran away to his wooden blocks. Nick only stood there, grinning. Rachel laughed and shooed him away as well.

Ben gathered her in for a longer and more thorough kiss then with his arms still around her, lifted his head and looked down into her eyes, suddenly very serious. "They've found Wiley Harpe."

Rachel felt the sudden need to sit down and reached behind her for a chair. Ben pulled a folded newspaper from one pocket and laid it on the table in front of her.

She scanned the article. "This is the Frankfort paper?"

Ben nodded.

Extract of a letter from a gentleman in Mississippi Territory to his friend in this town dated February 8, 1804: "There have been two of Sam Mason's party — which infested the road between this country and Kentucky — in jail at Greenville for trial. They were condemned last term and executed this day. One of them was James May; the other called himself John Setton but was proved to be the villain who was

381

known by the name of Little or Red-headed Harpe, and who committed so many acts of cruelty in Kentucky."

Rachel pushed the paper a little away from her and looked back up at Ben. "Tried, condemned, and executed."

He nodded again. "The story goes that he and May had been part of Mason's gang for a long while, and thinking to collect on the bounty, double-crossed the old river pirate, cut off his head, and wrapped it in clay to preserve it." Ben grimaced, doubtless remembering the scene he'd related to her from nearly five years before, of another certain criminal's head. "When they went to claim the bounty, someone recognized Harpe, and said he'd bear a particular scar on his chest from a fight in a tavern right about the time he and Micajah started their killing spree. So, they made him remove his shirt, and there was the scar."

Rachel shook her head slowly. "All this time." She traced the edges of the paper with her fingertips. "I wonder if Sally knows. Perhaps — perhaps now she'll feel released to marry again. If she can bear it."

Sally's trial had held no surprises, and at the end, the jury handed in a verdict of "not guilty" for her as well. She'd stood weeping openly in the circle of her father's and Rachel's embraces. They hadn't much to prepare for departing again for Knoxville, so early the next morning, they left, Ben and Rachel accompanying them. Sally took her last leave of Susan and Betsey the evening before. "I prayed and God delivered us, at least of Big," she declared to them. "The Lord is worthy of your trust for the rest of your lives, whatever that may be."

"Always the preacher's daughter," Susan said, but with less mockery than one might have expected. Betsey looked thoughtful and nodded.

A local planter, Colonel Anthony Butler, had offered to shelter and employ the women until such time as they decided to go elsewhere, and both Susan and Betsey seemed content with that.

After seeing Reverend Rice and Sally safely back to Knox County, Ben and Rachel lingered a bit to visit with family and friends then made a wedding trip to Virginia so Rachel could meet Ben's family. His uncle and aunt and cousins received her very warmly, but soon they both were eager to be away again. Their first destination after that was Daniel and Anne's, where the earliest days of their unconventional courtship had taken place, and then to Stanford, very briefly, where Ben made inquiries on what community farther west might be in need of him.

They settled eventually in Elizabethtown, where Ben set up practice as a barrister and rose quickly as a leader in the local militia and other business.

Wiley Harpe did not, to their knowledge, ever return to Kentucky or Tennessee. In the meantime, the Rices moved away from Knox County, and Rachel had heard no word since of Sally's welfare. She couldn't blame her old friend for wanting a quiet life, away from the public eye, though folk had been kind enough, at least as far as Rachel knew, after Sally returned home. But Sally's admission of envy of Rachel's good fortune in Ben still stung.

To think she'd had the audacity herself to envy what she thought was a good friend's happiness, at one time. Not trusting that God could similarly bless her, or even exceed her hopes.

Not understanding that even something that appeared to be a good thing could go suddenly, horribly awry.

A familiar pang of fear and doubt gripped her heart, and once more she looked up at Ben. Even after nearly five years, she still caught herself wondering whether things would yet similarly go awry. . . .

A somber expression etched his features as well, and he gazed past her as if his thoughts were completely elsewhere. What was he remembering? Did he grapple with questions similar to her own?

"Ben?"

He stirred, inhaling deeply, eyes no longer distant, but searching hers. She put out a hand, and he took it, drawing her back to her feet and into his embrace.

The babe in her belly kicked against the sudden pressure. They shared a chuckle, then Ben tucked her closer and sighed. "After all these years . . . justice is finally served for Thomas and the others. Finally."

"And God has answered us all," she murmured.

HISTORICAL NOTE

The internet is a repository of many things strange and wonderful, but most of the two dozen or so articles out there featuring the Harpes, plus a few books, draw from the 1924 work *The Outlaws of Cave-in-Rock* by Otto A. Rothert, who dug deeply into newspaper articles and original court records. He in turn often cites the works of historian Lyman Draper, who had much of the story from the lips of men who participated in the hunt. In cases where their testimony, sometimes given decades later, conflicts with court depositions, I took the word of the deposition as more accurate. I also thankfully have access to genealogical records, where Rothert and other early writers did not, and feel on the basis of those, a few of his theories are disproved.

On the true identity of the Harpes: Historians disagree on whether Micajah and Wiley were indeed brothers or only cousins.

Early records sketchily document two brothers by the names of James and William Harper who immigrated from Scotland to the American colonies in the 1760s. The younger was killed during the Revolution (possibly even at Kings Mountain). Some speculate that Micajah was son of the elder brother — possibly of an African mother, by descriptions of his personal appearance — and Wiley son of the younger, or that both were sons of one father but different mothers. Either way, it's my opinion that the story of the Harpes begins here, with the fathers, who sided firmly with the British, and whose sons William and Joshua were definitely "wild Tory boys."

Many historians paint all Tories as cowardly and murderous, but T. Marshall Smith, in his work *Legends of the War of Independence* makes a very important distinction between those who chose loyalty to the Crown out of principle (in this case, the fathers of the Harpes, being proper Scottish Covenanters) and those who saw it as an opportunity for avarice. (I'd argue that some chose rebellion against the Crown for similar reasons, but that's another novel for another time.) He's also the only source for the early years of the Harpes, accounts of which he claims to have gotten directly from the lips of Betsey and Susan. Being written in 1855, however, the whole thing reads more like a Victorian novel than actual history, so I'm not sure how much weight to give his work. Where possible, I tried to cross-check persons and dates through Ancestry.com and Find-A-Grave (oh so helpful to have actual census records and gravestones to verify names and ages and locations), but I had trouble pinning down solid evidence for parents' names or ages for either the Harpes, or Susan and Betsey. I also read his account of the kidnapping of both girls well after writing Susan's account in my story, which I'd built out of bare facts and speculation. Genealogical records say that Micajah was born in 1768, and Wiley in 1770, which would put the two of them at twelve and ten during the Battle of Kings Mountain, where Micajah's father was a likely participant and the boys possible witnesses, if not participants as well. This seems harsh and implausible to our modern minds but — from what I know of history, and even modern-day warfare on other continents — is still extremely possible. If the boys were participants in that particular battle at that age, it could certainly explain how their thirst for bloodshed found its roots.

The probable ages for Susan and Betsey are also much in question, as well as what year they were stolen from their homes. If the kidnappings took place near the close of the war, then they very well could have been only thirteen and eleven, as Susan states — and certainly no more than fifteen to seventeen, if it happened later. Were there witnesses to the Harpes traveling the wilderness, the girls in tow, tied to their saddles, or was that a melodramatic construct of Smith? One cannot be certain. But I used the names Smith supplies, if not the ages, for Susan's and Betsey's true identities.

Solid genealogical records on the family of Sally Rice I did find, the best in my opinion on Geni.com. Also, with the murdered Langford being variously reported as Thomas, Stephen, and John, I was determined to track down his family as well, and in the process discovered a well-established Virginia lineage where the name Benjamin proliferated — and this after I'd written my proposal and chosen that name for my fictional hero. So, my Ben becomes the orphan cousin of a fictional branch of the real-life Langfords of Pitt County (similar to what I did with the Bledsoes in *Defending Truth*), but other named family members are verified historical figures, with actual positions and histories as I found them: "Pitt Ben," the sheriff of Pitt County; Stephen, who indeed helped found the town of Mount Vernon, Kentucky — after having his lands confiscated at the end of the Revolution as a penalty for choosing loyalty to the Crown; Mary Todd, widow of Richard Todd and sister-in-law to Judge Thomas Todd, who served in some respect during at least the initial hearing and trial for the murder of Thomas Langford; and a probable connection to Jane, the daughter-in-law of John Farris and assistant keeper of the tavern where Thomas was last seen alive. (Some sources state she was Jenny Langford, given name Mary Jane, but her deposition as one of five witnesses for the hearing in Stanford and the trials in Danville was signed Jane Farris, so I went with that first name and not Jenny.) Many of the connections between the Langfords and the true identity of the Harpes' murder victim were made in discussions during genealogical research, the most detailed of which I found at Sherlene\'s G-LOG (https://sherlene .wordpress.com/), which chronicles some excellent and fascinating genealogical research by Sherlene Hall Bartholomew.

If I'd had time, I would have loved to find out whether original court records for either set of trials still exist. As it was, I had to rely on others' accounts of those, which in some cases included transcriptions. The events of Thomas Langford's murder and others are as true to historical account as I could make them, with very few and minor alterations. Most of these events are covered in great detail either in Rothert's work, *The Outlaw Years* by Robert M. Coates, *The Harpes' Last Rampage* by E. Don Harpe (who interestingly claims relation), and *America's First Serial Killers* by Wallace Edwards. Certain things emerge as "canon," with a few variations, depending upon whom the later writers took as most trustworthy from the earlier ones. Some side research on the internet uncovered a surprising new source not referred to by the others: a letter written beginning in 1808 by a woman named Sarah McClendon, who lived within sight of the crossroads where Moses Stegall placed the head of Micajah Harpe, and who remembered the Harpes' reign of terror quite vividly. Hers is the account which includes an encounter between them and her husband, wherein Micajah asks for a replacement for his lamed horse; the description of the women (including the rhyming nicknames); and the incident regarding her young neighbors, Helen (or Grace) Levi and Silver May. Sarah McClendon herself was one of those neighbors who sat vigil over Helen to make sure she didn't harm herself. Sadly, she also relates how the mother of "Dollbaby," the little girl found killed and dismembered by the Harpes after wandering away to pick berries, succumbed to grief and drowned herself, laying yet another death at the Harpes' feet.

The connection between Rachel and Sally is, of course, fictional. Although Ben and Rachel are properly my story's hero and heroine, Sally emerges as central — amid the spiritual warfare that almost certainly played into her eventual deliverance. When I first began researching and discovered that she was indeed the daughter of a Baptist preacher, my first thought was, *How could that have happened?* However we feel about it with our modern Christian sensibilities, it's very much a fact of history that many couples were intimate before the actual wedding, as attested to by the vast numbers of genealogical records where the oldest child is born six to eight months after the wedding. I first noticed this phenomenon in the record of my husband's family tree, which goes back to about 1850, but human nature is human nature, after all. After some study, I've concluded that premarital sex wasn't necessarily approved of, publicly, but that it might have been considered "allowable" if the couple was engaged — or perhaps it was more a matter of, having been found out, the marriage was carried through more speedily than it otherwise might have been. And so that seemed the most likely scenario to me where Sally and Wiley were concerned.

I was delighted to find a microfiche copy online of their marriage bond. Further investigation revealed that an H. L. White, who stood as witness for the marriage, was Hugh Lawson White, the son of James White, founder of Knoxville (which really was as wild and wooly in its early days as I describe — worse, really), and recently returned from law school in the East. Voilà, a handy connection for fictional Ben. I could find, however, very little documentation for details of what law school entailed, or for how the judicial system worked, especially on the frontier, so there's much that I tried to keep vague. (If there are any glaring errors, I'd love to hear them because I might need the information for future stories!)

An actual marriage bond existed as well for Micajah Harpe and Susanna Roberts, signed by one John Roberts — likely the

"Old Man Roberts" that many writers and people of the day referred to. Most writers presume, because Susan and Betsey both took Roberts as their maiden names, that they were sisters, and Old Man Roberts their father, but — after much reading and consideration, and digging around on Ancestry.com and other sites, it's my firm belief that he was actually the father of Micajah and that they all just took the name Roberts as an alias whenever they wanted to appear legit.

Also, the existence of a living older son of Micajah and Susan is pure speculation on my part but could be accurate. An account exists by a preacher of the time of an encounter with "one of the tribe of Harpes" who attends church almost by accident and later becomes a Christian. The preacher refers to him as a younger brother of Micajah, but — what if he really was Micajah and Susan's son? How cool would that be, after everything, for a child of theirs to become a trophy of heaven?

And speaking of children and birth control — yes, it existed prior to modern times but mostly in the form of herbal abortifacients. There are a handful of tried-and-true "remedies" for "delayed menstruation" that have been in use since Roman times, but one in particular I ran across years ago in, I believe, one of the Foxfire books, where an Appalachian woman described having a jar full of seeds from a particular very common roadside weed, and how if she swallowed a spoonful of said seeds every day, she never conceived. But the moment she ran out . . . So I thought it very likely, if Sally and Wiley were married in June 1797 but neither she nor the other women had babies until early 1799 — and then all in close succession — it was likely they were practicing this or a similar form of birth control.

So much was guesswork, in between events verified by newspapers of the day and court documents. For instance, the famous (or is that *infamous?*) river pirate, Samuel Mason, once a Revolutionary War hero, was possibly nowhere near Cave-in-Rock at the time the Harpes landed there, but it's known that Wiley later associated with him, under the assumed name John Setton (or Sutton). Tracking the Harpes for story purposes often proved difficult. So did deciding on a particular spelling for names. I already mentioned the difficulty with verifying Thomas Langford's first name — genealogical records are notoriously varied, and his family also goes by Lankford. Harpe itself is most commonly spelled Harp in contemporary writings, but I chose the "e" spelling for modern familiarity. Same goes for Micajah, which should be pronounced Mi-CAY-ah (and in one place is actually *spelled* Micayah) but during that time probably was pronounced closer to Mi-CAH-juh, which then led interestingly enough to the transliteration on his marriage record as McAjor (. . . what??). Wiley's name is spelled "Willey Harp" on his marriage bond, written in Hugh Lawson White's own hand, and suggests a different pronunciation for his name as well, but again I chose what fit modern legend, for familiarity.

Other figures in the account with various spellings: Tiel/Thiel (I went with the phonetic), Leiper/Leeper/Luper (it's Leiper in the 1810 Census though Ancestry.com says Leeper), McBee/Magby (it's on his tombstone as McBee), and Stegall/Stigall/Steigal/ll (I had to just pick one, but that would be why there is Stigall's Station early in the story, and then a different spelling for the man who actually ended Micajah's life).

The period abounded as well with certain first names. As a novelist, if I'd known I'd be writing this story, I'd have tried to choose different character names in earlier stories — Sarah or Sally, Susanna, Thomas, Elizabeth, even Micah — but perhaps my readers could take this as an example of unavoidable similarities of name in any era. (For instance, there were so many Benjamins in the Lang[k]-ford family tree, what was one more, albeit a fictional one?) Also, just as Sally is the common derivative of the formal name Sarah, several early derivatives exist for Elizabeth: Betsy, Bess, Liz, Lizzy, Eliza. I've used Bess and Lizzy in previous stories, and it seemed to me that the real-life Elizabeth Carrick, genteel daughter of the Presbyterian minister who started the first college in Tennessee, and eventual wife of Hugh Lawson White, should be none other than an Eliza, so that's what I've called her.

Yes, there were still herds of buffalo (really, bison) and elk in western Kentucky at this time, and flocks of the now-extinct Carolina parakeet, often referred to by settlers as parrots, all of which were actually native to the region.

There were so many little things I learned about the Harpes while studying them that I couldn't find context for explaining outright in the story. Such as, they had a liking for "good horses" — the term of the day for particularly fast or strong mounts — and it's almost certain that they'd have been motivated to try to procure one like Ben's Ivy, once they saw her in action. And much time is given to speculation over whether the women could have, or how they should have, tried harder to escape the Harpes. I would argue, again, that while Micajah still lived, such a thing was unlikely. Multiple accounts document the unholy influence surrounding the men — how sometimes even properly equipped search parties would encounter them in the wilderness then get spooked and run away. How much more would the women feel it impossible to cross them, and live? I feel that those who express incredulity at the women not being able to leave once they'd been in bondage have no real understanding of victim psychology. I didn't have any trouble understanding the terrible hold Micajah and Wiley exerted on the women, even to the extent of them choosing to return to the men over such great distances and encumbered with little ones.

So what became of them all, after?

Susan Harpe lived out the rest of her days in Kentucky. It's reported that Lovey grew to be an eye-catching but temperamental young woman who followed the Butler family to Texas, and her fate from there is a mystery.

Betsey Roberts (she kept her adopted name) also lived in Kentucky, where she met and married John Hufstutter then eventually moved to Illinois where they "raised a large family" and lived to a good old age. Her son Joseph Harpe, however, vanishes from historical record, except for it being reported that as a young adult he joined the army.

Sally Rice Harpe remarried at least once and died possibly some forty years later in North Carolina in the company of her younger siblings. She was harder to track — and no wonder, if she was trying to keep a low profile to protect her family from further recrimination. It is documented that her father and mother eventually moved to northern Alabama and are buried there. One account, given by the very eccentric man who served as their jailer in Russellville, Kentucky, says she was seen crossing the Ohio in the company of her husband, father, and daughter, some fifteen or twenty years later, but I have a hard time crediting this as fact. Still, it could be, but the daughter would not have been hers by a Harpe.

The head of Micajah Harpe did not, as legend suggests, get carried off by someone seeking to use it for occult purposes. Sarah McClendon writes in much detail how in the weeks following, Moses Stegall would return and shoot at the head he'd posted there, and eventually, when what was left of it fell into the road, made his mare tread back and forth across it. So — whatever fragments remained after that are likely buried under layers of time.

Wiley Harpe did indeed make his escape, apparently via the Ohio River, downstream to the Mississippi, where he became known as John Setton (or Sutton) and fabricated a whole new personal history for himself. (Including the claim that he'd immigrated from Ireland, to cover, I presume, for his strong Scots/Irish accent.) There is evidence that he did actually return to Tennessee, so it's anybody's guess whether he might have tried to reclaim Sally — although I expect if she had her family to back her up, his influence would have proven less compelling without Micajah also present. It seems likely, however, that he was responsible for the seduction and murder of another young woman from central Tennessee, while claiming she fell from her horse and was dragged to her death.

Moses Stegall met with a violent end a year or so after his wife's and baby's deaths, for his involvement in persuading a young woman to run away with him. Several writers speculate that he secretly had dark dealings with the Harpes himself, and that his act of cutting off Micajah's head was motivated more by a desire to silence the other man before he could be implicated, than revenge for his wife and baby. I tend to disagree and point to Sarah McClendon's account of how he kept venting his fury on that head.

John Leiper is a similar mystery. Otto Rothert relates a story of crime and woe connected with him, but again, when I dug into genealogical records, I discovered a census record with the name, details of family members, and a verified burial place. I think this is a case of stories getting confused in a time when we didn't have access to certain records, and it's likely that Leiper was more the upstanding citizen I've portrayed him to be. Also, I'd point to the testimony of Sarah McClendon, who as a neighbor, more or less, spoke very highly of him.

Lastly, at least three different accounts exist of Micajah's final days and death. I had to choose the most likely but least cluttered . . . which indeed could describe the entire process of separating probable fact from certain fiction surrounding the legend of the Harpes.

Regarding all that, the reader might be

tempted to ask, were the Harpes really as bad as I've portrayed them? Did they truly commit all the murders attributed to them? If court documents and eyewitness accounts are at all trustworthy, then absolutely. Did Micajah actually murder his own child? The births of all three babies are well documented, with it also being well documented that when the women were apprehended and brought to trial after Micajah's death, only Susan and Betsey had living children with them. If McBee's own testimony is to be believed (as recounted by Rothert and given credence by him for many reasons), then Micajah himself admitted it, although his exact words were, "a child of my own blood," which could include any of Wiley's offspring. Yet, from what we can gather of the men's sexual habits, it would not be surprising if Sally were shared between them at some point after her marriage to Wiley. It would, in my opinion, be more surprising if she were not. Either way, even the bare facts about the whole situation are horrifying. I tried to present the more gruesome historical events of this story with as little detail as possible (and in most cases, in filmmaking terms, "off screen"), but felt I couldn't avoid an on-screen recounting of the murder of Sally's baby — nor of the later incident that provided proof of the spiritual forces in effect.

Which naturally leads to the question of, how much is too much? I asked myself that countless times during the writing of this book. Prayed nearly without ceasing over it. Agonized over the things God will allow and still say, *"All things work together for good to them who love God. . . ."* Note, though, that it does not say "All things ARE good." And that often-quoted passage in Philippians 4, which tells us where to fix our thoughts, likewise does not say, "Think on things that are only excellent or worthy of praise, in and of themselves," but gives room for what I call the redemptive in things that, well, in and of themselves are less than wonderful. So it is my prayer that you, the reader, may find something redemptive in this story of the terrible Harpes.

For a complete listing of my sources, including more discussion of details, please see my website, shannonmcnear.com.

ACKNOWLEDGMENTS

Becky Germany — thank you for first suggesting the idea and once again inviting me aboard.

Ellen Tarver — thank you for both patience and perceptive editing, which made this story better and stronger.

Lee S. King — thank you for reading, my good and dear friend! And encouraging. And praying! I could not have done this without you. . . .

Corrie McNear — you've read every word, and often kept me going, once again.

Breanna McNear — same! Thank you for your fangirl faithfulness!

Jen Uhlarik — for prayer and encouragement.

Jenelle Hovde — once again, amazing beta reader, with absolutely invaluable insight and feedback.

Michelle Griep — crit partner extraordinaire, who ruthlessly hunts down all my repeated words and pet phrases.

Deborah Teitsort Richardson — for your zeal and dedication in providing last-minute research — it made a difference!

Kailey, Jeanne, Phyllis, Jenelle, Teri, Trisha, Brenda, Tina, Andrea, Susan, Paula, Renee — my official influencer team, and many others who have read and liked my stories and taken the time to write reviews. Thank you all so much for your faithful readership, and for being brave enough to tackle this story as well!

Troy — for believing in me all these years. You've endured every part of this journey the last three decades and more, from the long hours I'd devote to writing simply because I had a story burning to get out, to sending me to writers conferences without a word of complaint . . . and now, slogging through deadlines. (Yay! I have deadlines!) May we continue to be a living witness of God's mercy and grace.

And — of course — my glorious Lord and Creator. You, who blinds the night with Your radiance, once again answered my tearful prayers. You carried me through, gave me the words, and brought this work to completion. I am here for You.

ABOUT THE AUTHOR

Transplanted to North Dakota after more than two decades in Charleston, South Carolina, **Shannon McNear** loves losing herself in local history. She's a military wife, mom of eight, mother-in-law of three, grammie of three, and a member of ACFW and RWA. Her first novella, *Defending Truth* in *A Pioneer Christmas Collection,* was a 2014 RITA® finalist. When she's not sewing, researching, or leaking story from her fingertips, she enjoys being outdoors, basking in the beauty of the northern prairies. Connect with her at www.shannonmcnear .com, or on Facebook and Goodreads.